SOLOMON BULL

WHEN THE FRICTION HAS ITS MACHINE

Clayton Lindemuth

Hardgrave Enterprises
SAINT CHARLES, MISSOURI

Clayton Lindemuth/HARDGRAVE ENTERPRISES
218 Keith Drive, Saint Charles, MO 63301
www.claytonlindemuth.com

Publisher's Note: This is a work of fiction. Names, characters, places, and incidents are a product of the author's imagination. Locales and public names are sometimes used for atmospheric purposes. Any resemblance to actual people, living or dead, or to businesses, companies, events, institutions, or locales is completely coincidental. Stock trading techniques are described purely for atmospheric purposes. They do not constitute advice. If you try them as described in this book, you will almost certainly lose money.

Cover Design by Franco Antonio Nioi. Look him up on Fiverr. His handle there is franconioi92

Book Layout ©2013 BookDesignTemplates.com

Solomon Bull/Clayton Lindemuth -- 1st ed.
ISBN-13: 978-0692858158

Dedicated with love to Cindy and Joy.

Also by Clayton Lindemuth

Cold Quiet Country

Nothing Save the Bones Inside Her

My Brother's Destroyer

Tread

TWELVE DAYS to RACE DAY

I was not born to be forced. I will breathe after my
own fashion. Let us see who is the strongest.

Henry David Thoreau

That crunchy noise was a rattlesnake. Its fangs skewer my sole.
I leap a basin, searching ahead for ankle-breaking cobble. My
next step will crush the snake's skull and drive its fangs into
my heel. This very thing happened to a guy in the Revolutionary War
and they made the Gadsden flag in his honor.

Five miles of the run are packed away and salted, and this. I don't
want to suck snake poison from my foot. Not in the desert. The air is a
hundred and ten degrees and flat like ten-day cola.

Country and western line dancers lift their boots and smack their
heels. I attempt this while glissading limestone talus—but I'm slapping
a snake, trying to grab the fat reptile's neck. Sweat burns my eyes and
eight feet of serpent corkscrews behind me. I grab him by the throat

and fall, slide on rocks as I ease him from my shoe. Cuff his tail to keep him from wrapping around my wrist.

I chuck him. He twists in the air, lands in century plant and looks like a heavy metal band's logo until he slinks back to the trail. Coils. Stares. Flicks his bifurcated tongue. His tail sounds like bacon cooked right.

I pitch a rock and he gives me a head fake. Advances a foot. I watch his hips to know which way he'll go.

Voices approach around the bend, where the trail pitches to a streambed. Their voices are merry, young, female.

"Stop!" I call. "Rattlesnake!"

Quiet.

One of the girls soprano-whispers, "...pepper spray."

"Give the snake a minute to clear the trail," I call.

My palm bleeds. Sliding on rocks has misaligned bones in my back. It's going to take two hours of ice packs to get to sleep. I lift my butt and crabwalk away; twist to all fours as the snake slithers toward me.

I grab a rotten saguaro shaft and it crumbles. "Stay back, girls. This fella's got a 'tude."

I chuck another rock. The snake has moxie. Fine, I have a reptile brain too, except mine is surrounded by another three pounds of gray. We face off, me crouching, him coiled. My fingers are splayed. My knees are rubber and my thighs, after five miles pounding the trails, are Jell-O.

My foot feels hot, like the snake filled my shoe with sulfuric acid. He advances and coils again. He's a spring, ready to explode into fangs and venom.

I ease my fingers to a water tube that traces over my shoulder to my Camelbak, while slipping my arm to the lower half of the pack. I press the water bladder and squeeze open the mouth valve. Yellow Gatorade rains on the rattler. His head darts sideways, back and forth. He blinks. Flicks his tongue and breaks to the side. Disappears into a crag.

"It's all right, girls. He's gone."

They arrive around the bend, cautious, poised for flight. One points a pepper spray canister at me. Her finger trembles on the trigger.

I point. "The snake is off in the rocks, there."

They look at the fissure, then at the wet spot on the trail. The dribble of Gatorade on my shorts. One tries not to giggle.

Desert Dog is in twelve days. I paid a grand to enter. The prize is a t-shirt numbered with my finishing place and the honor of having completed the most brutal race in the country. An old Green Beret hosts it on his ranch, north of Happy Valley Road. The Internet chat is that he uses the event to recruit mercenaries. The winners sometimes disappear.

I want to know where they go, and I want the t-shirt.

Cal Barrett, race organizer, runs Desert Dog during the monsoon season. Rock climbing, running, mountain biking, aqueduct swimming, cactus walk. Barrett designed the course to shred a man, alternately take him to the threshold of heat stroke and drowning, give him a thousand reasons to quit, and see which iconoclast will stand center-arena and fight to the death for a t-shirt.

I've seen interviews before the Super Bowl. DeJohnDa was born in a bad part of town ... fought off the drugs ... his dog died ... his daddy beat him ... his mama prayed. He's bought her a house and a Cadillac and just signed a ninety-three-million-dollar contract, but golly if he doesn't win the Super Bowl, it's all for naught.

Hype. To quote Jim Morrison, who is dead: I think it's a bunch of bullshit.

I don't have a reason to win. My mother did a better job of raising me than I did of growing up. I've never been a victim. I have all my limbs. My worst addiction is caffeine. All I know that if I'm conscious at the end of the race, I better be holding the first-place t-shirt.

So I'm out running in hundred and ten heat. The Camelbak carries three liters of iced Gatorade. I dig the calories and salts, but the life saver is the ice right next to my core. Without my Camelbak, the twelve-mile run would be lethal. With it, mere torture.

I finish the last mile. Wobble to my Jeep, sit on the bumper, stretch my hamstrings. Glutes. Those chicks were young for me—bodies still made of elastic. Immune to hangovers. They know how to use their iPhones. And they thought the only snake on the trail was in my shorts.

I power down the windows and turn on the radio. Blast the air-conditioning. The black steering wheel is a hundred and forty degrees. I tilt the air vent at the wheel; sit on the gravel and stretch. Girls giggle a little way off and I know it's them.

Closer, the brunette says, "Was there really a snake?"

"A big one," I say. "Look at my shoe."

Brunette keeps her distance, eyes dubious.

"The snake bit my sole. I left a trail of venom with each step."

Brunette gives me a buzz-off look. I accept.

The steering wheel is touchable. I hang a towel on the seat and climb in. I'm at my apartment in ten minutes. The building manager has hung a banner stating rent has dropped from six hundred to four hundred and sixteen. I make a mental note. My lease is up in a month.

I glance at the pool. Three chicks, backsides broiling. My roomie Keith's car is in the lot. And since she's not at the pool, Katrina probably is too. Keith is nailing my girlfriend. I know, and they know I know. The topic lurks the way death lurks when there's a corpse. I'd break the silence but I'm waiting for my moment.

I open the door.

They're on the couch, opposite sides, but the middle cushion is dimpled like a dog was there twenty seconds ago.

Keith looks like Kurt Cobain would have if he'd gotten off the drugs, ate some kale and lifted weights. Same hair and face dropped on a linebacker's frame. Keith and I were roommates at ASU and miserliness has kept us renting the same apartment years after finishing our postgraduate work. We're skinflints: me, because I don't want much; and him, because he doesn't earn much.

He's a lawyer working for the state. Wants to save the world. Puts him at sixes and sevens with the people who don't want saved. Makes him come across a smidge haughty. Sometimes he does worthwhile work, like donating time and money to the battered women's shelter. Other times, frankly, he needs his comeuppance.

Katrina is a nine. She'd be a ten if she'd ever shut up about the dysfunction in her past. I rescued her, and now she's a bored prima donna. She was happy about the hurricane because it made her name cool. We've moved beyond each other, but Keith has kept us in the same orbit. By screwing her.

Things change. Brew. Like a jug of homemade wine with a balloon on top. Sourer and sourer. The snake incident needled everything... or maybe I'm sick of the games.

"Hey," I say. "Curious. You two have been beating guts how long?"

"What?" she says.

Keith exhales.

"Simple question."

She looks at him. "What's that mean?"

"Having sex."

She shrugs. "Two years?"

He shakes his head. "Seems like a lot longer. Why?"

"What's the big deal?" she says.

"Let's end it on this."

"Whatever," she says.

"Alright," I say. "Go pack."

I sit between them. Grab the remote. Flip the channel from the game to a channel on commercials. Katrina hasn't moved. Keith adjusts his crotch.

"I'm going to be doing a lot of training," I say. "The race is in twelve days. Let's end it on this."

"You were serious?" she says.

"Hey," Keith says. "I live here too." He faces Katrina. "Put your things in my room."

"That'll work," I say.

Katrina snorts. Big airplane hangars have weather systems inside. They're like Katrina's head—mostly vacant, with little mechanics scurrying around the ground floor. It can be sunny outside, but a storm will brew inside. Suddenly you're turning a wrench and it's raining. That's Katrina's head.

"You're not going to win this race," Katrina says.

"Thanks. Your nipple is showing."

She tugs her tube higher. "I'm serious. Why do you even try? You're going up against a bunch of mercenaries. Guys who look like Van Dammage used to. If the heat doesn't kill you, they will."

"Mind over matter," I say. "I can do anything. It's about learning the price and deciding to pay it."

"What about genes? Ability?"

"The mind is superior."

"Yeah, but not yours." Keith smiles.

A new commercial flashes on the tube. Senator Cyman's reelection campaign is in full swing.

"I hate Cyman," Katrina says.

"Hypocrite. He's on the take," Keith says.

"Didn't you date his daughter?" I say.

"Ash Cyman," he says.

Katrina studies Keith's misty face. He sees her and says, "Years ago. Undergrad days."

"Who's Cyman running against?" I say.

"Some schmuck real estate developer who's running like he wants to lose," Keith says. "Two weeks ago, he came out in favor of banning firearms. Just started making progress and he comes out against mom's apple pie."

"I'd prefer if both lost," I say.

"Cyman's a six-term incumbent. He's royalty."

"I could make him lose."

Katrina stares, then Keith.

"I could bring him down."

"Do you know something?" Katrina says. "I mean, do you *know* something?"

"Mind over matter. I can do anything."

"Fair enough, Lizard King," Keith says. "Bring him down. The nation will be grateful."

"I don't believe you," Katrina says. "The news just said he's up twenty-three points. You can't dent his numbers. If it was so easy, the other guy—Duane Hock—would have done it."

"Wait," Keith says. "You're a conservative. You'd be bringing down your own guy."

"No. I have no party. How about this for a disbeliever's special: I'll take ten points off Cyman's popularity in three weeks. Fair enough?"

"Ten points in three weeks," Katrina says. "You'll cut Cyman's lead to thirteen?"

"I accept," I say.

"Done."

"Good. You want to get your junk out of my room? I'm going to nap."

I wake like I've slept exactly six and one half hours, though it's only been three. It is midnight. With Katrina's things gone, my room is empty. On the flip side, Keith went to sleep wondering if formalizing his fling was worth losing his space. I can tell him now, it wasn't. Soon she'll park bags in his brain, too.

Katrina needed him. He was there for her, and now he'll suffer. He's got at least three other women who will question why his room has bras on the floor.

For me, I have a joyous project: bringing down a senator. Five years ago, while attending Arizona State, I picked up a couple cardboard tubes from the Phoenix Times that had fifty feet of blank newsprint left. Keith and I taped the paper over the dorm room's cement block walls. We got drunk and engaged in magic marker brinksmanship. I wrote Nietzsche and Derrida aphorisms, build your cities under Vesu-vius, and Keith wrote his favorite FDR and Sonny Bono lines. The New Deal... goes on and on and on...

One tube of paper remains in the closet, a blank slate waiting a pro-found message.

I swing by an all-night Wal-Mart and buy three cans of spray paint, red, white, and blue. People on Keith's side of the spectrum would hang me for buying at Wal-Mart. But I say put Wal-Mart in charge of Wash-ington DC—the whole outhouse. We'll have plenty of gasoline and health insurance will cost as much as a bag of chips. Everything will be bright and cheerful and thieves will be prosecuted.

Back home I don a backpack of paper, paint, and tape. A climbing rope and ascenders in case things get hairy. A Soloist belay device, be-cause I have one.

I board my mountain bike. My tires sound like a three-mile zipper. The air is hot, high nineties. The sky is devoid of clouds and the smog diffuses a fake borealis of ambient city light. I race along Interstate Sev-enteen's access road, north. Cycling brings insights. Ed Abbey advo-cated burning, chain-sawing, or using an acetylene torch to topple billboards. I say, we're accustomed to the ugliness, we may as well co-opt the signage to democracy's noblest purpose: shoveling political dirt.

The billboard is impressive architecture. Small from the highway, up close, it's a monster. Moths and bats flutter above spotlights spaced evenly along its twenty-foot scaffold. Though I anticipated pitching a rope and climbing with ascenders, the center column sports a ladder. I stash my bike a dozen yards away in a wash, deep in low-hanging juniper branches. Trot back to the pole. Standing at the base, after an approaching vehicle passes, I dash up the rungs.

On the ledge I learn that although the guys that put signs up here look like acrobats, they've got all kinds of room. I could build a campfire and pitch a tent.

A string of cars approaches. I lie on the metal grid as they pass, then wiggle out of my backpack. Remove my shirt, wrap it around my hand, and loosen each spotlight until I work in the dark.

I empty my backpack. Grab duct tape and line the guardrail with a hundred hand-length strips. I manufacture loops and stick them to the billboard face, then roll the paper across. A quick snap at the end tears the paper like foil. I roll two more sheets and I've covered nine vertical feet, or two thirds of the billboard.

In red, I script inner-city graffiti: BREAK THE CYMAN.

In blue: VOTE HOCK.

Leaning against the rail for as much perspective as possible, I wonder if I might reduce the subtlety of my humor. Will anyone be dyslexic enough to get it? I spray a few white stars so the whole thing looks like a giant campaign bumper sticker, and outline the C and H in white. Gather my gear, drop my pack to the ground, screw in the floodlights, down-climb, retrieve my bike, and drop head to pillow in twenty minutes.

Train, Train, Train. I wake with the Desert Dog race in my dreams. I slug my way to consciousness like a cat escaping a sinking burlap bag.

There's dead weight on my arm.

"Katrina? What?"

She mumbles.

"Nah, nah. Naaaaah! Wrong bed, baby."

I remember, now, the playboy bunny dream right before the Desert Dog race dream, where I was drowning inside a barrel of hair and boobs. I slip from beneath Katrina. Check Big Murtha for crusties.

Katrina did the wave on me.

It is five o'clock—the New York Stock Exchange opens in an hour and a half. I've got time for a mad bike ride through the desert. Slip on some spandex with the pads in the butt. Keith snores in the other room and Katrina mumbles. She flips over and the sheet pulls away. There's a blue streak on her breast and I check my hands. My index finger is bank robber blue from a leaky spray can nozzle.

I carry Katrina to Keith's room and dump her beside him. I'm the enforcer that keeps people true to her word.

By the time I get the paint off my hands I've lost fifteen minutes. I slam a Red Bull and two ginseng capsules.

Oh yeah. Here we go.

Finally on the bike; same route as last night. City-bound traffic trickles. My legs slam like a locomotive's main rod, up, down, metronomic.

Cars cloister at the billboard ahead. I thought it might be the road construction, but they seem to be slowing to read the billboard. A news helicopter hovers. A man points a television camera and a competing channel's bird stalks low on the horizon, coming quick.

A black Suburban sits on the shoulder below the billboard. Tinted windows. The kind of vehicle you see doing security for presidential motorcades. I saw a video on You Tube of one of these bad boys opening the sunroof. Some space-age Gatling gun telescopes through the aperture. A ninja-suited man thumbs the trigger mech and creates a dotted line of lead moving three thousand feet per second between him and the bogey.

I pedal past. No sideways glance to acknowledge traffic has slowed. Cyman's bodyguards are there, news choppers are above. But should I turn?

How would it look to pass without wondering why their panties are knotted? I'm the criminal and I've returned to the scene of the crime. Stupid. But since I'm here—look at it this way. If I didn't know I did what I did, would I notice the traffic? Sure. I'm an observant guy.

But would the average guy?

A few hundred yards beyond the billboard, I turn left and dismount at the curb. Fake like I'm tying my shoe. The sign is still there but a man in black climbs the ladder. Maybe it's the turret gunner. Cars honk as he attains the pedestal and begins tearing the paper. It was good while it lasted.

Onward. I set my mind to Desert Dog.

The race has been run during every monsoon season for the last six years. Monsoon, to take full advantage of the deadly combination of high temperatures and high humidity. Former Green Beret Cal Barrett designed the course with Vishnu in mind. I read an article where he said he was thinking of Robert Oppenheimer mistranslating the Bhagavad-Gita: "I am become death, destroyer of worlds."

Barrett said if he runs a race and no one dies, it isn't much of a race.

His hair is silver, straight and long. His thick, Scott mustache could stop a machete. He's got hams for arms and his chest is a beer keg. A tat of a trident-wielding devil adorns his forearm. His eyes say I've killed men, mostly because I like it.

I pedal shy of Barrett's ranch. This is where I train, where I saw the snake and the girls. I'll hammer out a circuit and be home before the New York Stock Exchange opens.

Barrett changes the course every year to keep it fresh, but the race consists of the same core events. The beginning six-mile trail around his ranch is just to loosen up. The last few years, whelps—as he calls contestants—circumnavigated his ranch on mountain bikes five times, or thirty miles. Then they ran the same six-mile trail. He starts the race at ten a.m., so the final legs will be at two in the afternoon, when the temperature is usually a buck fifteen and the humidity around sixty per cent.

Don't think you're going to conserve energy. Pace yourself. Rest when you need to. Barrett bought hives of Africanized bees to keep men scrambling through the rare shaded areas.

After the run, weak men have already collapsed.

Barrett owns land on both sides of the aqueduct from Lake Pleasant. The free style event that follows the six-miler involves climbing a mountain trail, scaling a rock face, sliding down burnt volcanic rock through Cholla beds, and climbing a ten-foot, razor-topped chain link fence. Diving into a fifteen-mile-an-hour aqueduct, and pulling one's whelp self out the other side, thirty feet away. This is where men drown. This is where lumberjacks suck their thumbs. The run continues along the aqueduct until Barrett decides it's time to cross again. No one knows—Barrett may not know—how many crossings he will demand.

The cement is slick and the current is fast. This isn't like crossing a river, where pockets of water move at different speeds. Where you can grab a rock and rest. And once you reach the other side, which is only thirty feet from where you started, you're liable to slide along, unable to claw your way out, for miles. Barrett places ropes along the way, and they are your only hope. If you miss them, you will drown.

Let's say you grab that one-inch hemp. Think a man like Barrett will have tied knots so your wet hands won't slip?

Get out of the water. Get in the water. Out. In. Out. In. You scale the chain link. Slice open your arms, guts, and legs. There's a group of Jeeps and trucks, two miles ahead. As you near them, you see Cal Barrett standing like Thor among men, and your heart races. This wasn't bad. You can do this. You cross the finish line, and Cal slaps your shoulder as you stagger along. Drop palms to your knees. Wheeze hot desert air to your starved lungs.

"Lap one!" Cal screams. "Get your bike, numbnuts! Two to go!"

ELEVEN DAYS to RACE DAY

We have no government armed with power capable
of contending with human passions unbridled by
morality and religion. Avarice, ambition, revenge,
or gallantry, would break the strongest cords of
our Constitution as a whale goes through a net.

John Adams

I jiggle the mouse and the monitor wakes. Log in. Pull up the charts. I've missed the opening bell but I don't trade the first fifteen minutes. It's all about probabilities and the only thing predictable about the first fifteen minutes is most times I don't have a clue which way a stock is going to travel.

Lot of stock jocks think they're chartists. Some are news hounds. The real suckers, the ones who crash a hundred grand in two weeks, take their cues from the chat rooms.

The pros manage risk. Though there's plenty of adrenaline, this isn't about the ups and downs or seat-of-the-pants decisions based on hunches, smashing keyboards, screaming into telephones.

This is about making sure a trade never takes you down.

There are two kinds of trades. Add their inverses if you play the market short, and you have four. I keep it easy. Just two on the long side, and only two ways to play them.

The momentum trade and the bounce.

With a momentum play, you buy a rocketing stock when it trends on a one-minute chart, and you only buy in the direction of the prevailing trend. Easy. You sell the instant it breaks the line or your four-period exponential moving average crosses below your nine-period simple.

This is Burger King. There's another trade so you can have it your way.

Trade two: the bounce. Climb aboard when a stock finds support. Doesn't matter if it breaks through the roof and jumps higher, or thumps its ass off a thirty-eight percent Fibonacci line. When the four crosses above the nine, press the buy button. Trust the probabilities. Screamers keep screaming.

Don't waste time trying to figure out which direction a stock is going to go. You'll never predict the breaking news on CNBC about the CEO of the company you just dumped your entire 401K into who just got filmed laying pipe in a goat at that special ranch outside of Seattle. You buy a stock, you better be willing to dump it cold.

There. Go forth and be a millionaire.

I've added three grand to my account this morning riding Dryships, Inc. It's ten a.m. and time for mac n cheese.

I'm stirring pasta, watching the timer on the microwave. I drain the water at exactly five and a half minutes because any man who tolerates limp macaroni... I don't even have to say it.

Keith's door creaks open and his head kilroys around the wall. "Solomon," he says.

I look. He shakes his noggin. I think he's cold, but it's just blue ink on his lips.

"Dude," he says, "you got to help me get rid of her."

"I tried last night, but you were high on the nectar. Don't come complaining of thorns." The microwave timer beeps and I splash noodles into the colander. Drop a quarter stick of butter in the pan, a dollop of half-and-half, cheese mix. Stir. Keith closes his eyes. He has that stoned look that comes from ten hours of sleep.

"She's psychotic," he says.

"You need her."

"What?"

"She'll teach you what she taught me. People can't be saved."

He grunts and returns to his room. I stir the cheese sauce and noodles, dump it all into a cereal bowl and splash a little gourmet Frank's Red Hot.

Chowin' down at my computer, I jet in and out of a few stock positions. Not bad. I've removed four grand from the ether. I siphon two thou in settled cash from my trading account to my tax account, and slip in a CD purchase just under the wire. I file quarterly, but allocate funds toward my tax liability daily. Uncle Sam never misses his split.

Uncle Sam is the neighborhood Mafioso that will take a ball bat to your knees if you don't give him half of everything you make. With your money, he lives in style, keeps his patrons' palms greasy. This age-old strongman social order is legal. Today, we dress it in red, white and blue, proud colors of civil religion, and call it government.

I launch a browser window and scan the Rudge headlines. My handiwork has made it big time. Rudge hates Cyman.

Hock Campaign Denies Vulgar Billboard

The story takes a full minute to load... must be getting a billion hits. I glance over the text. The ostensible beneficiary of the billboard's message, Duane Hock, is a moron. The Hock campaign has distanced itself from what it terms a 'vigilante supporter' with whom the campaign has had no prior contact and vigorously denounces. Making fun of a person's name is the worst kind of politics, and doing so when vital issues are finally making it into the public discourse threatens to derail the progress the candidate has fought—

Et cetera.

Secretly, they ought to be loving it. This is like when George W. Bush didn't realize the microphone was on and called a reporter an asshole. The base swooned because they knew most reporters *are* assholes. It fed the straight-shooting, stick-by-principles mystique that got him elected. Some say Rove planned the whole thing, knowing likeability is far more important than the capacity to say nuclear.

In a couple of days I'll check Real Clear Politics and see if the polls change.

Dryships is trading flat but that usually changes two hours before the close. I tilt my monitor forward and sit straight-legged on the floor. Stretch. My lower back is tight as two quarks necking. If I don't get some ice on it I won't be able to run this afternoon. About to rise, a knock on the door halts me.

"Yeah."

Keith opens the door, says quietly, "She's taken over my sock drawer and my underwear drawer. You've got to take her back."

"Keith. Be a man. Throw her out." This is not my conversation. I slip into running shorts while he grumbles. Pull on trail shoes. Log off the trading platform, lock the computer and force Keith to step aside as I close and lock my bedroom door.

"Uncool," he says.

"You pick that lock and let her in my room, I'll drive her fifty miles west and leave her face down in a hole."

He tilts his head. Eyebrows wrinkle. "Would you?" He follows me to the kitchen. "I'd chip in for gas."

I fill the Camelbak with ice and water.

"You can't kick her out," he says. "She's pregnant."

"You know I shoot blanks, right?"

"That's what you've always said."

I'm at the door, opening it. "Well, I'm sure you two will do the right thing."

"She won't abort."

"Yeah, wow, I honestly don't know what to do with that."

In fifteen minutes I'm at the trailhead. One more round of easy warm-up stretches. A valley spreads to my right. The aqueduct from Lake Pleasant zig-zags six or seven miles and splits the valley floor. At its most immediate point, on the near side of the fence, a man rides a horse.

His hair is silver.

I run like a cheetah with his backside soaked in habanero salsa. After fifteen minutes of shale that tinkles like glass, I'm thirty feet behind.

"Mr. Barrett!"

He ignores me. I give the horse a wide berth and trot alongside.

"Mr. Barrett, I just wanted to say hello, and that I'm looking forward to Desert Dog."

The horse lopes easily; his head like a buoy on a lake with syncopated waves. Barrett keeps his eyes forward. I tell myself tough guys are often loners.

I pull ahead a little and his head swivels.

Telltale white lines drop from both ears to a shiny purple device clipped to his shirt. The baddest mercenary in Arizona is listening to a purple iPod. Offsetting this mildly effeminate fashion statement, his horse bears a brand of a coiled rattlesnake—like on the Gadsden flag.

I wave.

He nods.

"I'm looking forward—"

He pulls a bud from an ear. His hand looks like a chewed-up leather dog toy. He flashes a grin. "What?"

"I'm looking forward to Desert Dog."

He nods, begins to put the earphone back in.

"How's the course shaping up?"

He drops his arm. Looks at the sky and exhales. Glances at me with eyes like the scales of justice.

"Or not..." I say. "Just thought I'd say hello."

"You'll know we're in the End Times when a woman is the CEO of Apple."

"Excuse me?" I stumble on a barrel cactus.

"You notice the size of these things?" He indicates the iPod clipped to his lapel, about the dimensions of a decent beetle turd. "Smaller and smaller. Soon, the only way to carry them will be under your skin. And don't think for a minute the government isn't already gearin' up software, waiting on the day."

"Right."

"Damn right," he says. "You've heard of the mark of the beast, right? How we're all going to have computer chips? Think how much easier full compliance will be when the people who are most capable of rebelling form lines and shell out money—pay the government—to implant the chips that will enslave them. Our enemy is *clever*."

"What's that have to do with a woman CEO?"

"You ever hear of the Garden of Eden?"

"Uh."

"Uh-huh. Wha'd they eat, and which one ate it?"

Nietzsche said Adam ate the apple, and quickly blamed Eve. Philosophy, I think, would antagonize Mr. Barrett. "The woman ate an apple," I say.

"Eve."

"Right."

"Apple. iPod. Clear as a bell."

"Yes sir. Well, I thought I'd say hello."

He returns the bud to his earlobe and gazes straight forward.

Break the Cyman. Vote Hock.

Rudge has taken the photo of my billboard graffiti from the lower left side of the webpage and turned it into the banner shot. The caption is HMMMM...

Interestingly, in the bottom right corner of the photo, in the distance, a cyclist with long, straight, black hair approaches with his head down.

I follow the link. Doomberg has picked up the story. The headline: HOCK CAMPAIGN FURIOUS ABOUT MAVERICK SUPPORTER.

This is going to be more difficult than I thought. Duane Hock's campaign manager is dipped in stupid. If he knew how to play it, my billboard could have turned his campaign. All he had to do was deny any involvement, wink, and let Cyman rage. Instead, Team Hock insults every potential voter who thought he must have ice in his veins to pull a stunt like that.

I pause. There is something rather nihilist about helping an intellect as far left on the bell curve as Hock win a senate seat. He's two standard deviations down the dumb side, and I'm working overtime to make him my representative against The Machine.

But it is fun. A happy convergence of agnostic politics and prankish daredevilry.

The challenge is that Hock's posturing doesn't ring true. People saw my billboard and thought Hock had it on the ball. Now he has seemingly turned on himself, just when it appeared he was lugging cannonballs in his boxers. He'll be seen as intolerably dishonest or intolerably stupid.

Voters will abide a lot of dishonesty and stupidity, but the upper limit can't be broached. As soon as a politician resembles a guest on Jerry Springer, he becomes a guest on Jerry Springer. We've been inoculated against the dishonesty and thievery and stupidity of our ruling class... We've turned our backs on our duty to kick the thieves out of office and hang them from a scaffold... but we have all the time in the world for Wife Swap and Duck Dynasty. Hence we don't actually notice the political elite until they become entertainment.

Keith thinks the right stew of government programs can set things aright.

I, on the other hand, believe we are tumbling down the waning slope of democracy toward bureaucratic tyranny. Until something nixes our ability to bury our heads in entertainment, we will allow our leaders to tap shoes in airports, screw interns, pageboys, and hobos at truck stops. Take bribes with impunity, raise taxes, start preemptive wars, monitor every single email or telephone conversation...

When the iPod is miniaturized enough to slip inside the hollow of a needle, I'm bugging out, regardless of who runs Apple.

I drop my sweaty shorts and tank top to the bedroom floor, wrap a towel around my waist. Katrina made her jab about men with Van Damme bodies chasing me, but the fact is, I could kick Van Damme's ass from here to the lawn chair. I don't have the movie muscle, and my abs won't put you in the mind of corrugated steel. But I bring ten years as a karate black belt, and ten thousand years of Blackfoot wiliness to the fight.

Van Damme is getting old.

And let us not forget he is French.

Twist the knob all the way to the hot side. Mom always said a shower should be as hot as you can stand, and I took her literally. With shampoo in my hair and my eyes closed, the curtain drifts inward against my legs and the temperature changes.

My first thought is the ninja in the black Suburban.

I open my eyes and they burn. Douse my head. The curtain loops tinkle across the aluminum pole and cold air washes inside. There's a hand on my stone sack and—this is critically important—it is a woman's.

Katrina.

"I thought we ended this yesterday," I say, twisting and breaking contact. My elbow brushes a breast a little more determined than the pair I recall mounted on Katrina's ribs. I wipe water from my eyes and open them.

"Whoa!"

She smiles. She's a bombshell—some alchemist mixed an anime girl with oxygen and lightning.

"Who are you?" I say.

"Rachel." She reaches for the soap.

"Uh—pleased to meet you?"

"I just always wanted to do an Indian."

"Nothing against profiling," I say. "But you're out of luck."

"You're not an Indian?"

"Oh, I'm Indian."

"You don't find me attractive?"

"Take a look at Big Murtha."

She takes Big Murtha in her hand. Soaps him. He becomes Bigger Murtha. "Then what is it?" she says.

"This doesn't happen, and so this isn't happening. I'll step aside and let you do some other Indian." I take her shoulders, ease her away, rinse the soap from my rocks and think of that Ninja again. I spin. She's still there, smiling.

I blink. Still there.

I slip out while the shower's still on and soak the floor.

"I live in building C," she says, now behind the curtain. "I was at the pool when you came home from your workout."

I think Rachel is soaping herself. A neon green bikini is on the floor. I peek out the door and though I can't hear over the shower, the apartment is quiet like Keith isn't around.

Katrina sent her here. She's psychotic enough to need this kind of proof. Me telling her the relationship is over isn't enough. She needs me to make it with one of her friends.

"Tell Katrina it's over."

"Is Katrina your crazy girlfriend?"

"She's not my girlfriend."

"Well, you know what I mean. The three of you. It's kinky-cool."

"You don't know what you're talking about." Toweled off, I lean on the sink. "Which apartment are you in?"

"Uh— D'."

"But what number?"

"Seventeen."

There is no seventeen. "Oh, great. Well, the towels are in the closet, here."

"Thanks," she says.

I'm already in the hall. I slip Keith's door open. Katrina's bras litter his dresser. Underwear on the lamp. Jeans discarded across the bed. His bureau drawers are open. I look in the living room and kitchen, empty. Check my room. The computer monitor is on. My desk drawer is ajar.

Rachel isn't just the neighborhood slut.

I slip back to the bathroom, cautious as I near the door. I don't know where she might have hidden a weapon—well, I do, but—

The shower's still going and I halt at the jamb. Glance at the mirror, then the shower. A trail of water leads to the open window. No way. This is a second story apartment. Unless Rachel truly is a ninja, she's behind the shower curtain.

And where the hell did she come from? I haven't seen her around the pool—and I watch the pool. Who sent her? Cyman's crew can't be that sharp, even presuming some photo of the billboard showed my face. I haven't angered Barrett, yet, I don't think.

"Come on out, babe," I say. "Gig's up. Who you work for?"

Silence.

"Come on. You've got nowhere to run." Brandishing fists at head level, I step inside the bathroom. Reach for the curtain and snap it open. The shower is empty. I look at the ceiling. Spin. Jump to the window.

A very naked Rachel sprints across the lawn clutching her bikini, strings trailing like kite tails. She jumps into a black Lexus and I'm twisting now, knowing the futility, but giving chase anyway.

I reach the lawn. Still in a towel. A pair of guys stand by parked cars, grins about to break open their heads.

"Which way did she go?" I call.

"Left," one says.

In the future, I'll know where to look her up.

Left.

NINE DAYS to RACE DAY

"Yes, this is an age of moral crisis. Yes, you are bearing punishment for your evil. But it is not man who is now on trial and it is not human nature that will take the blame. It is your moral code that's through, this time. Your moral code has reached its climax, the blind alley at the end of its course. And if you wish to go on living, what you now need is not to return to morality--you who have never know any--but to discover it."

John Galt in "Atlas Shrugged"

This morning's run was a bruiser. Before leaving the apartment, I checked Real Clear Politics. Thinking about the results of my billboard experiment, I slipped on a stone. Twisted my ankle, scuffed my palms, pulled Cholla needles with my teeth.

Cyman has expanded his lead by a point. Not much, of course. But the polls include five days of data. A one-point move overnight implies a five-point move five days after the billboard hit the news—minus the "forget effect," and barring, of course, the bone jarringly stupid Hock doing something else to speed the destruction of his ratings in the interim.

I'm going to focus on Cyman. Two reasons. Negative advertising works, and if I try to make Hock look good, I have every faith he'll wind up looking dumber. I need to remove him from his campaign while eliminating Cyman as a viable candidate. Even as emasculated as Hock becomes, voters will hold their noses and pull the lever for him.

I have a feeling about that.

My next project will require help. While attending ASU, I met a few crazy rock climbers in Sedona who hailed from Northern Arizona University. We climbed and stayed in touch. Years after graduation, they're still bumbling around Flagstaff, Sedona, Prescott, Williams.

I fire an email to Paolo, the center of the storm.

Paolo; My new house will require eight sheets of plywood. Two pallets of cement blocks, and enough cement to stick them together. S.B.

I'll bet an iconoclast like Barrett could arrive at a few original ways to destroy a politician's ratings.

Then there's the naked Rachel to think about. A man likes to think he's prepared at an instant to do his duty for the propagation of the species. Part of me feels guilty for not pounding her to the shower wall, and sorting out her alphabet soup agency entanglements while drowsing on the sheets, afterward. Priorities.

You see movies where the woman pulls a dagger from between the mattresses...

I kick away. My chair rolls to the bed. The sheets are loose; I flip them back. Lift the mattress.

There's a knife the size it would take to gut an elk.

Haft about four inches, blade six. Sharpened to a razor's edge; the point and two inches on the spine are also sharp, and curved like one of those Arabic blades made famous on Disney's Aladdin. And on those videos where Islamists don't behead people.

If I touch it, I destroy fingerprints.

Here's a mind bender: She's an assassin and I lucked out of getting killed. But what if she was legitimate? Above-board? What if I'd caught, disarmed and quarantined her until the police arrived, and they said, *kindly step over here so we can kill you.*

How do you know? Especially since I just tried to take down a senator?

Blood rushes in my head. You train in the way of the starry-eyed novice to be a bad ass. Pushups on your knuckles. Sit-ups 'til you puke. Punch a tape-wrapped board until the callus is like shoe leather. But seeing the blade that was intended for your back, *coitus interruptus*, shoots a shiver that starts like a big bang somewhere in your core and ripples like seventy-thousand football fans doing the wave. They chuck popcorn and spill beer. They punch each other in excitement. Your ribs slap each other on the ass.

The blade reflects the striped mattress. I see a smudge.

I drop the mattress. Corny, but I check the closet and under my bed. Draw the curtain. Then go to the kitchen for a plastic baggie. They're all used, dirty on the counter. Do I risk the peanut butter smudge? I turn the bag inside out. Soap and scrub. Dry with a hand towel. Place on the sill to bake in sunlight.

Cal Barrett is the kind of man who would have a useful contact.

Rachel was clever. How many witnesses, you think, got a glimpse of her license? Zero. They were all wishing they were seat leather.

Inspiration: I'll go to a hobby shop. Buy a junior detective fingerprint kit. At least I'll preserve the evidence. Then—who knows?

If she had time to rifle Keith's room, snoop in mine and cache a weapon, did she plant a listening device? Video? Would it make sense to record killing me?

I sit at my computer but can't work knowing the blade intended for my back is... behind me.

After logging out of my trading account I lock the computer. Get in the Jeep. In twenty minutes I'm at the Metrocenter, a mall that covers more acres than God originally zoned, but they get away with it because God threw up his hands and said, I guess if I'm not doing anything about the pedophiles, what's a zoning infraction?

I park beside a chick magnet, a Geo Tracker that's dying of radiation poisoning. Paint flaking, discolored. Inside, the dashboard is like a giant broken blister.

Stride to the hobby shop. Balsa planes. Trains. Remote control Hummers.

There, alone on a shelf beside rocket engines. LATENT FINGER-PRINT KIT.

The plastic case looks like the ones the FBI guy carries to the crime scene on TV. The sticker shows the contents: tape, dust, a compact disc with the initials, FBI. Enough cards to lift twenty prints for a mere thirty bucks. I race home, ignoring skanky mall chicks, bad Phoenix drivers, the scorching heat. My legs are jittery. I need a good eight-mile run to settle them. Metabolism is running a little hot.

I slow, swing tight to avoid a black sedan leaving the lot.

Passing the pool it hits me. Black Lexus! Stomp the brake. Reverse, three points, and I'm motoring on Happy Valley.

Left...

The Lexus is a quarter mile ahead, sweeping the bend toward interstate seventeen. Times like this I'm glad I opted for the fourteen mile per gallon 5.8-liter v-8. I flood her veins and she roars.

The Lexus makes an erratic lane change. Rachel saw me pull in, out; knows I'm on her. She takes the onramp to Seventeen south, races past a sign that says the construction speed limit is twenty-five. She's going eighty. I'm touching ninety. My bottom line is simple. She wanted to kill me. I want to kill her. But in society, we make concessions. I'll settle for running her into a concrete barrier and then tying her to my luggage rack.

She merges, swerves into the left lane. A semi slams his brakes. Squeals tires. Other cars weave and swerve. They're going fifty-five and I tap the brakes down to seventy to avoid an old orange Chevy Luv farting eggy white smoke. I swerve to the passing lane, zip ahead around a tractor trailer. The Lexus swings back to the right lane and exits on Pinnacle Peak. I slam the breaks. The Chevy Luv has been tailgating me. He bumps my bumper.

Rachel's gone, and I never saw her license plate.

I'm pissed sixteen shades of red. I'm going to get her fingerprints. Knock on Cal Barrett's door and appeal to his desire for Armageddon. His hatred for the State. The universal desire of all men to stand on the mountain and full-throated roar, I'll take no more!

The Deer Valley exit comes and I loop back to the apartment complex. Race up the stairs and find my door hanging open. A two-thousand-dollar stereo sits within eyeshot of anyone walking by. A collection of four thousand antique CDs. A curved flat screen television the size of some kids' bedrooms.

I enter with caution. Promise myself that by sundown, I will own a firearm and it will never leave my presence. I circle slowly, taking everything in. Nothing appears to be missing, but the kitchen smells like the garbage needs taken out.

I creep to Keith's door. Listen. Slip by, pause outside my room. The door is open. I slide around the corner, low, in case someone is waiting with a fist or a gun. My room is empty. Computer is still locked. But the mattress is upended and the knife is gone.

Paolo calls me while I'm researching Cyman on the Internet. "Two pallets of blocks? What kind of cryptic crap was that?"

"Let's drink a beer."

"I'll be at O'Fallon's 'til they close."

"See you in two hours." I swipe the phone off.

Keith and Katrina are on the couch watching television. She holds a bowl of spaghetti and he makes wonder bread sammiches out of his.

"Make sure you lock up, tonight," I say.

"We always lock up."

"Well, don't forget."

"Right."

"Going to Flag. Be back tomorrow."

Keith's eyebrows go wild. "Oh, wait. I'll walk you out."

We shuffle down the stairs and he lingers at the Jeep. I'm still thinking about Cyman's past, but Keith has an I-need-a-friend look.

"What's on your mind?"

"I don't think the baby is mine."

"Why?"

"She talks in her sleep about you. She saw everything slipping away and set a trap."

"Trap me?"

"No. Your money. I'm going to get a DNA test when the baby's born. If she has it."

"Totally within your rights."

"You're not worried?" he says.

"Not at all."

"It could be yours."

"I doubt it. But finding out I can have kids would be like a paraplegic finding out he can walk. It isn't going to break my heart."

He nods, dazed. "I'm not ready to be a father. The world's too unjust."

"Ahh. Life is hard and then you die. Don't be a candy ass. Every other human being in history has lived in squalor and mortal fear of the local strongman. You live where you get to choose between varieties of fake sugar."

He nods, thinking, not ready to accede.

"You and Katrina would do that baby a favor if you didn't kill it."

I close the door and leave him standing at the curb with his head down.

The road to Flagstaff flies out my rearview. I don't listen to radio, and though my iPod is plugged into the Jeep's stereo, it is off. The wheels thrum. The engine drones. I climb the hill at Bumble Bee thinking about babies. On my left the sun sets at a lookout aptly called Sunset Point. I descend the other side toward the Prescott exit thinking about my people. Assimilation. Humiliation.

Light rain spatters my windshield as I crest the plateau leading into Flagstaff.

Of course, I have almost forfeited the right to think of them as "my people." I am like Jack London's White Fang; I belong to a dispossessed class who begin as one thing and evolve into something else, and endure most of their lives unable to be either. I turn the comparison over in my mind, and wonder if I am not more like London's other dog, Buck? The domestic dog who heard the implacable call of the wild?

What is the Indian, anyway? A gene pool? A tomahawk? A defeated nation? A culture that struggles to adapt, without losing its soul?

A resurgent people?

A fascinating pedigree at a social event? Oh you're *indigenous*. So cool.

Edmund Burke said example is the school of mankind, and they will learn at no other. Ed could have been Blackfoot. We were a conservative people. Tradition. We learned from ourselves, history, earth. Our ancestors live not in some quasi-religious glitchy schlitcky, cross your knees and hum sense. Our ancestors are here.

But me? At ASU I wrote papers about the evils of assimilation on a Macintosh computer. There's only one thing I want. Desert Dog. When I win, I'll be a Blackfoot version of Nietzsche's Overman.

I'll walk between raindrops.

Water trickles across my windshield. I coast into Flagstaff and ease by Northern Arizona University. In town, the rain lets up but the smell lingers—that living, reassuring smell of fresh rain. After swinging below the railroad tracks I count three streets, turn left, and because my ancestors love me, a parking space waits in front of O'Fallon's. Backing in parallel I see Paolo inside the bar, supping on a pitcher of Guinness.

At the entrance I absorb the noise after the neutral sizzle of rain. The smells. Tobacco and deep fried chicken wings. The floor sticks to my sneakers.

Paolo hefts the pitcher and salutes me. He drinks. I drop into the opposite seat. Lean conspiratorially across the table. He belches. Smiles.

"Firewater?" he says, and offers the pitcher.

"Ha! Wow. Just brilliant. Any of the crew around tonight?"

"Marz lined up a sweet gig cooking breakfast at the Holiday Inn off the Williams exit. He starts tomorrow and wants to go in sober." He rolls his eyes. "Yeah; I know."

"Where's Layne?"

"Sedona. Probably grilling a frankfurter about now. He's backpacking the McKenzie trail since those clowns on the news spotted the mountain lion. He took a little fold-up crossbow and tipped the bolts with rattlesnake venom."

"Cliff?"

"L.A. Hand-delivering a karaoke CD to some recording contact he found on the Internet."

"Yeah?"

"So. You need cement blocks and ply? Building a house?"

"You still with Morton Construction?" Paolo does construction, but his heart is in video graphics. Layne too, but more with still life. Trees.

"A miracle. They laid off half the company."

"Von Mises said there's nothing that can stop the collapse that follows a credit expansion."

"You ever notice you quote a lot of white people?"

"Touch not the poisonous firewater that makes wise men turn to fools and robs the spirit of its vision. Tecumseh."

He grins wide, points, "AAAHHH! You know I love you. But that's beer!"

"When you die, you go back naked, like you came."

"Whoa." He drinks from the pitcher. Five seconds. Ten. His eyes swell and his face contorts as he pursues the final swallow. Some things deserve a fellow's best. He lands the empty pitcher on the table and belches.

"What's going on?"

I pull a slip of paper from my pocket and read faint pencil lines. "I need two pallets of cement blocks, eight sheets of plywood, eight four by fours, and enough cement to lay the blocks."

"Anything else?"

"Labor. You and the boys, Sunday night."

"Night?"

I hold his eye. His face glazes. I don't know if it is the Guinness or some deep genetic Italian glee waxing at the prospect of mischief.

He smiles. "Could I go to jail?"

"You could get shot, play your cards right."

"Materials will cost you. Two hundred bucks for the blocks. Close to three for the ply."

"Can't you get some cheap plywood?"

"Not that will hold you."

"It doesn't have to bear any weight."

"Half-inch work?"

"Sure."

"Still, you'll total four hundred, easy."

I open my wallet. Snap five sheets of cheddar and lay them on the table. His eyes follow my wallet.

"Stupid to carry paper like that."

"Maybe." I push the cash to him, sticking a bill in a circle of condensation. "Sunday night."

"Sunday. You spring for the party afterward, I'll round up the boys."

"No substitutes. It has to be us five."

"Of course." He slips four bills in his pocket and waves the other at a barmaid.

I zone out. A woman climbed into my shower and tried to lure me to bed so she could kill me. She returned while I was away and took the knife she'd cached. The only reason my name could have topped her dead pool list was that I spray-painted a Juvenalian barb about a senator on a billboard. And I'm planning another strike? Why?

A dare from a woman whose opinions have the significance of a frog fart.

Is this quest to monkey with electoral politics my boondoggle? Did Katrina strike a chord, and now the project runs on steam bottled up over twenty-seven years of watching—let's be frank—a race of conquerors drive itself to self-indulgent madness?

Paolo is talking at me and I haven't heard a word.

"What?"

"I said, how do you know I'm not going to have a moral problem with your project?"

"Good one."

I stand as a pair of headlights swings into the space that just opened behind my Jeep. Someone else is keeping the Gods happy. "I'm out of here. Sunday, brother."

"Hey," Paolo says. "We got to do the blood brother thing."

"You know that's Hollywood, right?"

"But it's cool."

"In the day of AIDS, you want to swap blood?"

He slips a knife from a sheath that hasn't left his hip in nine years. "It's time."

He asks once a year, always drunk. Some guilty white people want to be Indians. Some want to be black. Others want to be women. Only men with grease or field mud on their hands seem content to be white.

"Study blood diseases." I smack his shoulder.

Paolo's been on blackout drive, his euphemism for being a functional alcoholic, for six years. He gets more insistent about the blood-brother thing each time he mentions it. I bet on Sunday night he'll have a length of twine in his pocket, in case he gets to slice my hand.

The ritual isn't valid. Blood was important to people starving on lichens and mice.

I step outside and the cool, humid air hits me, urges me to sleep in the back of the Jeep with the sunroof cracked. I know a place I can pull off the road, right after the Mund's Park exit.

Circling the Jeep, I see the woman in the vehicle behind hasn't exited her... black Lexus. I stride to the door. She rolls tinted glass down and I see her eyes, mouth, cleavage, and a nine-millimeter pointed at my belly.

She smiles. "Get in the passenger side."

"No luck finding an Indian?"

She flashes teeth.

"If you shoot me from there, you'll have a hole in your door."

"And you'll have a hole in your belly."

I glance up the street. At the bar. Paolo watches, nods. From his angle, he sees her face and gleaming teeth, not the gun.

"You're thinking too long," she says. "Get in the car. I won't shoot you. I promise."

"Yeah, but I've seen you drive. I'd rather die from a bullet."

She slips the nine in a holster that shouldn't fit on her thigh and remain invisible under her skirt. I see the pooch of her panties and I could kick my moralistic ass for not having tagged her when I had the chance.

And then she pulls an I.D. from her bra.

"That can't be comfortable," I say. "If it says 'sex police,' I'm going to be disappointed."

She flips it to me through the window, powers up the glass, and exits the Lexus. Slams the door while I hold the badge under a streetlight. The photo is she and the badge says TFI.

"The gun was to get your attention. I'm one of the good guys." She takes three steps into the street and stops.

"What's TFI?"

"Office of Terrorism and Financial Intelligence. Come on."

"You're kidding me."

"I'm with the Treasury. Let's walk. What I'm about to tell you is secret."

"What you're about to tell me is total crap. Treasury agents—"

"What?"

"Aren't hot. They don't shave bare. They don't Mirandize a guy in the shower while they soap his gonads."

"I didn't Mirandize you. I fondled you. Because I'm trying to recruit you."

Paolo is in the bar making a blow-up face with his mouth against the glass.

"Recruit me? With a knife in my back?"

"I don't know what you're talking about."

Time for me to shut up. Talk to people who plant knives and pull guns, whether they're gangsta or banksta, you get what you deserve.

"Are you ready to listen?" she says.

I sit on a bench and pat the space beside me. She looks left and right and sits. Cagey. The badge looked real, but any ten-year-old with a Mac and a laminator could make one. And who the hell ever heard of the TFI?

"Does the Treasury approve your methods?"

"You mean when I introduced myself in the shower?"

I nod.

"That wasn't a method. That was me."

"Mixing business with pleasure?"

"You're sharp like New York Cheddar."

"You're tits and ass. Like tits and ass. Where is this going?"

So much for waiting on her to say more than she should. I'm too eager to find out what she knows. Is this about Cyman? Have I broken some day-trading rule that the SEC polices with heavy artillery? Have they mistaken any of my money transfers as some kind of laundering or terrorist-financing operation?

"Well, this has been swell." I stand and she grabs my hand with speed that reminds me she somehow down-climbed my building in the buff, wet from the shower. She's a ninja, all right. She's one of those folks, like me, who can catch a dollar bill before it drops its own length. Chuck Yeager, Rachel, and me.

"Stay," she says. "Your country needs you."

I laugh. I can't help it. Full-throated braying. She faces away.

"I'm serious."

"You should have thought about being serious before you stashed a knife under my bed, snuck into my shower, busted back inside to remove the blade, tailed me to Flag, pulled a gun on me, and flashed a lame-ass T-F-I badge. Rachel."

She flinches. "Are you nuts? I tried to seduce you. You freaked out. I ran."

"In the buff."

"Uh, I was naked in the shower. Hello?"

"Why'd you come back today?"

"To warn you." She reads my face, which I consciously paint with yer fulla crap. She stands and offers her hand. "Come."

I walk with her. She angles across the street to a coffee shop. Buys a pair of mochas and claims a computer at the back. She sits on the barstool. Pulls up an Explorer window.

Logs into... the Treasury.

still NINE DAYS to RACE DAY...

All men dream: but not equally. Those who dream
by night in the dusty recesses of their minds wake
in the day to find that it was vanity; but the
dreamers of the day are dangerous men, for they
may act their dream with open eyes to make it possible.

—T.E. Lawrence

I look over her shoulder as she navigates to the Treasury's version
of corporate white pages and types Rachel N. Brenner. Her photo
flashes on the screen. Date of birth, 3/12/85. Blue eyes. One hun-
dred-twenty-five pounds. Mostly curves. She swivels to me.

"So," I say. "What's the TFI's mandate?"

"Financial crime."

"What does the TFI want with me?"

Though the coffee shop is almost deserted, she surveys the emptiness. Closes the browser window, erases the history, cache, cookies,
then uninstalls the browser.

"They're not going to like that."

"They have no choice." She pulls a blackberry from nowhere and fires an email. "I'm telling them to reset my password because I've accessed Treasury's intranet from a real-world computer."

My loins ache to hear truth in her words.

She finishes. "Let's go outside."

We walk. I drop a half-full mocha into the trash. The air is full of mist like the chic cafes in Phoenix dispense from white PVC pipes at the height of the monsoon. Except at night in Flagstaff, it is decidedly cold. We tramp along a deserted sidewalk toward a church. Rachel is silent, maybe waiting for me to say something that will give her an edge. Inform her how to play me. I'm thinking the same, of course. Her beauty is an asset. She might overestimate her strength if I allow her to think it works on me.

I take her hand, swing her face to mine, clutch the small of her back. Kiss her like I paid cash.

She responds tightly at first, then warms. Gets into it. Gasps a breathy moan that I'd buy as unintentional if she hadn't already tried to manipulate me with sex and a gun. No, Rachel, like any woman who connives, knows those whimpers are siren songs to men. I'll trust nothing.

The kiss evolves and in two minutes we've created a new species of desire. She pulls my lower back and somehow rotates her inner thighs out. I feel her pulse—no, mine. We separate and I hold her gaze. My face feels tight—I read her eyes and know the face she beholds is mad, possessed. I want her. I want her to know I want her. I want her to think I've forgotten about the chance of a six-inch blade winding up in my back. Let her proceed like the match is won, and let's see where she stumbles.

"We should go somewhere private," she says. "Where we can talk."

"Talk."

"I was thinking about a motel a couple blocks away."

"Do we walk or drive?" I say.

"Drive."

We return to her car. "Where'd you go to school?" I say.

"George Mason."

"Economics?"

"That's right."

"How did a libertarian school turn you into the Sheriff of Nottingham?"

"It didn't." She slams the door.

I slip into the leather seat. The dashboard glows a citrusy orange, which somehow fits Rachel. The tach flashes to four grand and she swerves to the street. I hang onto the armrest and slap the shoulder restraint across my chest. She burps the tires; the car surges. She whips left, gasses it, another left, a right, and in three minutes she's negotiated the surrender of Flagstaff. We pull into a Day's Inn. She slips a card in the door slot, we get the green light to enter.

She closes the door and embraces me. Pushes me against the wall and slips the security chain through the slot. Her other hand reaches between us, plumbs the gorge between her breasts and releases a clasp that does nothing. Her bra isn't about support—it's about appearing conventional. I nose to her neck and her hair smells like a meadow of flowers. My mind shifts to single-track territory. I need to rattle her, if only to rattle myself. I push her away.

"So you want to recruit me?"

"Talk later," she pants.

"Now."

She sighs. Turns. Reaches for the nine holstered on her thigh, and as I inhale and prepare to drop her with a palm to the base of her skull, she removes the holster and rests it on the dresser. She sits on the edge of the bed. Puts her hands together at her knees and leans forward.

"You paid a thousand dollars to Cal Barrett," she says.

I'm silent.

"Cal Barrett is a terrorist."

"I'm sorry. No."

"We believe Cal Barrett funnels cash to extremist groups throughout the country. Home-grown groups. Are you familiar with money laundering?"

"Uh, gee, Rachel..."

"Money launderers follow distinct steps to insert black market money into the legitimate financial system—"

"Are you saying the one thousand dollars I paid him was black market money?"

"No. We don't know where his money comes from. With most of them, it's drugs, or cigarettes, or guns. Fencing stolen merchandise. With Barrett, we don't know. One of the ways we find criminals is to search out the middle-level transaction. After a launderer inserts money into the financial system, he'll move it around and try to create a complicated paper trail. The more transactions the better. Everything from buying cash value life insurance to sending and receiving a thousand wires from bank to bank. That's how we isolated Barrett. We've got computers that do nothing but apply algorithms to financial records from all the major institutions. Barrett's engaged in so many red-flag transactions, 'layering'—we call it—that we had to investigate him. The problem is we can't get close on the ground. He's coy, financially. He's even worse, in person. We can't get an asset in."

I recall an Internet news story I read about him a month ago. "Former guerilla soldier. Everything is about security."

"You admire him."

"I want to win his race."

"We need someone who can get inside. He likes you."

"He doesn't know me."

"He knows more about you than I do," she says. "And I know a lot."

"We met once. He doesn't know me. He's psychotic, by the way."

"You mean when he said a woman running Apple would signal the End Times?"

"...Right..." I say. "How...?"

"Remote listening devices and telescopic microphones. At any given moment, we have three agents snooping around his ranch. We picked up your conversation. We even know what he was playing on his iPod."

"Of course you'll tell me."

"Baby, It's Cold Outside. Over and over. He sang along for six miles."

"So if you heard that conversation, you know I haven't had any interaction with him."

"Ah, but he knows you. Why do you think he was out there, that day, when you just happened to be running? Could it be that you've run at the same time every day for the last month?"

"Coincidence?"

"Hardly. He knew you'd seek him. We're trying to figure out what he told you." She levels her head. "And why you wanted to talk to him."

"You taped it. You know what he told me."

"But we don't know what he really said. He was communicating with you."

"If he used a code, I missed it. I thought he was a nut."

She says something I miss. Instead, I remember thinking shortly after meeting him that we're tumbling toward tyranny. And... when Apple makes an implantable iPod, I'm busting outta jail.

"We need you to infiltrate his organization. Find out where his money comes from. Put us on the right track."

I'm reluctant to turn my back to her, but I have to think. I face the sink built into the far wall and watch her in the mirror. She's facing the television. It's hard to think when you could be moments away from poking Jessica Rabbit.

I expected Cyman to show up in the conversation, but unless Rachel is sixteen times smarter than me, this discussion has nothing to do with the billboard.

"Well?" she says. "In or out?"

"Are you investigating me?"

"Only insofar as necessary to understand Barrett's interest in you."

"What is his interest in me? What does he know? What's he done?"

"He may be trying to kill you. He may be trying to recruit you. He's like Colonel Kurtz in Apocalypse Now. We know he's nuts. We just want to get him before he grabs the machete. He's formed the roots of a militia, but we don't know where they are. He moves money, but it disappears into legitimate cash. His money shows up and then disappears and all we have is the middle. We don't know the source or the destination."

"Maybe he doesn't think you have the right to know. Besides..." I finally turn to her. "Treasury can touch anybody."

"You think? We've got superhero agents working for Elmer Fudd execs. Our mainframes speak Cobol to computers that *hablo* FORTRAN. Treasury is more spaced out than the White House. More dysfunctional than Congress."

"I can't quite get my brain around it," I say. "You're talking like Treasury is the third branch of government."

She smirks.

I'm quiet.

"That's everything," she says.

"Tell me again, why you joined me in the shower."

"Sex."

"I've heard good things about it," I admit.

She stands. "We have a shower, here."

"I don't know if I can get it up for a chick who might kill me."

"What are you talking about?"

"Come on. The knife."

"What knife?"

"The one under my mattress, back home. The one you planted before dropping in on my shower."

"I don't know what you're talking about."

"The one that disappeared, right after I saw you leaving my place the second time."

She turns and touches her index finger to her chin. "He *is* trying to kill you…"

"Oh, come on!"

"Barrett! Don't you see?"

"You're out of your gourd."

"He's recruited your girlfriend."

"Ex."

"You nailed her the night you dumped her. That creates ambiguity."

"How did you know—"

She tilts her head. Lowers her brow.

"She snuck into my bed," I say. "Look, I dumped her. What's she have to do with Barrett?"

"How long have you known her?"

"A year and a half."

"What'd she do before you met her?"

"She was a stripper."

"What else?"

"She sold drugs."

"What else?"

"There's more?"

"You really don't know?" Rachel hesitates. "She's Mossad."

"*The* Mossad. The baddest intelligence agency on the planet Mossad?"

"That's right."

My guts are having a hard time holding it together. My lungs are set to explode. My thighs prepare for a come-to-Jesus smackdown. "She. Isn't. Jewish!"

Rachel is unperturbed. "Not now. But think of her. Can you see her nose?"

"This is ridiculous. You want to take a shower, or what?"

"A shower. But you need a gun. Either your girlfriend or Barrett is trying to kill you. Get a gun." Her face slackens as she thinks. "Oh, this is brilliant. This is good."

"What?"

"I'm going to put you in touch with just the right person. Tomorrow morning, there's a vagrant that sleeps on the bench by Babbitt's. It's because of the way the sun hits from eight to eleven. You go to him and ask him to help you score some weed."

"Pot?" I step to her. Unbutton the top of her blouse.

"That's right. Give him money. Don't stop until he tells you about a punk at the Exxon out toward Crater Mountain. Go to him, and ask where you can get a gun."

"Convoluted, don't you think?"

Her blouse hangs open. I tug the tails from her skirt.

"We have to lay the groundwork. You can't just go to a dealer and say give me a gun."

"Why?" I unzip the side of her skirt. It falls and she steps forward.

"He'd shoot you."

"Why don't I go to the gun shop?" I reach to her back. Slip my fingers beneath elastic.

"You want to risk the background check will take days?"

"A well-regulated militia being necessary to the security of a free state," I tug the fabric over her hips, "the right of the people to keep and bear arms shall not be infringed."

"Tell that to Congress."

I toss her to the bed.

It's a strange walk back to the Jeep. Because I'm alive.

I did what I should have done at my apartment when I met her. I kept her away from the side of the mattress, her purse, any place she might have hidden a knife, gun, ink pen, or cannoli. I reflect on life as I walk in the cold drizzle, how nice it is to be alive and young. And to be with someone who is alive and young. And animal. Lust. Nothing like cold air. Nothing like that vacant, empty, totally wasted weakness in your loins, suggesting to the deeper self that if suddenly life ended, you did your part. The swimmers have swum.

I unlock the Jeep and sit. Glance through the glass at O'Fallon's. Paolo sits with a half-full pitcher of Guinness, his rear end half-slid off his chair. He studies the foam as if the pattern contains a map to riches. Concerned for the five hundred bucks I put in his pocket, I enter the bar. Squeak across the hardwood floor and slip into a seat opposite him.

"You okay?"

He lifts his head. "Life is bad."

"Don't be a dumbass. Let me take you home."

"I live upstairs."

"I know. Time for bed."

He nods, slowly. "You didn't introduce me to your girl."

"That's because I just met her."

"Dude," he says. Lifts his pitcher and chugs. Eructs. "She's hot."

"Let's get you out of here." I reach but he ignores me.

"I'm fine."

"You don't look fine."

"Blackout drive. I'll get there."

"You going to remember Sunday night?"

"I love you, man." He pulls the knife from his hip. "Blood brothers," he says.

The woman behind the bar nudges a man.

"Put the blade away, before you get your ass thrown out."

The man walks along the bar to the end and turns the corner toward us.

"Come on, Paolo." I take his elbow and he points the knife at me. His eyes have an edge like the blade that wiggles a few inches from my nose. The burly guy slinks behind Paolo, and I stay him with a look.

I back a few inches away, double-slap Paolo's wrist. The knife clatters across the floor. I pick it up, then Paolo.

I leave him in his room, passed out.

I need to think. South of Flagstaff on Seventeen I take the Mund's Park exit.

About five miles back a dirt road, past the golf course and the always-fashionable A-frame cabins, I cross the ditch at the first opportunity and park in the forest with my grill pointed for a quick getaway. I open the sunroof, spread a self-inflating sleeping mat and bag in the Jeep's cargo bay.

Small animals move over the needles and leaves. An easygoing breeze, the kind you'd like to make friends with on a warm day, wavers branches. Stars fight through the blackness for a perch on the sky.

Katrina is Mossad? Might as well tell me she's the president.

I don't know what game Rachel plays, who she works for, what her agenda is. I have no reason to believe anything. She's like a stock chart, making promises that suddenly reverse. One minute she's a woman in black leather, or nothing at all, ready to slink to the bedroom and blow your... mind. One minute, hell. Every minute.

And when she's holding a nine-millimeter at your belly, her eye glints like Madeleine Stowe. She's tough as nails, defiant. The kind of woman it's hard to pry from the mind, especially with the forest whispering lonely poetry.

I slip into my sleeping bag, zip it half way. These thoughts are residual weakness: sentimentality born of having been a writhing, sweaty, shuddering mess a half an hour ago, and being alone, among the stars, animals, breeze, and trees, now. Knowing she's in her bed, cuddled against a pillow, thinking whatever game-thoughts she thinks to keep her crazy game sane.

I can't be with a woman and not think about destiny. The point of it all. Winding up on a rocking chair in sixty years, clasping arthritic hands and giggling at tumbleweeds. Every chick I poke earns full consideration; I'm adamant about that. I weigh Rachel's merits and demerits: Beautiful, witty, steely, crafty, investigated me, pulled a gun on me, planted a knife ...

Rachel. I don't think you're the one.

It takes three minutes to drain beside a tree. Shivering, I return to the vehicle. Pull a protein bar and a toothbrush from the backpack permanently cached behind the driver's seat.

Sit on the hood.

I promised I'd get a firearm, and after last night, I'm prepared to keep my word. If Rachel speaks truth there's trouble around the bend. Barrett, Rachel, Katrina, and Paolo—who to trust? None. Not to mention the senator with the Suburban and the ninja turret gunner. The senator, to whom I'm about to land a body blow.

Von Clausewitz said don't fight your enemy so long that he learns your M.O. It is early for such concern. But still, the senator will quickly discern from attack # 2 that his challenger, Hock, has nothing to do with anything. Hock ought to be prosecuted for oxygen theft. Cyman will understand a rogue adventurer has taken Hock's cause.

What will he do to prevent further attacks? The political equivalent of carpet-bombing. He will use the power of his office to find me and silence me. He will call his buddies in the IRS, Treasury, Rachel. He'll trap me in a corner and the sunroof will open. A big-ass gun will telescope above the roof. That's the way Cyman plays politics. To win.

So I've got to hit him hard and fast. The billboard was cutesy, a girl-punch. He felt it like he'd feel a frog's kiss. Unremarkable, except it's a kiss from a frog. With the next jab, I need to drive nose cartilage square into the brain. Knock him down for good.

Figuratively.

But I don't know enough to bring him down. It is axiomatic that because he is a thirty-year senator, he's dirty. But I don't know the dirt, and I can't deliver the deathblow until I do.

Barrett. Will I infiltrate his organization? He might deserve a warning. I drive back into Flagstaff. Saunter cool into a gun shop.

"I'll take this one."

"Two forms of I.D."

"I.D.?"

"That a problem?"

"Well, let's see. We have a second amendment—"

"Don't start. Law's the law."

"You read Aristotle. Good. Humor me. I have the I.D. But hear me out. The Second Amendment says—"

"An Indian's gonna lecture a gun store owner on the Second Amendment?"

"That's right—are you with me?"

"Yeah, I'm with you."

"The final safeguard against tyranny is the citizens' ability to band together and overthrow their government. Right?"

"Yeah, whatever."

"Government and citizens are forever at odds. Right? We want rights. Government wants power. They're mutually exclusive. Opposites. You want me to fork over my I.D. so the other side knows I'm interested in defending myself against them. Does that make sense?"

"Two forms of I.D." he says.

"Giddyup. How the hell did your race defeat mine?"

I rest my driver's license and social security card on the glass counter, above a coffin-handled bowie knife.

"Let me see that Springfield. The .45."

He puts it in my hand. Shiny, like someone took a steel brush to the bluing. I snap the action and it's ragged out. Flopping it back and forth, the parts rattle.

"Need something tighter than that."

"Puts you in a different price range."

"And one other thing. I need to do this friend to friend. You know? I'm not waiting three days."

"Can't do it. Friend."

"Yeah, but you have a buddy somewhere, right?" I look around the store. The man browsing the targets is a likely candidate. First, no one browses targets. Second, he's a bum. Kind of rough. The sort of fellow one would suspect of disenfranchising the federal government from its excise.

"I don't know what you're talking about."

"That's him, right?"

"You some kind of cop?"

The hippies aren't out yet, but there's always a man or two asleep behind a dumpster, passed out, wrapped in newspapers. If you talk to them they'll confess they're trying to avoid the Trump Administration. Probe for details, they'll tell you about the secret detention camps in Oklahoma—where Blackwater keeps indigents in labor camps reminiscent of Auschwitz.

Cars pass. I consider Rachel's logic. Why hippies? Find drugs, you'll find guns. Rachel said to see the guy on the bench, and he'd refer me to another person, and the other person would refer me to the guy with the gun. The circuitous route would prevent me getting shot. If I had come to something as dim as this through my own thought process... I would have done it. Life is messy. Things don't make sense from one moment to the next, and the most improbable route looks like a sure thing in the rearview mirror. Sometimes the only reason you cross the finish line is because you kept trying different tacks along the way. Success is about how many times you pick yourself up of the ground, and all that. But her mapping out visiting the hippie then the drug dealer then the arms dealer beforehand—and me being gullible enough to follow her directions—that exhibits the worst kind of hubris. I sense a trap, but shucks, I'll punch my way out.

There's a burnout on a bench, asleep. From a few feet away his hair calls to mind a fishnet with trapped seaweed. Smells about the same. His tennis shoe is open at the toes. His piggies are a crusty black and blue that suggests he is not long for this world.

I tap his foot with my shoe and watch to make sure none of his toes falls off. His eyes open slowly. I'm not sure I'm looking at sentient intelligence until he blinks twice, clears his throat.

"Wha?"

"I need your help."

"My help?" He smiles. Throws his legs off the bench and pivots to a seated position. I can almost hear his bones creak. "Do tell," he says.

"My guy is in Phoenix and I need a dime bag."

"A who?"

"Dime bag. You know. Ganja."

"Wha?"

This isn't working. I pitch him a twenty for his trouble. 'Thanks, bud."

"Exxon, top of the hill."

He nods north, and I peel him another. His eyes warm. His shoulders sit square, his chin retracts with dignity. He has information, and

I pay him for it. Our exchange elevates my skuzzy friend. We could be media execs paying for polling data, or some chemical companies' research and development liaisons, buying and selling the newest secrets. It's none of my business how the homeless maintain self-esteem, but I'd rather be the guy buying information than the one slipping him a single without condescending to look at him.

"Need a name."

'Talk to Spanky," he says.

"That's his name? He isn't going to punch me, right?"

He grunts. I'm driving in two minutes. The road rides like a mishmash of potholes and cobble, though it is merely eroded blacktop. I fill my tank at the self-serve and watch the half-asleep man inside. The machine fails to print a receipt. I step inside.

"Can I get a receipt?"

He taps a couple of keys in slow motion.

"You Spanky?"

His eyelids half-cover his eyes. He nods. A twitch originates at his temple and jerks half his face to the left. His nametag says Henry. Probably has a surname like Spankovich or Spankinatra. It could be as bad as Spanker.

"Friend of yours told me you could square me away."

"I dunno, man."

I look around the store. Over my shoulder. "You want to burn a cigarette on the step a minute?"

He closes the cash register. Pulls a hard deck from his breast pocket. Opens it. The front, middle smoke is upside down, for luck. He takes the one next to it and follows me outside. I open my wallet, retrieve a twenty.

"I need a name."

"Who?"

"I need a piece. Today. And not some ragged-out revolver from Pancho Villa days."

He nods. Buries his fingers to the second knuckle in too-tight jeans pockets. He looks back and forth, up and down the road, into the store and then across the road to the trees. Looks skyward for satellites.

"You got any more money? Cuz I could really use a little more, and if I'm going to sell out a friend, and all, you know…"

"I'm not a cop. I'm a customer. Stop smoking dope before you lose your last three brain cells. C'mon. Help me out."

"Whoa."

I slip the twenty to his hand. "I don't think it's worth more than twenty."

"You can find him at Milkin's—the fender shop. Diagonal from Schlotzsky's, way back off the road, you know?"

"What's his name?"

"I dunno." He says. Reads my frustration. "Seriously. I don't know. No one does. He's got pony tails like that country guy."

"Willie Nelson?"

"Yeah."

I rap his shoulder. "Appreciate it."

I'm back in the Jeep, bracing against the road. The chick I made the two-backed beast with last night, who may be trying to kill me, wants me to infiltrate an organization headed by a man who, although kooky, by outward appearances has his mess together. I sit at a red light. Drift forward with another twenty mind-wandering folks. Cal Barrett heading a militia seems in keeping with the reputation he's established through interviews with online magazines. But the government's only evidence is that they can't see what he's doing. This is not evidence. Some hide their activities from law enforcement because they are criminals. Others hide their activities because it is nobody's business. You know—the right to privacy the Supreme Court found waiting patiently to be discovered in an emanation from a penumbra of the Constitution? Rachel's accusations don't yet overrule my concept of Cal

Barrett as a man who—within his rights—finds government too dangerous to welcome to his hearth.

Maybe Cal Barrett has absolved himself of government. A one-man secession. He can do what he wants out there, for all I care. A man who listens to Baby It's Cold Outside in the September desert can't be all-bad.

I wonder if he likes the Dean Martin version.

I see Schlotzsky's on the left and turn right. Weave around a few cars, cross a parking lot that seems more junkyard than the zoning Nazis probably want, and stop at Milkin's Auto Body. Clouds of orange dust billow across the pavement like a rock concert's dry ice haze. A man in black denim, a wife-beater, and hi top sneakers holds an oscillating sander to a fender. He's wearing a Soviet-era single canister gas mask picked up from Jim's Army Navy up the street. His braided hair falls past his shoulder blades. He won't see me until I tap him on the shoulder.

I hesitate.

He's working on a '72 Fastback with more putty than metal. Science-minded motor heads could study plate tectonics on this gem. He'll blow his wad on cherry bombs, chrome rims and eighteen-inch drag slicks, then spend his last eight bucks on grey primer. Then the first time he hits a hundred and ten and drives over a nickel-size rock, the body will disintegrate into a cloud of dust.

I circle the work in progress. He glances. I nod as if stirred by his artistry. His head synchronizes with mine, and we nod together, briefly communicating as only men near cars can.

Except everything I convey is false.

Nietzsche said dissembling was the original form of communication. One primitive sees another and puffs up to warn his challenger off. A man inflates his chest in response to the same brain chemicals that animated the frightened monkey. We are all born liars and have to learn truth. Because the real world will kick your ass if you don't meet it prepared to do likewise, and a good lie can spare bloodshed. Thus spake Nietzsche, who is also dead.

He turns the sander off and rests it on the putty. Slips the gas mask to the top of his head.

"Sweet," I say.

"Yeah. Man." He leans, looks beyond me. Queries me with his eyes.

"Friend of yours said you was the man to see. Friend at the Exxon, north of town, top of the hill."

"That so?"

"Looking for a forty-five. Stopping power." For the first time I see his wife-beater t-shirt has a faded decal on the front.

My new friend wears a Desert Dog t-shirt. The unmistakable pit bull with a chain coiled around his neck, looped around and around for weight, with the visual effect of stretching his neck like one of those crazy African women with the gold rings elongating their necks like giraffes'.

The dog has a big # 2 on his chest. Willie Nelson, here, came in second.

When I look up from the logo, his eyes are on mine. He's waiting for a secret verb or handshake, a Masonic twitch to let him know if I merely dig the decal—or if I'm a member of the clandestine clique.

"Running this year?" I say.

Side-to-side headshake. "Never seen you there."

"First year."

He waits. His face says, how long are you going to waste my time?

"You know Cal?"

He squints. Nods. "You?"

"Ran into him on the ranch a couple days ago. He said the funniest thing, you know."

"What'd he say was so funny?" Willie steps toward me. His shoulders are bulbous like a surgeon has implanted grapefruits under the skin. He's got a steady air about him and I wonder if he doesn't do more than buff paint and peddle pistols for a living.

I wonder if like Katrina, Rachel, and Barrett, he is something entirely different than he seems.

"Cal was listening to an iPod. He said when they make them small enough to implant under the skin, it's the End Times."

"You a religious man?"

"I am Blackfoot."

"Barrett sent you to me?"

"Nah. The pothead at Exxon. Barrett's just the happy coincidence that keeps you and me civil."

"And what you want?"

"Glock."

"Smith and Wesson .45. Seven hundred."

"It shoot?"

"Poly frame but shoots like steel. Twenty-four ounces. Five-pound trigger that feels like three. Perfect balance."

"Seven hundred?"

"You want it for five, do the background check at Mo's."

"You got it here?"

He studies me. "Bad guys waiting around the corner?"

"I got a lot of work to do. Where do we do this?"

"Meet me here in an hour with cash." He lifts his sander.

EIGHT DAYS until RACE DAY

Use humility to make them haughty.

Sun Tzu

I
t is not lost on me that Rachel machinated our introduction. Willie
is not what Willie seems.

I pause behind my steering wheel before starting the engine.
I've got cash in my pocket but Willie has to go somewhere to get his
gun. I feel his stare. I need to micturate, but this arms dealer could be a
lucky break. If he's wearing the second-place Desert Dog t-shirt, he
might know who earned the winner's tee, and where he went.

Or do the winners go to Flagstaff and work at an auto body shop?
Or back to their stockbroker jobs? Plumbing jobs? Cable installers.
MBA programs. A horde of tough guys waiting for the call, one if by
land, two if by sea. When they see the lanterns in the steeple, they lift
a canvas bag from the closet, assemble in the shadows and fight under
Cal Barrett's steely leadership.

My mind wanders many barren subjects, seeking gold.

Maybe Cal Barrett's a genius. One thing I've wondered—idle, vain thoughts—is what the biggest challenge facing a modern revolutionary would be. Superior weaponry of the U.S. Government? The fact we live in a police state? The piss poor quality of the average man's education—can't name Abe Lincoln's Treasury Secretary or even Jefferson's second Vice President?

I draw the conclusion that the biggest impediment would be finding men fit enough to fight. Look at the office rats around you, right now. Could any lace up a pair of jump boots and run ten miles? Strap sixty pounds to his back and trek a mountain trail with four thousand feet of vertical gain? Live on stale crackers and roaches for a week? No. The average American sits an extra ten minutes in his car waiting on a parking space to avoid walking thirty feet. He gets inside and waddles to a motorized cart. Complains he has a gland problem.

Young people are fit and athletic, sure. But the mules who carry the nation's debt, who would lend legitimacy to an uprising—the men who would band together, organize, lead, are in their late thirties, forties, fifties. They may grow pissed, but more likely, they grow tired.

And the few who might otherwise be up for overthrowing old regimes have flamed after decoys like War For Oil, Global Warming, Ferguson and the War on Women—whatever sleight of hand it takes to keep one half of the population perennially pissed at the other. If I ruled the world, I would ensure the men who could overthrow me were too fat to walk the Wal-Mart parking lot, or were otherwise deployed chasing a fairy like their carbon footprint.

There is one man running the world. He has undermined his natural enemies. He is a genius. Opposing him is another madman, genius, destroyer. Cal Barrett. Why? Because he's building an army of supermen, one at a time.

Desert Dog.

I twist the ignition and drive from the lot. Schlotzsky's is empty. I pull onto the road, circle a block and park in a residential area behind the auto shop. Watch through maples and chain-link fences.

Willie leaves the shop and follows a footpath through a runoff area littered with plastic bottles and hubcaps. He crosses into the neighborhood a hundred yards away, trots to a house with sooty white siding and a collection of rusted bicycles on the front porch. He's inside maybe three minutes and emerges empty handed. Probably tucked the nose of my new Smith and Wesson in the crack of his ass. He retraces the route back to the body shop.

I wait five minutes. Exit. Mosey along the sidewalk, cross the street. Pass the sooty house. The lights are off. I cross the lawn like I'm supposed to be here—Nietzsche's dissembling, in action. I listen at a side window. Peer into the kitchen. Circle to the back window. There's a small pennant stuck to the glass with plastic suction cups. A yellow Gadsden flag bearing a coiled snake and the words, *Don't Tread on Me.*

I feel my heart beat and somehow, my sense of self seems centered an inch behind my eyes. I twist the handle. The door is locked. I push, creating a tiny aperture between door and jamb, insert a Capital One and wonder if there is poetic significance that I'm breaking into a man's sanctum with a credit card.

Quietly, I push open the door. Samurai-step inside. Willie is a neat-freak. The blender base has no residual protein powder. The dishes are segregated in the drying rack as if he washed plates, cups, bowls, in groups. Largest first, smallest last.

The living room has a television and a massive weight-lifting contraption with six workout stations built into one frame, drawing off the same iron-tablet weights in the center. He's mounted old Bose 301 speakers in the top corners of the walls, each aimed at the machine in the center of the room.

I check the bench press. Three hundred and fifty pounds.

I don't know if some deep, ancestral knowledge bubbles to the surface or whether I've just become a candy ass, but I want out of this house, now. Maybe he's coming back because he forgot the firing pin or a magazine. Maybe he saw my Jeep. Maybe the whole thing was bait. Rachel, who the hell knows, could have—

Footfalls on the front porch. I dart down the hall as a key grinds into the lock. Slip into a bedroom, then a closet, then behind clothes, then shrivel as small and short as I can, then will my skin black. Mind over matter.

Footsteps in the hallway, into this bedroom. Pause. Too long. A bureau drawer slides open and from the turkey-gobbler bark, I'd guess it's a humidity-swollen runner. If fate ever provides an above-board opportunity for me to tell the guy, I'll suggest he take a little sand paper and a bar of soap to it.

The room is silent and I wonder if I have somehow missed his leaving. What is he doing, that he makes no noise, whatever? Listening? Smelling? Studying his biceps in the wall mirror? Or does he stalk the closet?

I wait. Envision the room I glimpsed before finding shelter. A curtained window faces the road. To the left is a desk with topographical maps. Wall hooks support rock climbing equipment, hexes and cams, ropes, shoes, a crap ton of daisy-chained webbing. The bed is a single, and the blanket is O.D. green wool.

The drawer closes and footsteps diminish. The front door slams and the house trembles. The walls carry the tinkle of Willie resetting the dead bolt.

That means he's on the inside...

I hesitate. He may have eased back to the bedroom entrance. He may have a pistol barrel pointed at his closet. He may—

Swing the closet door open. Clothes slide along the rack. I smile at Willie and...

"I have some explaining to do."

He doesn't bother to hold a gun on me. When a man bench presses three fifty and sees a wiry Indian, his confidence waxes. I'll cave in his temples before he grunts and frowns, but I read genuine curiosity on his face.

"Freaking loco," he says.

"Partly."

He steps backward, clearing my exit. I stumble on a boot, lurch, catch support on the jamb. He leans on his desk, crumpling maps.

"You know Cal Barrett," I say. "I need to know more about him."

"Wrong answer." Willie reaches behind his back and his hand returns with my Smith and Wesson. Straight from his sweaty ass crack.

"Hold on, amigo. I got to get a message to him. He's in for trouble with the Feds."

"That so?" He points at my head.

I've read folks with above average reflexes can dodge a pistol bullet, but I doubt five feet gives me enough time. "Listen. I got a Treasury agent trying to recruit me who thinks I know Barrett. Some sub-agency no one's ever heard of. Wants me to infiltrate his group. If I do, she's going to know about it. I need someone else to get word to him."

"Why do you care? Why not give the Feds what they want?"

I gamble. "I know Barrett's mission. I'm simpatico, brother. When I saw your tee, I had to know if you were inside or outside."

"Inside or outside?"

"He recruits from Desert Dog. Some of the winners make it, some don't. Just because you've got the t-shirt, doesn't mean you've been selected. I had to get in the house and see."

He lowers the Smith and Wesson. "So what do these Feds want you to find out?"

"They think he's a terrorist. Can you get word to him?"

He tilts his head, neither agreeing nor disagreeing. His brow gives away nothing. "Lift your shirt."

I expose my midriff.

"Turn."

I spin.

"Seven hundred."

I pull my wallet. Count off seven bills. He flips the .45 from grip to barrel and hands it to me. "It's loaded," he says.

I pass him the bills. "You got a box of bullets laying around?"

He pulls the dresser drawer open. It sticks.

"You might sand that down and rub some soap on it," I say. "It won't sound like a turkey trying to get laid."

I hit the highway south toward Phoenix. The sun crashes through my sunroof and warms my face and I remember wisdom memorized when I was young and weak. Unsure of my skills, in the way of all eleven-year-old boys. Ponca Chief White Eagle said,

When you are in doubt, be still, and wait; when doubt no longer exists for you, then go forward with courage. So long as mists envelop you, be still; be still until the sunlight pours through and dispels the mists—as it surely will. Then act with courage.

I take 89A toward Oak Creek Canyon and Sedona.

The Smith & Wesson is on the seat beside me. Horace Smith and Daniel Wesson started the odyssey that resulted in my .45 in 1852. In a hundred fifty years we've gone from the first rim fire cartridge pistols to missiles that shoot down missiles.

I consider the state of the Second Amendment, for a moment, as Cal Barrett might. Would he consider it relevant? Technology has advanced the standing army's weaponry so far that for practical purposes the right to keep and bear ought to be redrafted to the right to hunt deer and mount Sharps rifles over knurled mantles—provided of course they have a trigger lock.

A man like Cal Barrett would say the balance is gone. When state of the art weapons were flintlock and cannon, government feared its citizens.

What does government fear now?

Nothing.

My take is that the Second Amendment is good to have around, but if things ever go so far you have to wage war on your government, you're probably going to break some laws anyway. What's a couple gun laws on top of sedition? They hang you harder?

Besides, if any group ever launches a successful overthrow, they won't do it with rifles. The weaponization of the desktop computer and the cell phone will make missiles and nuclear bombs irrelevant.

I look at my new .45.

Beyond the Oak Creek Canyon overlook the road begins a series of switchbacks as it descends to the bottom of the canyon, then follows Oak Creek between the steep walls. A few miles from the top, the gorge widens. Campgrounds and restaurants sprout in clumps like fungus on the underside of a rotted log. Driving with traffic, I watch the terrain, pass an old road I've never seen that looks like it was built for wagon wheels. It runs parallel for a hundred yards before rejoining 89A.

I continue through Sedona on 179 until I reach Bell Rock and park at a pull-off where a pavilion shelters a giant historic map. A machine dispenses Red Rock passes—parking permits—that amount to a tax on tourists looking at big red rocks. It isn't enough that sightseers spend their dough buying Made in China Navajo Indian trinkets and Indonesian Mexican blankets. Don't worry, Sedona provides valuable services with your money. They crisscross the land with trails so people who can't walk the Walmart parking lot can at least get far enough into the wilderness to throw a snickers wrapper to the cactus spines.

I divest myself of a golden braid of urine behind the pavilion and finished, keep driving.

While I'm not wondering at the insanity of teenage Honda Civic drivers, I muse about how Rachel said Barrett's money is disappearing. The way she said it doesn't make sense—just popping on and off the radar. Once money is laundered, it is in the legitimate financial world. It is traceable. That's the whole point of laundering money—to get ill-gotten cash into legitimate circulation so no one questions why you're buying a million-dollar house and paying with a truckload of crinkled singles. If Barrett is inserting dirty money into the financial system, Treasury knows where it goes once its in the system. Period.

I descend the final slope to the Valley of the Sun. Ahead, a blanket of smog protects wary Phoenicians from skin cancer.

Either Rachel is lying because she thinks I won't understand, or she doesn't want me to know what Barrett is really up to. What target could be bad enough to get her to enlist a skeptical civilian?

Alert for a black Lexus, I swing into my covered parking space. My eyes linger at the pool, partly visible through the hedges and fence. Women lounge. I step out of the Jeep and a girl I've seen several times wiggles her fingers at me. Hmmm. Treasury?

Bound up the stairs and enter the apartment. Keith sits on the couch with a slightly stoned look.

"Hello." I walk past him, down the hall, and hear his steps follow. I open my bedroom door and he grabs my arm.

"Solomon!" he says.

I turn. Something in my Blackfoot nature rebels at opening a door without looking inside.

"We have to talk," he says.

"Sure." I spin back to the open door. Katrina's things have invaded, have displaced the peaceful locals. Her clothes cover my bed. Some have crawled to the bureau and I catch them stealing into drawers. Some have raided my closet, deposed shirts and jeans, and hang proudly in the center. Her baubles are on my dresser. Her makeup kit is on my desk—where my keyboard usually sits.

"We had a fight," Keith says.

"In here?"

"She was in a hurry to get her stuff out of my room, and wasn't very neat about putting it back in yours."

"What the hell is wrong with you?"

"What?"

"I ended—damn! You got onions the size of snow peas."

I dig a packing box from behind a file cabinet in my closet and expand it. Fold and interlock the flaps. Hurl a leopard patterned bra and panty combo inside. "Why hasn't she just gone?"

"She doesn't have her old place anymore."

"What?"

"They kicked her out. That's why she's got so much crap here. Half of it is still in my room."

The sign out front—the one I saw the other day—comes to mind. Rent at $416.

"Here's the deal, Keith. You don't pay rent. Katrina doesn't pay rent. This place is in my name. You and I go way back, and—"

"Don't start—"

"I've always treated you like a brother. But it's over. I'm packing all her stuff. I'm going to the office, and I'm going to lease a second apartment. I'm going to pay the deposit and the first month's rent. And I'm going to haul all her crap to the new apartment. And then I'm going to ask you nicely to haul all of yours to *your* new apartment."

"And if I don't?"

"I'll murder you in your sleep."

I cast underwear, bras with blue paint, jeans, shorts, halter-tops into the box. Shoes. More than I've ever seen her wear. When the box is almost full, Keith vanishes.

On a whim, I lift the mattress. There's a knife waiting for me.

Still EIGHT DAYS 'til RACE DAY

"All machines have their friction; and possibly this does enough good to counterbalance the evil. At any rate, it is a great evil to make a stir about it. But when the friction comes to have its machine, and oppression and robbery are organized, I say, let us not have such a machine any longer."

Henry David Thoreau

I drive to the hardware, buy a lock and change the deadbolt on the front door. The building manager won't know for a while. I'm kiting information.

It is time to run.

Desert dog is important because I must win. Now Rachel—the Treasury—an organization I would prefer to see scaled back to 1789 dimensions, wants me to risk my Desert Dog tee to spy on the founder and infiltrate his group. Let's say I get cute and make a misstep, and Barrett figures out I'm working against him. Something not beyond possibility, since I just told Willie Nelson about Rachel. How am I going to run the man's race after that?

When you focus on one thing to the exclusion of all else... when you set a physical goal and work unbendingly toward it... you don't stop on a dime.

When your sense of self is linked to an objective, your worth hinges on achieving it. You can't flip to a new currency without figuring the exchange rate. You can't say, okay, I'll measure my success as a human being by how many dandelions I mow, or how many flies I swat. It can't be artificial. Meaning is in short supply. Relevance is so easily undermined in this nihilist's paradise that I can't vanquish the idea I'm being asked to jeopardize the only thing that is truly important.

If I do, then what? Study Derrida again? Mope for a few years that nothing means anything? Humans assign value whether their targets merit it or not. You persuade yourself things are important when deep down you know they aren't. And when miracle of miracles you find a project that consumes you, that you throw yourself into with every passion you can muster... something that makes you loathe to retire at night and energized at five a.m. the next morning—even though it is futile—try to swap that passion for mowing dandelions or swatting flies.

Relevance makes things matter. Relevance to identity. Maybe it's the only thing that matters.

I don't merely love the physical abuse that promises to elevate me above being a shadow of my ancestors. It isn't competitiveness, the desire to prove to these desert late-comers that a man born of the land, who embraces and loves it, eats cactus flowers for breakfast and needles for lunch, will receive from the desert the strength to outdo those who would pillage and pollute it. It is not that.

It is that in a world where nothing matters, *feeling* something is a high-octane mental exercise.

I run. My feet pound the ground like jackhammers and the recoil jars loose thoughts that cling to my mind like barnacles.

We create and sustain relevance by belief alone. When enough men pretend, we forget we pretend. We enter the trance, every one of us a zombie convinced the fabric of belief is reality.

When something produces a strong illusion you give your life to sustain it because the alternative to the illusion is the reality of nothing.

What would a calculator do if it realized math wasn't real? It would say I was designed for something, by God. You say there is no math, but I've got nothing else. It would calculate still, regardless, and eventually forget that anyone suggested such an idiotic thing as math isn't real.

I run a different route this time, following a blacktop road that leads to a reservoir the size of a football field, surrounded with razor wire. The roof is flat, corrugated metal. There are many such reservoirs located around the city, invariably located above the population. Some mountaintop is bulldozed flat and, because of the elevation, the facility is invisible to all who live around it. Curious places.

My knees reject running, but a few hundred yards into the uphill route, they no longer protest. The stiffness in my back, exacerbated by falling with a snake in my heel, and worsened by Rachel's bumping beauty, gets stiffer still. I stop and bend over at my waist for a minute before continuing.

From the top I see the valley, the aqueduct, and Barrett's ranch on the near side, closer to the interstate. His giant fenced yard of rocks and cactus. The guard posts, like outposts on the Great Wall of China, except manned by cameras. Barrett has stables and garages. It isn't a house so much as a compound. The house is tremendous, of the hacienda type, but with a three-story tower at the far end. It is a desert green color, like some rocks have a dusty, faint shade yearning to be emerald but ordained to be dirty foam. It blends.

Is this where the winners go?

The place is deserted. Next time I'll bring binoculars. A camera may be trained on me right now. I wave, a smallish, trite gesture. Stretch my back. Touch the earth. The earth is real. Don't need a convention of believers to sustain that. Maybe that is why it is so easy to believe in Desert Dog. It is an expression of the living. It is a rock rolling downhill. Water flowing over a ledge and gurgling in a pool. Grass waving in a breeze. Things doing what they are suited to do, and justified in the action by the action.

Crowfoot said, what is life? It is the flash of a firefly in the night. It is the breath of a buffalo in the wintertime. It is the little shadow which runs across the grass and loses itself in the sunset.

I lean, stretch my stomach. Turn right. There, beside my Jeep, partially obscured by the crazy modern-architecture shade-thing—what would normally be a gazebo, but instead is some miscreant art student's self-expression—is a black Suburban.

I picture a turret. Envision the glitter of metal under the vehicle's tinted sunroof. The most up to date version of the Gatling gun, maybe they call it Vulcan, these days. I don't know it's there, under the sunroof. But with Treasury chasing me, and my mind fresh from exercises exploring Cal Barrett's worldview, it's a comfortable daydream to imagine a machine gun or rocket launcher built into the Suburban. I visualize diving into rocks for cover.

Distance and tinted glass prevent identifying the form sitting behind the wheel. Maybe he waits for me to return; maybe his buddy is working on the undercarriage of my Jeep.

Rachel said she and her TFI agents had listening posts, and they heard my conversation with Barrett. I doubt they would have been so conspicuous as to use a Black Suburban. Plus, the Suburban was stopped at the billboard I painted. What would Treasury care about a billboard?

I run.

In the distance, a band of coyotes chirrup and howl. Their voices are beautiful if not terrifying. They sing mournful notes that seem to say times are tough, can you help a brother out?

The trail zig-zags to a plateau above me and circles behind the lot where the Suburban waits. A dry streambed will allow me to approach, unseen, within twenty meters. On top of the mesa I see thirty miles in any direction. I can't fathom giving up Desert Dog to make TFI chick Rachel happy. I am on top of the world. Wind in my hair. Sun on my back. Sweat on my skin. Feet working like they ought to, synapses firing, dancing over rocks, cactus quills, gravel. I sprint. One, two, three hundred yards, glide over gravel and cactus, jumping sideways, sliding, leaping. At bottom I circle, hit the dry streambed and tear a new record back to the lot. It's been all of six minutes. I crouch behind juniper and marvel at the strength of my heart.

No one hides under my vehicle. The Suburban sits; a shadow occupies the driver seat. Moving left I see the window is down and a cigarette-wielding hand dangles near the side mirror.

Her finger flicks ash. She looks better in a Lexus.

But Rachel doesn't smoke. Or have that much hair on her arms.

I stand, approach. The vehicle starts and the reverse lights flash. The wheel twists. I approach on the side, my hands open and loose at my side.

A skinny man with an effeminate mustache looks at me from the driver seat as the Suburban backs. Stops. Rolls forward. The man's forehead is high and wide, his chin narrow. Niles Crane, but much less masculine.

"What do you want," I say.

He ignores me. The engine roars. The muffler has a throaty rattle that sounds simultaneously tinny. Tires crush gravel against blacktop and the vehicle's shadow darkens my shins.

He's got a globe-style compass on the dash. I can't think of the appropriate judgment.

Tires squeal; the Suburban rocks around a corner and is gone. I look, and turn, and think. Was his goal harassment?

Of me, or Barrett?

My run was shorter than usual. There's a nine-mile loop around the back of the hill that is always fun, but I'm curious to see more of Barrett's compound, a half mile away. I trot, then walk. With Rachel's group lingering in the hillside, I don't want a face-to-face with anyone, least of all, Cal Barrett.

I'll just get close enough to get a feel for the organization.

The guard towers and high walls easily call to mind images of men in bandanas brandishing Chilean Mausers or AR-15s. Plywood covers the gate, dissected so a half sheet will retract with each side. A message is scrawled across the face. I squint as I approach the gate, feeling like the coke-bottle kid at the eye exam. With heat-wavering air between the words and me, reading is impossible.

I weigh my inherent respect for a warrior who doesn't truck with government against Treasury's accusation that he finances terrorism. All war is atrocity, but the victor assigns the labels. The truth that decides the matter is whether the atrocity that caused the terror was justified, and it is impossible to be anything other than subjective about it. I'm kosher with nukes on Hiroshima and Nagasaki. Not kosher with a nuke on Phoenix. Maybe Washington. I guess it would depend on whether the wind is blowing toward the Atlantic that day.

The question is not whether Cal Barrett wages war, but what I would do in his shoes?

States, of course, are free to designate other states enemies and murder their citizens. Common defense against such marauders provides the deepest motivation for individuals to band into polities—and the strongest justification when these polities take human life. Some country attacks, neighbor joins neighbor and drives the invader's ass back across the line. Not just legit. Honorable.

But today, an enemy doesn't have to arise from a different country.

And if we've got to shred The Constitution to save it, why that's in The Constitution too.

Cal Barrett being labeled a terrorist is likely an example of perfervid and hortatory oration. Rachel propagandizes on a Goebbels scale, hoping her accusation tenders enough visceral emotion to outweigh my desire for proof. Government dissembling relies on key words that tweak social prejudices. Fears. Same principle that powers word-association tests, and the implacable hunger of politicians for poll-tested sound bites. Rachel was hoping the word terrorism would make me eager. I would, after all, hate to be terrorized.

I'm a few yards from the gate and the letters resolve:

The Fourth Amendment: The right of the people to be secure in their persons, houses, papers, and effects, against unreasonable searches and seizures, shall not be violated, and no Warrants shall issue, but upon probable cause, supported by Oath or affirmation, and particularly describing the place to be searched, and the persons or things to be seized. So piss off.

Does Barrett anticipate media gathered outside his compound? I dig the cocksurety. Braggadocio. The in-your-face element that almost instructs law enforcement to seek a warrant on the assumption he must be hiding something. Like the old joke about beating your wife even though you don't know why, on the premise that she does.

Anticipating Waco II, Barrett has installed an electric wire along the top of the wall, presumably charged by an on-site generator. On the left and right of the gate, two towers rise twenty feet above the dusty drive and appear to be modeled after prison watch posts. Three hundred and sixty degree views from superior elevation. A camera silently swivels to me. I point at the sign. Thumbs up. Return to the Jeep.

Back at the apartment, Katrina has discovered she doesn't live in my place anymore. She sits at the door. Her eyes follow me as I climb the concrete stairs. She springs to her feet.

"My key doesn't work," she says.

"I thought Keith would have told you."

"Told me what?"

"You and he have an apartment on the other side of building F. One-twenty-seven B. Bottom floor, facing the wall between us and Safeway."

"What's that mean?"

"It means that a few days ago, when I asked you to move your belongings, I was serious."

"But Keith said I could live here."

"Wasn't his to give."

"You're kicking us out? Just like that?"

"Just like that. Call it the nexus of two converging factors. One, you irritate the living hell out of me. Two, you've been sleeping with my roommate for two years."

She smiles. Katrina has a talent. Boobs don't have muscles, but she can make hers levitate. Girls without jobs have time to figure out how to animate their boobs. Katrina's struggle against her V-cut top, and if they ever learn teamwork, they'll be free.

"But don't you want to have sex?"

"Don't you feel, even the smallest bit, like a prostitute?"

"Solomon."

"You should get a job. A different job. Be productive. You'll feel better."

"You know I can't do that."

"I know you make excuses—"

"I can't think very well..."

"—since you dropped out of school. And I know that until you take responsibility—"

"They did it to me!"

"Responsibility for how—"

"THEY DID IT TO ME!"

"For how you live afterward, you'll be nothing but a wasted opportunity."

"You said you'd take care of me!"

"I tried to make you understand—"

"I can't. I don't want to. I can't hold it together. I'm not responsible for what happened."

"Yes you are. It's the only way you'll ever be entitled to defend yourself. No responsibility, no authority."

Her lip quivers. Maybe it's time to rip gauze and tape from the wound.

"I didn't make six men wait for me in a parking lot," she says.

I nod.

"I didn't make them drag me into a van."

I touch her shoulder. She shrinks.

"I didn't make them..." she chokes on a sob. Tears stream.

She doesn't need to continue. I happened along that night. Heard her wails from the van over the bass of the gangsta noise they had turned up so loud it made my pants vibrate. I tried the driver's door and it was locked. The van rocked from side to side. I thought it was one crazy-big dude inside, only one.

I open the rear door and the dome light pops on. They're in back and it's a mini movie set. Six guys, all in the buck, and Katrina.

She screams when she can.

The guy with the camera swings to me and I take him out. The camera lands on a seat and films me delivering surgical missiles of chi on the other five. I use whatever I can against them, mostly the sides of my hands and the heel of my right foot. Three are hospitalized, one is dead, and the other two are released from the E.R. once their plaster casts set.

I was free that night. The videotape caught everything. Incidentally, I saw the tape on You Tube a few months ago. A cop must have burned a backup of the evidence.

According to film, in some societies, when you save a person's life, that person becomes your servant. Katrina has never been particularly moral, from what I have unearthed of her past, but she has barnacled herself to me with some quasi-inverse-indebtedness. I stopped pitying her, but can't overcome her. I can't kick her to the curb because I feel guilt—simply by association—with every human that has a dick and has done something wrong with it.

Some shrinks will tell you that victims of sexual violence can go two ways. The saner ones build a wall and avoid intimacy. It takes a lot of love to climb the wall. The wall never comes down.

The others go a different way. They cultivate violent appetites, always seeking to obtain the power of the ones who tormented them. This is the child of an abuser who later abuses his own. The rape victim who sportscrews her way through an entire fraternity, spreading Aids to all.

This is Katrina.

Tears roll down her face and drip on her boobs, which rest like lazy honeydews under broad green leaves.

"I didn't make them gang rape me," she finally chokes out.

"No, but you sold them drugs and stripped for their money. Being responsible doesn't mean that you relieve evil people of culpability. It only means you recognize your choices have consequences. It's convicting, but it frees you."

I speak slowly, trying to make polysyllabic words tender. I must sound intoxicated with myself. All she wants is a hug and for me to take her inside, and tell her she doesn't have to think. She can throw a frozen dinner in the oven and survival is guaranteed.

She wipes her face. "Is this a pep talk? When you're kicking me out?"

"No. This is just the way I think. I wish you thought this way. You're squandering the only chance you get."

"Chance? At what?"

"Think about this. Your entire life is a series of yesterdays. Was any worth a damn?"

She braces against the guardrail and I imagine she throws herself over—but it is only two stories to the ground. She'd break her leg, maybe.

Her chin quivers, and goes white and dimply. She exhales. Smiles. "One last poke?"

"I paid your first month's rent. You can use me as a reference for a job. I may know a few people who are looking for help. But you've got to move on."

She smiles like she's still learning how. "Okay. Yeah," she says. She turns.

"Hey?" I say.

"Uh-huh?"

"Are you Mossad?"

She blinks twice, smiles with teeth. "You know me. I'm Katrina."

She rattles down the stairs and I can't tell if she has been profoundly affected by my humble attempt at truth and grace, or if she has merely digested that I'm no longer her meal ticket.

My apartment is so clean it looks empty. The pillows on the sofa are gone. Didn't realize I didn't own any. The sneakers that guarded the closet, so I would have to battle them to get a broom or a trash bag, are gone. The cheese grater has vanished from beside the toaster on the counter, and the toaster is gone too. Remaining, however, is the oppressive certainty that I could have handled it better.

There is no perfect place or time to make a stand. The point of rebellion, when Camus says the rebel realizes he prefers any outcome above continuing the situation he rejects, can happen any time. It will not be opportune or convenient. If it was, it would be change, not revolution.

Everything leads my thoughts to Cal Barrett. Has he reached his moment of rebellion?

I'm in my room, eyeballing the mattress. Beneath should be the incredible disappearing knife. Through tempestuous change, the fingerprint kit I bought is still beside my computer desk.

I shift to the bed. Reach for the mattress. Lift. The knife is present.

I shove the mattress from the box springs. It drops halfway and hangs with sordid determination, like a drunken woman whose torso has fallen from the sofa, but her legs point skyward. I land the case on the box spring and flip the latches. I dust the blade and handle, but nothing sticks. The other side is equally reluctant to give up a print.

I question whether you-know-me-I'm-Katrina is sharp enough to wipe a blade for prints.

Occam's razor, if I understand it, requires me to conclude Rachel has planted the knife. It is the only elegant solution.

I'll have to ask her.

FIVE DAYS 'til RACE DAY

Freedom had been hunted round the globe; reason
was considered as rebellion; and the slavery of
fear had made men afraid to think. But such is the
irresistible nature of truth, that all it asks, and all
it wants, is the liberty of appearing.

Thomas Paine

I usually don't answer the door when I'm trading, but having com-
manded Katrina to go forth and prosper, I half hoped the plaintiff
at my door would be she, asking for help completing a college ad-
missions form, or better, a job application.

Instead, Rachel smiles, ducks under my arm into the living room.

"Very tidy," she says. "Report your progress."

"Why are you here?"

"Let's get something on the table. Our professional relationship requires you to recognize my authority. That means when I ask for a progress report, you oblige."

"This brings up so many areas of disagreement. Where should we start?"

"You went to Barrett's gate. Why didn't you make contact?"

"I'm not playing your game."

"I don't think you've fully registered what Treasury agent with a gun means—"

"I went to the gate. No one answered."

"Did you knock?"

"I waved at the camera."

"Do you think Cal Barrett responds to *cute*?"

"I wasn't looking for a response. I wanted to read the sign. Have you read it?"

"On the gate—of course."

"Did you recognize it? I mean, the source material?"

Her look warns me.

"I wonder if you have a good enough reason to pursue him. You haven't shown it to me."

"You have to trust me. As an extension of a highly-revered founding institution of the United States government."

"Yeah. I—hmmm."

"We have cause for suspicion. We know he's laundering money."

"You said that. But once money is laundered, it is easy to track. It's the source of the dirty money that's generally the problem. Why is it the reverse, for you?"

"I can't divulge—"

"You're the government."

"Don't start that egalitarian drivel. I'm Treasury. Responsible for the world's reserve currency. You have to find out what Barrett's doing."

"I don't care what he's doing."

"I don't believe that. I've heard you talk to him. And I've seen your room. You're in awe of him. Why else would you be training for his race, and fail to answer your country's call?"

"What about my room?"

"You're a secessionist."

"I didn't realize that."

She clenches her jaw and whatever smidge of friendliness she's allowed to dwell there disappears.

"You're going to help me. The IRS can be hell auditing a day trader. All those transactions to reconcile, one by one. And the SEC can be a royal pain in the ass in how they regulate trading accounts. They put you on a Patriot Act watch list, that wouldn't be too good for your livelihood."

I stare.

"Am I communicating with you? Let me be blunt. Your trading accounts? TFI has its finger on the delete key. This is national security."

I sit. She can destroy me. When she's not scaling walls or seducing spies, she's liquidating wealth.

The sad reality is, I know she can do it. Most stockholders don't realize how tenuous their ownership claim is. They control nothing. They can prove nothing. Instead of paper certificates, their ownership is an electronic ledger entry. If the right people get together and decide your assets no longer exist, or ought to be transferred to a government holding account, it's done with a few keystrokes.

"So first you try sex," I say. "Then you appeal to patriotism. Then you try sex again. Now you've progressed to blackmail. Is that what this is? Coercion, I guess."

"Whatever it takes."

She spins. Exits. No time to parse the exact measure of threat she has delivered. Feed her information about Cal Barrett, or face financial extinction.

Survival dictates I consider caving. Another side of me urges noncompliance. This side rejects government interference in anything I am competent to sort myself. Such as wearing seat belts, or withholding patronage from restaurants that are smoke friendly. Or trading unsettled cash in my IRA. Instinctively, I want to call after Rachel as she takes the concrete stairs two at a time, and tell her to go to hell, and take the Treasury with her.

Instead I stand inside my apartment and wonder why my life seems to be coming unglued the more entangled with government it becomes.

I sit at my computer and jiggle the mouse. I've been stopped out of RIMM at a minor loss. I pop a new browser window and coast to Real Clear Politics and check the poll numbers. Cyman has expanded his lead to thirty-six points.

My effort tonight will not overcome Hock's inveterate stupidity.

But if I am going to avoid losing everything I own, I'll have to continue a plan that will get me closer to Willie—by taking one more shot at Cyman.

Behind me, a mantle of smog grays the city. A column of smoke rises into a red Phoenix sunset and I think of hell. Traffic eases after the Cave Creek exit. The speed limit increases.

Someday I'm going to leave the city for good. Build a cabin in the mountains. I'll trade a few hours each morning, smoke ceremonial ganja on the porch the rest of the day. Amazon will deliver my groceries and everything else I need by drone. I'll find a woman and make babies.

On my right, a plain of green grass stretches across a hundred thousand acres of emptiness. Every year when the heat and drought of summer comes, the grass turns into yellow tinder and patiently waits for a bolt of lightning. A brown mountain range borders my left. I cut right at the Sedona exit.

The air is cooler, even though it is mid-afternoon. The reddish dirt sprouts pale, maladapted bushes that suffer silently as succulent cacti taunt them. A mile from the highway, a string of cars presses close behind me, anxious to see the famous Red Rocks.

Past Sedona, deep into Oak Creek Canyon, I pull over and let the cars behind me pass. When the road is clear of witnesses, I pull onto a logging trail I've highlighted on a contour map. Out of habit, I hang a Red Rock Pass from my rearview. If arrested for crimes against the state, at least I won't be ticketed for parking illegally. I don a camouflage hunting outfit, complete with hat, gloves, and mask. Grab pole diggers with handles wrapped in the same camouflage tape as my turkey gun, and start digging.

The air is humid and rich with the mysterious scent of green things. Oak Creek gurgles below and mosquitoes hover in jagged flight paths, each moment taking them deeper into the carbon dioxide-rich jet stream of my exhalations. I stand with my back to the road facing a two-tone rock wall, where the red of Sedona gives way to the white of the north canyon. Both colors meet and are perfectly framed in this narrow glade. The beauty is several magnitudes beyond speech, and I stop every few minutes to grin.

Tourists will soon begin their nonstop bidirectional flow along the scenic route. I drive the pole diggers into a tangle of roots. A bead of sweat finds a gap between my shoulder blades and shirt, and hides there. I pace twenty yards and dig the second hole, happy to be farther from the road and masked by vegetation.

I have time before the boys join me. Opportunity. I drive to Flagstaff and swing into the body shop where Willie Nelson works. He looks up from a Chevy S-10, rapidly ignores me.

"Yo Willie!"

He keeps sanding. His shoulders look like giant ball joints for equip‑ment that would normally be made of metal and exist in a factory that smells of oil and ozone. I come to his side and he cants his head, pulls his mask over his face, and while the oscillating sander buzzes free and spits a cloud of fine dust into the air, yells "No returns!"

I shake my head and squint. He squints. I squint, but exaggeratedly.

"This would be easier in English than Bonobo," I say.

He switches the sander off. "What?"

"I got a job for you."

"What kind of job?"

"Security. A side thing, one night only."

"When?"

"Now. All you got to do is sit on the curb with a cell phone, a mile from the action."

He glares; his distrust nears perfection. "Why?"

"I'm going to break a law. One of the obscure ones. It's not covered by the Ten Commandments. I pay well. Hundred bucks an hour."

He shakes his head. "I only bust laws that shouldn't be laws."

"Very reasonable. This falls more in the mischief category. If the state had a sense of humor, it wouldn't be a crime."

He waits. I explain.

"Cyman?" He says. "I'm in."

He dumps his sander into a bin, peels the mask from his crown and smacks dust from his thighs.

"Wait a minute." He grabs a piece from a toolbox, checks the breech. "Let's go."

"I don't think you'll need that."

"You don't get to decide."

"Any chance your name is Willie?" I say.

"Bernard."

"Go by Bernie, do you?"

"I go by Bernard."

The road passes in silence. The boys are waiting ahead a few miles at a small state park.

"What tribe?" he says.

"Blackfoot."

"Ah," he says. "You got all kinds of reasons for mischief."

"If insult was stored in a person's genes, sure."

"It is. People on our side can't afford to forget. Because *their* money doesn't forget. They pass it from one generation to the next, and all their status and secrets with it. All the rules. Vested authority. It's like in the Old Testament, when they had an entire tribe of priests. They're so special, they think it comes from God."

It strikes me odd that Bernard is a street intellectual who finds a parallel between Washington and the Levites. And also odd that the patter the "ruling class" designs to appeal to him—the Civil Religion, the patriotic claptrap on the radio, the pandering drivel they condense into poll-tested promises, cradle to grave, give us your money we'll give you simulated prosperity—doesn't appeal to him.

He has rejected not just the edifice of artificiality, but its scaffold as well:

(You don't have to think about anything. And the fact you'll never be more than a couch potato—you'll learn to love it. We have some really-super-interesting programming for you called "reality television" and we feature schmucks you can laugh at. You don't have to achieve anything to feel superior. You don't have to build a better mousetrap, work like a dog, save a dime, invest wisely—we'll simulate your success by supplying an idiot to look down on. Just fix your eyes on the tube and pay your taxes.)

I digress.

"They dicked with your people, but good," he says.

I wait through generic commiseration. Non-Indians like to care. Like metropolitan whites imitate blacks, or emasculated men empathize with women. No one knows the other side, but it is important to honor the other's victimization.

"January twenty third," he says.

My ears perk.

"Eighteen-seventy. Massacre."

"What do you know about the Piegans?"

"I know that the power elite recognize terrorism because of its own dealings. I know the chief came out waving a white flag, that the military was at the wrong camp, and butchered two hundred women and children. And I know the rest froze to death marching to a fort."

"You expect me to exact retribution?"

"For that, and a thousand other offenses."

"Well, I'm assimilated. American. Blackfoot to me means the same as Italian to you."

He snorts. "Right."

We pass Oak Creek Canyon lookout and begin the winding descent. I downshift to third and then second and let the engine keep us safe and slow. My headlights become useful as we descend a thousand feet into wooded gloom.

"What kind of work do you do for Cal Barrett?" I say.

His eyes betray a glimmer of surprise, then harden.

"Keep Barrett at arm's length. If he asks a favor, do it. If he says something funny, laugh. If he makes it clear he doesn't like you, make sure you're never on the same side of the street. In fact, if Cal Barrett don't like you, it's better for you if you don't exist at all."

"You work for him directly? Or just heard things."

"Privacy is important in my line of work. Discretion, you know? But I will tell you this. Barrett's on the right side of things. And the fact that you know who he is—nothing's an accident."

I pull to the side of the road. "You got a cell phone?"

He taps his pocket. We load our numbers in each other's contacts. "I'm going live at eleven. Call me if any northbound traffic comes. If you can block the road with a log or something, it would be great. Anything to give me more time to work."

"What work?"

"I'll be a half mile up the road laying cement blocks."

The new moon has yet to rise above the canyon walls. Black stillness amplifies the bubbling creek. The steep rock and ponderosa canopy mimic being inside a gigantic, breezy cave. As planned, the boys wait for me in two trucks.

Each is loaded with a pallet of cement blocks, pre-cut ends, four bags of Quickwall, five sheets of plywood, painted with slogans, and five four-by-fours. A bag of half-inch bolts rests on the passenger floor.

I ride a short way with Marz.

"Where's the turnoff?" he says.

I point. We chug along. He spots where I broke the vegetation and stops the truck. I hop out and confer with Cliff, Paolo, and Layne in the second vehicle.

"This is time sensitive. Work fast; we're done in a half hour. Got your phone?"

"Got it." Layne says. "Let's make this happen."

Layne has my map, but basically, he's driving a hundred yards to where I emerged from the logging road earlier, and relocated an orange pylon from nearby construction.

I jog back to Marz's truck and ground guide him into the woods.

"Let's go."

Marz jumps from the cab, grabs a plastic bucket from the bed and heads to the creek with his flashlight. I place a battery-powered lantern on the ground, pull on leather gloves and transfer cement blocks to the tailgate. When it will hold no more, I drop to the ground and line the blocks across the road. Marz returns sloshing a bucket of water on his pant legs. He pulls a mixing tray from the truck, dumps a bag of Quick-wall, adds water.

The fiberglass blend adheres to both sides of a cement block wall and eliminates the need for mortar between the blocks. The walls are stronger than those built with traditional mortar, but I'm more attracted by its speed of application.

I have three rows stacked before the mix is ready. Marz trowels the surface-bonding cement on the wall as I swing blocks from the truck. Sweat drips from my brow and I glance south, behind me, to the likely source of traffic.

"This is going fast," Marz says.

"Two minutes and I'll be out of blocks."

Marz slaps a trowel of mix on the wall and works it until the application is an eighth inch thick. He cuts another blade of the cement, applies it, mixes a second bag. I finish laying the blocks as Marz resumes trowel work and shifts to the wall's back side. His progress slows; the wall forces him to trot around for mix.

I fetch another bucket of water and mix the last two bags of Quick-wall. The ground is soggy and the leaves are limp with yesterday's rain.

Paolo works on the logging road. His red flashlight is like the distant monocle of a schizophrenic monster. He mounts pre-drilled four-by-fours into the holes I dug earlier. I charged him to stand them, align bolt holes, tamp dirt, and hang plywood. Each sheet has a number on the back, and they go up in order.

My cell phone vibrates. Writ across the blue backlit face: "Willie."

"Yeah?" The static is loud and the signal dies. I close the phone.

"We may have trouble," I say. Marz slaps a trowel of cement to the blocks. The phone vibrates again.

"Yeah?"

"Cop coming your way! He'll be on you in a minute!"

I close the phone. "Cops!"

Headlights flash. Marz ducks behind the wall. "So much for your lookout," he says.

I stand in the high-beams. The car pulls forward and lurid blue and red lights flash.

"Don't dig out your thermometer," Marz says. "We're cooked."

Yet I hear him continue with another application of mix. The police car door opens, slams shut. A wiry silhouette crosses in front, hand on holster. I keep my hands in view, but not up. Not like I'm a bad guy doing something wrong.

"You can tell your partner to come around where I can see him."

The voice is familiar. I hesitate. We face each other, me in the light, and the lawman cloaked in a swirling police-state-effulgence of red, white, and blue.

"May as well do as he says," I say.

Marz joins me in front of the block wall. He rubs wet cement from his hands.

"Beautiful night, officer," I say. *Where have I heard his voice?* "Nice and cool."

"It is at that. I hear it's gonna rain by noon tomorrow."

"We could use it."

"Looks like you're building some sort of barricade here."

"We are."

"What for?"

"We want to block the road."

"Uh-huh."

I place his voice. It belongs to the kid everyone picked on in high school. He'd just sit there and take it. I wasn't usually a bully—but Stu was such a mild, inviting target, even relative weaklings like myself worked out our aggressions on him. Once on a school trip to a dairy farm, I taunted him. Realizing his worst response was a bleat, I punched his head. I was maybe eight years old; I didn't yet know how to punch. The damage was to his ego. I hit him until he'd slunk so low in the bus seat that when he looked up at me it was like hitting a dog with big round eyes, and I quit. Disgusted with shame. Then and now.

"Stu?"

"Yeah."

"It's good to see you."

"I guess you're still a liar, Solomon Bull."

The years have stretched Stu into a wiry man. He stands with poise. A weapon is on his hip. Sweat drops from my nose and it tickles. I am trained to overcome weapons, but I don't know if I want to commit to the consequences of kicking a cop's ass.

I nod at him, friendly. The situation prohibits sudden moves. The forest towers damp and oppressive; neutral until one of us makes use of it. The police car lights glare angrily, but my heart stands strong with me before the bulwark.

"You have anything to do with that billboard in Phoenix last week?" he says.

"Although I was delighted to see it, I don't know anything about it."

"Well, who ever done it riled things up. Cyman is Arizona's own. Circles far above mine call it sedition. Got cops on the lookout for suspicious activity all over the state. Suspicious like a cement block wall across 89A."

He pauses. Waves to the fresh tire tracks through the grass at the shoulder. "So you're running a detour, huh?"

"That's the sum of it."

He walks to the five-foot wall, slides his hand across the top. "Using that new cement. Is that working good?" He exposes his face to light for the first time.

"Goes on pretty quick," I say. "Gets its strength from fiberglass."

"That so? Yeah. Well. I wish I'd a busted you doing something else." He is silent. Winces, sighs, shakes his head. He closes his eyes in a slow-motion blink, and I see my chance. The part of me that works at a sub-cellular level, that moves before the brain says jump, is already in motion... but before my muscles get the command I stand down.

Stu is capitulating.

"This wall's gonna be knocked down by nine a.m., at the latest," he says. "And nothing you say is gonna get that other clown elected over that son of a bitch, Cyman. It's like he don't even want to win."

"But a couple thousand cars will drive the forest road in the mean-time. And they'll understand."

Stu releases a deep breath and rocks from side to side. "I'm on my way home. As of, let's see, ten forty-five p.m., you wasn't here."

"Uh. Yeah, Officer Stu."

"I hope that forest road is clear."

"It's open."

"Take it easy." Stu gets into his vehicle. The lights stop flashing, and he courteously flicks his headlamps to low beams. He swerves to the forest road, spits gravel, leaves Marz and I with urgent doubts to discuss.

"That'll test your pucker power."

"I may have had an accident."

I call Cliff on the cell. "There's a cop coming through. Get out of sight and let him pass."

"We're already in the trees."

"He won't give you any trouble. How close are you to being finished?"

"Ten minutes. We're putting the cement on the second side of the wall. Are we busted?"

"I don't know. Not yet. Finish up when he's gone."

Marz and I watch taillights disappear on the detour route. Vegetation rustles. Paolo emerges rubbing his neck. "Mosquitoes." He faces me, searching for an explanation. "I take it you knew him?" Paolo says.

"As a small child I was unfriendly toward him. Regrettably."

"We're cooked."

"So the question is whether he's going home to bed, or whether he's calling for backup," I say.

"Backup. He was surprised and didn't know what to do. Didn't know if there was more of us, so he played it cool. I bet he's a half-mile up the road making a radio call."

"Do we try to finish?" Marz says.

"Try? Get the spray paint. Put 'DETOUR' and an arrow on the wall. Paolo, I'll help you with the four by fours. I'll get Cliff and Layne to paint their wall, then start bolting the plywood."

"Let's go!" Paolo grabs a pair of four by fours on the truck.

"Cliff?" I say into the phone.

"Yeah."

"Has he passed?"

"Just now."

"Stop with the cement. Paint the detour arrow, then start bolting plywood. Finger tight. We'll meet you in the middle."

"How much time do we have?"

"None." I close the phone with one hand as the other swipes the bag of bolts from the passenger side. I balance the first sheet of plywood on my back and join Paolo. He tamps dirt around the second four by four. I position the plywood, slam a bolt through the hole, lift it into place and run back to the truck for the next.

Marz has painted DETOUR, rinsed the mixing tray, and struggles to lift it to the truck.

"You done?"

"Gimme a hand."

We toss the tray into the bed and Marz hops in after it.

I drive through weeds. The undergrowth gives way to rutted forest floor. I turn my headlamps on—the risk is small and the need urgent. The lights bounce from the sign Paolo has just finished bolting.

Government for sale: Prices Reduced! Ask for Cyman!

I find the next pair of postholes and stop with the headlights blazing over our work area. Paolo drags a pole from the bed and erects it before I return with the next sheet of plywood. Marz follows with a second. They tamp earth while I secure the sign.

I drive forward. Ahead, through tree limbs and leaves, diffracted headlights mark where Cliff and Layne assemble the same signs in reverse order. We repeat the process. The third sign is up. The fourth. We meet Cliff and Layne after the fifth.

"Everything done on your side?"

"Done," Layne says.

"We should find a place out of sight to wait. We meet a parade of cops while we're driving out, we've got nowhere to go," I say.

"Let's go back to the park where we met up. The parking lot is set back off the road," Layne says.

Cliff throws his puke green 1981 Chevy into reverse and, spinning wheels, races a hundred yards back to the cement wall.

I follow with Marz. At the park, I pull a cooler from behind the seat and pass a beer to each. "That was some good work tonight."

"Damn but I'd love to see what happens," Paolo says, and throws back a flask.

"Do we have a plausible reason for being here with Quickwall on our clothes and empty pallets in the trucks?" Layne says.

"I could sleep right now," Marz says.

"I don't think anyone is coming," I say. "Of all the improbable, incogitable brain-benders, is it possible that cop just went home?"

"In cog what?"

"I'll be back in a few minutes," I say. "Let's meet uphill. Cliff—you know where we had the Easter party a couple years back?"

"Right."

"See you there in twenty minutes."

They're swigging beer as I leave to fetch Bernard. Badass Bernard has some 'splainin' to do. A hundred bucks to leave me hanging—not going to happen. I pull over where I dropped him off, but he absent. A drag mark across the road shoulder leads to a massive, half-rotted log barricading oncoming traffic. The log is half a cabin. Bernard is an ox.

A hand taps the passenger glass and the door swings open. Bernard lurches in. I'm relieved to see him, since this whole operation was about earning a little more trust.

"Did you have enough time?" he says.

"Cop's lights were in my face when I hung up."

"Damn." He shakes his head and as the dome light glows down to nothing, he bends to the lower seat well.

"What happened, Bernard?"

He is quiet. "I let you down."

"How'd it play?"

"I drug the log to the road. When the headlights came, I ducked in the woods."

"Yeah."

He hesitates. "I twisted my ankle. I couldn't call until the cop got around the log, and I couldn't move until he left. When he was gone, I couldn't get cell coverage. I stumbled down the streambed a hundred yards and finally caught a cell tower."

I turn on the dome light. "Let's see."

His ankle looks like a rotten pumpkin with veins.

"I won't take your money," he says.

"Course you will. If I don't pay you, the next time I come around, you say, no."

"Next time?"

"I want to talk with you about Barrett."

"Nothing more to say, amigo."

Not a good time to press him. "Do you have insurance through the body shop?"

"No."

"Then I'll take you to the emergency room."

"No. I'm cool."

I pass him a beer from the cooler. He takes the can, considers it silently as I kill the light and put the Jeep in gear.

"Thanks," he says, and places the beer against his ankle.

FOUR DAYS 'til RACE DAY

The character inherent in the American people has done all that has been accomplished; and it would have done somewhat more, if the government had not sometimes got in its way.

Henry David Thoreau

I watch television. The news flashes to the first plywood sign—again. Channel fifteen has cycled through all the slogans twice. The news reporterette gravely intones that the cement block walls were torn down before more than a few hundred cars were forced on the detour. Rudge links to a local blog with a slideshow of the signs.

I want to celebrate, but criminals get caught when they take their bag of blue money to the bar and buy the house a round.

My front door rattles like it's making out with a fist.

I check the peephole and Keith's face has been turned into a Christmas tree ornament. He combs his hair with his fingers and raps again. I swing open the door.

"Solomon! Turn on your television!"

I wave him in.

"Did you do that?"

"What?"

"That!" He points.

Clearly. I smile.

"It better work," he says.

"How's Katrina?"

"Depressed. She took all her money—about two hundred bucks—and bought lottery tickets. She's broke."

"Are you serious?"

"Heart attack."

"Who was it that said lotteries are a tax on the stupid?"

"They fund valuable programs."

"They're like eighth-grade bullies shaking down Special Ed kids for lunch money."

I watch the television. The clip is like one of those videos your uncle films from his fifth wheel's dashboard as he tours the mountains. This one banks right after a cement block wall with a detour arrow. Follows a muddy, rutted logging trail into the forest. Pans to a giant plywood placard, then one after another:

GOVERNMENT FOR SALE: REDUCED PRICES! ASK FOR CYMAN!

FALSE INCOME TAX RETURNS: 2001; FRANKING SCANDAL: 2004

SEXTING INTERN: 2006; XANCO SOLAR POWER BRIBES: 2009

BANK BRIBES 2010, OIL BRIBES 2011, GAMING BRIBES 2014.

VOTE HOCK. HE HASN'T SCREWED US, YET.

The other five signs are the same, in reverse direction for opposing traffic.

"You think that'll bring him down in the polls?" Keith says.

"No. Hock hasn't impressed me as ambitious or intelligent enough to capitalize on the free press."

"Your last line isn't a blazing endorsement."

"Anyone who gets his politics from a billboard ought to be shot."

"Still, it's like Hock doesn't want to win."

"I'm about to call it quits. It's a losing battle. A bet I shouldn't have made."

Keith's face twists. "I'm going to bring someone to meet you tonight. Don't drop out of the game, yet."

Cyman's chief of staff pens a response to the allegations by noon, citing no charges were brought in any of the cases quoted by Duane Hock's desperate vigilante, and the senator did seek counseling after the Senate censured him for ethical lapses. The senator would ignore these spurious, hateful charges, were it not for the critical nature of the present election. Keeping Senator Cyman in office is more important now than ever. The upcoming election will be The Most Important Election of Our Lives.

The population of Arizona turns over so rapidly, few voters will remember the sins I've enumerated on plywood. Most of the people who voted a dozen years ago are now old timers. Back then they lived in states where it snowed. Today's middle-aged people were barely cognizant of politics in their thirties, and the folks now in their thirties spent the 2000's trying to sober up. Twenty-somethings? Who cares? They don't vote. That's why they'll work their entire lives to pay off their grandparents' debt.

Challenger Duane Hock, action hero cool guy that he is, has a blog. Ole Ice-Veins outdoes himself.

Again, we find in these troubling times we must distance ourselves from an unsanctioned supporter whose efforts to help this campaign amount to a detour to the low road. We condemn both his guerilla communication and his Stalinesque zest for misinformation. Duane Hock promises a new kind of politics, where ideas are more important than shoveling political dirt. Where the courage to face troubling times is only surpassed by our willingness to see the best in our enemies and stand side by side with them to confront the challenges of tomorrow...

You're writing a blog, jackwad. Don't refer to yourself in third person.

I coast from Hock's webpage to Rudge. There's a story, but no photos on the front page. Matt must detect waning interest in Arizona's internecine squabble.

Screw it.

I've got things to ponder. Katrina's knocked up and I haven't given her more than ten seconds of thought. What if I'm not shooting blanks anymore? Is it possible that with enough organ meats, organic cabbage and broccoli, a fella can, I dunno, load live ammo?

My legs are nervy from needing a run. I haven't for a week scaled the rock face that will be part of the Desert Dog route.

Rachel was clear that I will lose my money and my capacity to make it if I don't quell my anti-authoritarian streak and join up with the Treasury. And Bernard tells me the man Rachel demands I investigate is so well connected, there's nowhere to run if he sours on me. I'm living the medieval paradox of the unstoppable force meeting the immovable object. I'll be sure to write a paper about how it all turns out—from a Native American viewpoint, with an authentic indigenous voice—but let me make a prediction. The unstoppable force passes through the immovable object, and they both go on like before, one immutable, the other unstoppable, both stained blood red. And anything between them in that instant of contact gets atomized with nothing but a moment's torture to mark his sorry life.

I drive to the desert by Barrett's place and the skinny man in the black Suburban swerves out of a Circle K gas station and tails me. He's being obvious. Right up on my bumper. He doesn't rear end me or wave a handgun out the window, but he wants me anxious.

Normally, in a situation like this one heads toward civilization. One seeks witnesses. Instead I drive to the desert, where it is easy for a body to disappear.

His body could disappear as easily as mine.

Pulling into the trailhead parking lot it occurs to me that my .45 is in the glove box. I bought it and haven't thought of it since. I pop the box open as I swerve into my regular space. The Suburban parks beside me and I slip the shifter into reverse, just in case. Power down the window and wait as the runt with the French tickler mustache lowers his passenger window.

I'm waiting to see a gun barrel, a group of guys in black suits and Oakleys—the cool ones from the nineties.

He smiles. Says nothing. I glance at the rearview. It doesn't feel right. Confrontations are supposed to be about clashing muscles, bracing wit, gnashing mental teeth.

Gayboy smiles at me. He shakes his head sideways in a tut-tut manner ...

And my passenger window implodes.

An aluminum bat bounces from the doorframe and a man in a black suit coils for another swing. I stamp the gas and the Jeep lurches backward. He misses my back window and hits the one he just shattered. I grab the bat as he stumbles; he reaches for me and slams into the jamb. The bat clatters outside.

He huffs and disappears like a missile hit his rib cage. I brake hard, glance to the Suburban, the rearview, all around. Sit up high and the man with the bat is rolling on the ground with another man whose arms look like I-beams. I'm out of the vehicle, .45 drawn on the Suburban. Taillights flash; reverse lights go white. The engine roars.

The men on the ground are on my right, in front of the Jeep. One is Willie Bernard, dropping a pile of hell on my attacker's front porch. He's on top, wailing fist to face; each blow sounding like a sledge hitting steak.

The Suburban jumps and I dodge right, swinging my .45 around and pointing inside. I hesitate, and the Suburban cuts the front wheels. I track the man's head with the front sight post until the Suburban's fender bounces me to the Jeep and its wheel clips the tip of my shoes.

I re-aim the .45 at his windshield... but I think I'll survive and my brain can't squeeze the trigger.

Frenchie backs away. Rocks to a stop. Guns the engine and swings the front wheels. I hear grunts and the Suburban jumps behind my Jeep and stops while the man who brought the bat, bleeding from his face and ragged at his elbows and knees, jumps inside. The Suburban squeals around the entrance loop and speeds away.

I'm still pointing the .45, now at an innocent saguaro cactus across the parking lot, standing with its arms comically raised. My hand shakes. I should have blasted glass. I should have leapt to the hood of the Suburban and driven my fist through. I should have been a super hero. I should have sounded off like I had a pair.

I should have pulled the trigger.

Bernard sits on the ground. His ankle is wrapped in an ace bandage. He heaves for breath and rubs his knuckles.

"I was here..." he says. He breathes heavily, grabs the baseball bat from the blacktop. His knuckles pinch white. "...because Barrett helped with my ankle last night."

My self-directed frustration keeps me from hearing him, and then his words register. He has anticipated an intelligent question, the very one I would have asked as soon as my heart rate dropped back to a single standard deviation above trend. It isn't strange that he answers this question, but his direct manner makes it hard to discern if he is a friend motivated by protecting me, or if he's a passing rogue whose temporary objective coincides with mine.

For the record, I've always been suspicious of the Zig Ziglar guys who try to get what they want by helping me get what I want. Stop pretending. Read *Atlas Shrugged*. It'll change your life.

"You were in the area," I say.

"Barrett's place is over there." He nods. "I was outside, stretching my ankle."

"Barrett's a doctor?"

"So who were these guys? And why didn't you blast a hole through that window when you had the chance?"

"I don't know. I should have. But it was a senator's bad man."

"From last night? Cyman?"

"Nothing else makes sense," I say.

"The guy with the bat wore a silk suit."

I offer my hand and drag Bernard to his feet.

"He lost a couple teeth. All the front ones." Bernard hops a few feet, favors his ankle.

I brush glass off the passenger seat; give up. "Get in the back and I'll take you to Barrett's."

"Yeah."

I discover reaching for the ignition that my hand trembles and the keys jingle. I miss the slot and Bernard slams the door.

"Exciting, once it's over," he says.

"Is that it?" I start the engine, brush glass from the seat.

"That's it," he says.

I leave him at the gate, which motors open as I put the Jeep in reverse. I glimpse Cal Barrett through the opening. He watches Bernard and then his eyes cut to me. I waive, but maybe there's a glare and he can't see. He turns around and enters his house as the gate closes.

I turn around.

At the opposite side of the mountain, accessible through the back of a new housing development, I drive to the periphery of a network of dirt bike and quad trails. Even now, their buzz saw engines decorate the air with noise and exhaust; their knobby tires pulverize the desert a few square inches at a time. I park among trucks and trailers with my broken window partly hidden against a juniper.

I'll rattle apart if I don't run.

I tuck the .45 into my Camelbak and strap it on. The water in the tube is warm, but after the first gulp, cold enough to provoke an instant headache. Got to keep the core cool.

I run.

Oblivion.

When I tore the .45 apart, I planned to learn how to rapidly reassemble it. My goal was to do it blindfolded, upside down, under water in fifteen seconds, but all I've managed is to create a mess of levers, pins and springs with no idea how they fit back together.

Rapping sounds at the door, the kind that provokes an instant response—even from the innocent. I leave gun parts scattered on the tabletop. Last run I went all out. My knees wobble, my hips feel like gelatin.

I look in the fisheye. Open the door. Keith glances to his right, smiles, and reaches. I can't see who stands beside him. "Got a minute, Solomon?"

"Uh."

"It's okay," he says to whomever stands at his side. "This is him."

Keith shifts partly aside and a woman steps before me. The distance between her and perfection becomes hazy as I try to peg its dimensions.

She is sublime. Her eyes are slightly smaller than a doe's. Her nose has a gentle bump in the middle and a subtle lift at the end. Her cheeks are high, her brow intelligent, her hair fine like the mist of a thousand-foot waterfall. She takes away my breath, and the forlorn purse of her lips makes my soul weep. Instantly. I see her in a wedding gown. Rosy and pregnant. Playing with children in a sunny meadow. With silver hair, on a sailboat. In a rocking chair, holding my hand.

Entering, she looks at the sofa, clasps her hands, contracts her shoulders in that famous diminishing move all girls learn young. Her modest bust, which I suddenly imagine stretched tight against her ribs as she arches her back in a fiendish frenzy of pleasure, disappears under the folds of her blouse. She sits, crumples her hands and looks at them, then me, then Keith.

"This is Amanda Cherubini," Keith says.

"Your name," I say. "Little angel, right?"

She looks at Keith. Crosses her legs, and I notice her attire is surely not what the Almighty has prescribed his angels should wear.

But to this assimilated Blackfoot, raised by a pious Christian woman whose husband—my father—was murdered after rabblerous-ing against the Bureau of Indian Affairs, Amanda is a perfect angel. I never bought the wings and white robes.

Her skirt is red leather. Her top shimmery white. Her heels are I believe what the ladies used to call FMP's. Her thigh, though, is telling. The flesh immediately above a woman's knee exposes her habits. Amanda's is tanned, muscular, but not ripped. The flesh tone stretches to a gazelle's graceful thigh and waits until your eye has traveled a mile before disappearing below red leather. One can only muse about following.

I soak her in while assuming an opposite seat. Originally disposed to question why she is here, I am now thinking of ways to prolong her stay. I glance to the entertainment center and my eye rolls over DVD titles: First Blood, Braveheart, and beside it, There Will Be Blood. Bottom of the cabinet, right side, my gaze flits to a copy of You've Got Mail that Katrina forgot. And then I smell her. Nothing overpoweringly sweet or wretchedly floral. Recalls rain and wine. My loins ache.

"You did the billboard?" Amanda says.

I glance at Keith.

"She's not a cop."

I clasp my hands. "I don't recall."

"I don't have time for this." She stands. "Keith, I told you not to waste my time. I ought to charge you for the hour."

I rise. "Whoa, Miss. No need to run."

"Run? I stopped running a long time ago. Either you did the billboard or you didn't."

"I did."

"Why?"

I open my hands, like I'm about to plead. "I wish it was something more noble, but it was a bet. That's all."

She looks at Keith and her jaw sets forward as she weighs my line against what Keith has told her.

"Keith, I've missed part of the drama. What's up?"

"Amanda hates Cyman. She's trying to destroy him."

She glares at him.

"That's fine," I say. "Of course that makes sense. He's a politician."

"You don't understand," Keith says. "She's really going to bring him down."

"How do you two know each other?" I say.

Keith looks immediately at the floor. "Sunday school."

Amanda's lips twitch at the edge. She says, "We grew up together. Then he volunteered at a shelter and recognized me."

"A shelter?"

"A shelter." Her posture is stiffer, and her voice has a New York tone. "So you did the thing in Sedona last night?"

I nod.

"Funny."

I grin.

"But worthless. Nobody cares that he's a crook. He's a politician. It's a given."

"I was limited to using public domain dirt. Google."

She stares straight into my eyes. Through me to the wall behind.

Keith says, "That may not be the case any longer. Go ahead, Amanda."

Rapping sounds at the door, jackhammer insistent. Amanda's flaring eyes scorch me. I look at Keith and point down the hall to his old room. When they disappear behind the closed door, I look through the peephole.

Rachel sits where a moment before, Amanda was, and the contrast is bold. A lioness has replaced my gazelle. Are this one's senses sharp enough to smell the other? I should throw her out, but I feel off balance. Unsure of what I stand to lose or gain in the next few seconds. Defensive but poised, like Ralph Macchio on one leg, no can defend.

"I saw your little incident with Senator Cyman's men," Rachel says.

"Why didn't you help?"

"Well, I wasn't there. My team reported the details—and they weren't going to blow their cover. They knew you were armed."

"That really helped."

"My people tell me that's what saved you."

"Well, no—" I halt, but from her sudden look I know why she's here.

"You were saying?" she says.

"It was my steely stare that did it."

"Who joined you in fending off the attack?"

Lying is no use. She has reports of my helper. "A guy named Willie."

"Willie?" She smiles as if she gets the inside joke. "How quaint."

"It's a nickname because of his hair. I don't know his name. He's the one you sent me to—for the gun."

"You must have made progress, for him to arrive like your knight in shining armor."

"Find a less-gay analogy."

"What did he say?"

"He was stretching an ankle injury. Why don't you just listen to the tape?"

Her eyes flit away like sparrows from a field, disperse, and circle back to me in a new attack. "You must infiltrate Barrett's group. I've warned you of the consequences."

She wrinkles her puny cat-nose. Presses the sofa cushion with her flat hand. "Someone is here—a woman." She looks straight ahead. Her neck stiffens and her eyes are steady as if she draws her consciousness inward, reassessing her setting.

"We hardly agreed to exclusivity," I say.

"I've had my Indian," she says. More quietly: "Who is she?"

"Treasury needs to know?"

"Treasury needs to know everything. If something is about to inter-fere with your mission—"

"You'll remove it? Is that it? Let's you and me get one thing under-stood. You lay a hand on her, I'll gut you."

Her mouth falls; she leans back. The lioness has been clapped by a two by four.

She recomposes. Her eyes glint like the blade she left under my mat-tress. "Solomon. Since we are dispensing with the veil of lust, let me assure you that if my agency or I desired you removed from this case, it would be so. If we desired you gone from this city, it would be so. If we desired you gone from this earth, it would be so. I represent the agency that makes the paper the world calls money. Think before you threaten to disembowel me."

I meet her hot eyes with cool ones.

"I will debrief you in three days," she says. "If you don't have anything worthwhile to report, your stock accounts will vanish. Your checking at the credit union. I will leave you nothing."

Though vernacular English offers several perfect rejoinders, I share none with her. I don't believe her.

"I had hoped to win your help with a carrot, not a stick," she says.

"Something you should learn about the unassimilated Blackfoot, Rachel. Don't bend him unless you want to kill him. He won't let you do one and not the other. If your brain worked as hard as your tits, you'd know that."

She stands. "I've been clear. There are consequences to your inaction. I've appealed to your patriotism, your sense of adventure, your passion. Now I appeal to the little man inside you, the one who fears. Three days, or I will destroy you."

She closes the door and my eyes linger where her calves were, as if the curve was burned to my retina. I sit in silence and as the exchange settles into the past, its ramifications ripple through the future. Will she threaten Amanda? Will she eliminate me from afar, surgically, as the central government has perfected in recent years?

I haven't gutted a squirrel. Would I gut her?

And who the hell was I talking about—the unassimilated Blackfoot? In truth, I'm as emasculated as a Native American can be and still pee through a pipe.

Keith's bedroom door creaks open. He approaches warily and Amanda walks behind, shoulders square, regal. I imagine several ladies-in-waiting lifting her gown from the floor. Her collarbones give me a chill. Her jaw.

"You were about to say something before we were interrupted," I say.

"Who was she?" Keith says.

"Not important."

"If you knew what I am about to tell you, you would disagree," Amanda says. "Who was she?"

If I knew what I don't... I suppose a lot of things would be different.

Amanda exemplifies how to appeal to a man. Excite curiosity. Hint the adventure, the secret. Hint her body might follow her mind. Or perhaps it only works on an already-infatuated man.

"She works for a secret arm of a well-known government agency, and wants me to infiltrate a group of terrorists."

Amanda stands. Walks to the door.

"Come on, man!" Keith says, glaring at me. "Amanda! He's joking."

I leap from the couch and beat her to the door. She stops abruptly, deep in my body space. Her breath is like crumpled mint leaves. Her hair shines like polyurethane silk. There are those lovely mounds, pressing close enough to challenge my bottom peripherals.

"It is the truth," I say. "I'm not going to say any more about it. If you have something to lay at my feet, do it. Otherwise, it was a distinct pleasure to have seen you. Meeting you wasn't as nice."

Her face changes slowly. Her jaw hinges dimple while her eyes become slits. I ease out of her way. Turn for one last look at the full ensemble before she disappears, and find she has faced me.

"Keith," she says, "I need to talk to him alone."

Keith nods. Leaves.

"What is it I can do for you?" I say.

"I don't want Cyman dead."

I nod.

"Just destroyed."

"And you've come to me because of my bet with Keith?"

"He mentioned it."

"So how did your dog get into the hunt?"

"Is that a Blackfoot colloquialism?"

Her dress says prostitute by her vocabulary says something else. I've judged too soon, but isn't that the way we're built? Ingrained prejudice that stems from the deepest "knowledge," true or not. Back in the day, anything that was different was worthy of fear. Anything outside the realm of the known could swoop in and cause damage. Saber-toothed tigers and all. Now we pretend to get along, and societies grow to huge sizes because we get along to the degree we are similar and police up the rogues among us who would prefer to be different, the killers. But that cellular knowledge punches through all we do. Wherever we see the unknown, first we shrink, then we draw our swords and step forward.

"It is a southernism," I say.

"It's dumb."

"How did you know I'm Blackfoot?"

"Keith."

"So what's the evidence? What's the senator done that only I can expose?"

She stands. Drifts toward the kitchen. "Do you have popcorn?"

I follow. "What line of work are you in?"

"I hook."

"Does your occupation inform your view of Cyman?"

"He's been a client."

"Interesting." I don't know how else she would have referred to him, but "client" strikes me as more dignified than the professional relationship merits.

"Interesting if you like sick."

She lifts a big boiling pan from the rack suspended over the kitchen island. Opens cupboards until she finds coconut oil, and pours it. I dig a bag of popcorn from the cupboard and a stick of butter.

She's thin, but not waifish or fragile. Her eyes cast a spell that is cute in the way feminism is sometimes cute. Defiance for a cause that makes meta sense, but not when fixing a flat tire in the rain, or when the house is burning. I play along.

"I decided earlier that my stunt in Sedona was my last," I say.

"He scared you off pretty easily." She dumps kernels into the oil. Flips the burner on high.

"It wasn't that easy," I say. "I waited until he smashed my window and tried to run over me."

"You wouldn't quit so easy..."

"If your information is as good as you say—"

"I won't tell you until I trust you. But if I tell you everything, you'll never be the same. You may kill him, instead of his career."

"That's quite a buildup, and I've got a lot on my plate. Why don't we enjoy the popcorn and end it on that?"

Kernels pop and startle me.

"Because if you let me go without learning what I know, you won't be on your guard, and they'll kill you."

THREE DAYS to RACE DAY

A wise man will not leave the right to the mercy of chance, nor wish it to prevail through the power of the majority. There is but little virtue in the action of masses of men.

Henry David Thoreau

Amanda is at my door, ready to leave. It is nine p.m. "You should stay," I say, and swallow over my dry throat, and wonder how I could sound more pathetic. Two emotions conflict. I want to fly to Washington and beat Cyman to death with a tire tool.

Concurrently, I want to close my arms around Amanda. Make her understand she will never feel that kind of pain again. She is nearer, and I'll try the latter first. God forbid she leaves; I'll be driving to Sky Harbor Airport tonight.

"Stay? How?"

"As in, sit on the sofa and talk." I pull her hands and she drags her feet, leans away, smiles through haunted eyes. Telling me her story has emptied her. Emptied me. I don't understand the species of depravity she related. Part of me keeps her here because I am in a fog, miscomprehending and mis-imagining. I don't believe her. I do believe her. There is evidence, she promises, for most of what she has said. Enough to earn my trust for the rest.

"Tell me whether you'll help," she says.

"You knew I'd have no choice. But there's nothing to do tonight. So rest."

"I can't rest." She walks from the sofa to the table, spins, returns. "He could be doing it right now to someone else."

I hesitate. "Show me, again."

She faces the wall. Lifts her top, exposing the nubs of her spine. Her blouse accordions higher until a series of welts and scars and blisters stare back at me.

"He did all of these?"

She lowers her head.

"Over how long a time?"

"Months."

"Why did you wait this long?"

"Until you painted your billboard, I didn't think anyone had the courage or the craziness to take him on. I realize painting those signs was just a prank to you, but to me, it was a clarion call. Don't you realize the reputation he has?"

"You don't speak like a woman of the night."

"How do nocturnal women speak?"

"All I have to go by is television and prejudice, but they tend toward five cent words."

"Does it bother you more to see my back, or to hear what I said about the Indian boy?"

"You don't need to stoke the fire."

"You don't look like other men. You look like a hunter, but not a brutal one. Does that make sense?"

Shall I frighten her to death and proclaim I am her slave forever, and that all my tough nonchalance is an act because I know no woman respects a man who needs her? "How do you know about the boy? Specifically."

"Cyman... I was with him and he was impotent. No matter how much he burned me. Those are the blisters. Six of them, I think. He dismissed me, and went into the bathroom. I waited while he made a cell phone call. He hadn't paid me, and I get paid for showing, not... anyway I overheard him insist on the phone that there was money in it if they hurried. After I got my money, I waited in the hotel bar where I could look across the lobby. I wanted to see the competition. I watched for an hour, and only normal folks came by."

"How did you know none of them were in your line of work?"

"You develop an eye. Only one made me suspicious, an older white guy with an Indian boy. Navajo. Wide face. The older man tugged him along, like he was dragging a dog. And the boy wasn't dressed well enough to belong there."

"So how do you know..."

"I caught the same elevator. Went two floors above Cyman's. I talked to the boy but he was silent. The man stared at me. They got off at the senator's floor, and when the elevator door closed, I stuck my foot in it and glanced down the hallway. Cyman's bodyguard was waiting at the door."

"The one with the mustache?"

"Right."

"What'd the old man look like?"

"He, uh. Why? He was tall. He wasn't an Indian."

"No reason. I want to know all I can."

Men start out evil, and if they don't erect in their youths a moral framework that will defeat their demons, they will succumb. From all I have learned recently about Cyman's character, I believe he paid the man to bring the boy.

There is little that can be done with this kind of knowledge. I'm not built to ignore wrong on this level. It isn't sport. It is life or death. No second chances.

"Did you see anything else?"

"I was afraid to wait in the lobby for the old man and the boy to come back out. Cyman's bodyguard is Géraud. He's like a weasel with a gun. He saw me stick my head out of the elevator."

"I've met Géraud."

Her eyebrows arch.

"He tried to run me over this afternoon."

I lean on the sofa. She continues to sit stiffly upright and though I surmise she does this because of the wounds on her back, it contributes to her elegance.

"Have you shown those to anyone?" I say.

"No."

I walk to the bathroom, load supplies from the cabinet to my folded arm. Return. "You're going to have to trust me. Turn around and lift your top."

Redness glows on her cheeks, a single second of vulnerability, and then fades. She obeys me the way a president obeys a child instructing him in patty cake. Her distance and poise define her. She has made all men into dirt to ensure she walks above them all. If I break that, I ruin her; but I cannot tolerate being lumped with pedophiles. She'll learn to make an exception.

I study her blisters. They are from cigarette cherries, and the black marks mean he placed the ember directly to her skin.

"Ugh." The syllable escapes me. "Why?"

"It makes whores buck," she says, her New York edge slicing the air like a scythe.

I daub antibacterial ointment to a gauze pad. "When was the last time?"

"Yesterday night."

I stick the ointment-laden pad over three burns and she shivers. Cut the tape and press it to her. I cover the remaining burns and count the scars.

"Why do you keep going back to him?"

"It is easier to deal with the burns than everything else he threatens."

"You never told anyone?"

"How would I prove it without laying the groundwork? Without working with someone like you?"

"What else did he promise?"

"That he would see to it that my father found out. That he would have the IRS audit my father's business. That he would have his city hall buddies revoke my father's business license. That he would..."

"What?"

"Send film."

"He filmed you?"

"He says he did."

Her wounds are covered. She holds her top at her armpits. I touch her fingers and motion downward. She is facing away. I rest my fingertips on her shoulders and press my thumbs to her neck, lightly, in small swirls, and the wind leaves her like I've tripped a valve. Her chin dips and she shudders. Leaning forward, I reach across her front and position myself to her side and embrace her.

"I will destroy him," I say.

"Don't kill him," she says, and sniffles.

I shift to her front. Drape my arms lightly around her. Her back is taut as if she resists my hug. But as I wait and continue to hold her, and my breathing paces hers, she wilts. Finally her head leans to mine and rests, and her shoulder presses my chest, and she shivers. She weeps silently, and her shivers are shudders.

"You never have to go to the streets again," I say. "Shhh."

I am become Keith; saver of worlds.

We sleep on the sofa, her on her side, me on my back. She has taken the night off in favor of snuggling with a man who has promised to destroy her tormenter, and she repays his promise with succor. She sleeps and my arm sleeps but my mind rambles through a wasteland of murderous thoughts. I wonder how many ways it is possible to take life, and try to create a hierarchy of the most frightening, as that Indian boy must have been frightened, and painful, as Amanda suffered pain, so that I can synergize and maybe kill him several ways at once, all the most frightening and painful.

I settle on bathing him in sulfuric acid while bouncing a slab of granite from his testicles.

It occurs to me that all our progress as a species is worth nothing—all our progress on the political plane, developing and testing the concept of self-government, expanding political freedom and suffrage, is nothing—without conquering sexual predation. If our society does not protect our weak; if we do not shackle and execute the beasts among us, there is no freedom except freedom of the strong, disguised within a new political order. We may have flourishing cities of technological marvels, but if bands of the abused wander those gold-paved streets, we have failed.

While Amanda sleeps I wonder what motivates a judge to release a man who has proven the inability to control himself. Is it the idea that nothing is so terrible that a deviant can't be rehabilitated? Is it that in our desire to flatten the moral plane and equalize all peoples, we have sacrificed our willingness to identify what is truly evil?

Do we even believe in evil, anymore?

The microwave clock melts minutes into hours, night into morning, and still I wrestle demons. My arm tingles; her head nestled in my shoulder cuts my circulation. She sleeps. Her exhalations are tiny and light—like a doll might breathe. I look at the divine sculpture that is her face and before her beauty can sweep me into forgetfulness and sleep, I recall the fact that launched my hatred this night: a man who was elected to protect the people took his deepest erotic pleasure from watching this delicate creature writhe in pain. And when she failed to sufficiently arouse him, he replaced her with someone *even more helpless.*

The juxtaposition of his office and his nature creates such a stark absurdity that it leaves me, after hours of meditation, unable to comprehend.

Amanda wakes to the enticing aroma of bacon and eggs.

"I'm vegan," she says.

I fix her a pea protein smoothie with banana and rice milk. She drinks and I wolf down a double helping of cholesterol and fat. She beholds me with knowing eyes as if I am part of the problem... and my intellect empathizes. For if we are nothing but souped-up chimpanzees, no matter how artistic or logical, we are beasts. The medulla controls the essential organs, the heart and lungs. Evolutionists assert that subsequent parts of the brain brought later functions. Our adeptness at consciousness and solving moral dilemmas is akin to having a DVD player mounted in a car. An afterthought that makes the ride more pleasant, possibly, but not something that gets you there faster, or safer.

Amanda watches me. Does she reduce me to a chimpanzee? A beast?

She finishes her smoothie and avails herself of the bathroom. She emerges in a few minutes and sits on a kitchen chair. Her eyes are now distant. Calculating. Her jaw has a new firmness.

"I want nothing from you," I say, lying. "But I do want something *for* you. There is an empty bedroom here. I'll move the futon—"

"I've got to go."

"We have to work together," I say.

"I'm confused."

"I'm not. I promised I wouldn't kill him, and I won't. But I will destroy him, and I'll need to know what you know. I'll need you."

"What will you do?"

"I'll shine a light into darkness. I want video evidence."

"What will you do with it? Bribe him to step aside?"

"I'll end his career and make the world protest if he remains a free man. But that's going to take some time. You can stay here in the spare room. Did you tell anyone you were coming here, other than Keith?"

"No one."

"Where do you live? Alone, or with a roommate?"

"Alone. Seventy third and Union Hills."

"Cyman's man—Géraud—has been watching me for days. He may already know you're here."

"If I go back to my normal routine, they'll think I've decided to look the other way."

"You're not going back to your normal routine. You never have to hook again."

Her eyes turn to brass and her cheeks alabaster. "Excuse me?"

"It's over. We nail him and then figure out the future. In the meantime, you have a room. You have food."

"I have bills. Are you going to pay my rent?"

"Yes."

"Then I'm just going to be hooking with a single client—who likes snuggling more than screwing."

I must have inadvertently hit the frosty bitch button.

She says. "I'm not a charity case. I take care of myself. I answer to no one."

"I'm not asking you to answer to me. I'm telling you that..." What am I telling her? That I'm so struck by pity and rage and a desire to take her for myself that I'll take care of her forever? "Look. You're doing something that hurts you. Let me help you."

"Bring him down. That's help enough." She slips into her heels, writes her number on my grocery list, and leaves.

I wait nine seconds and chase her. Catch her at the bottom stair. She spins as I approach, and does that diminishing move, curling her shoulders inward.

"Wait," I say. "What do you make in a night?"

"What?"

"What would you have made last night, on the street?"

"I don't work off a street."

"How much?"

"Six hundred."

I peel six one-hundred dollar bills, fold them once, and place them in her hand. "I enjoyed the evening very much."

She looks at the bills, shakes her head, passes them back. I hide my hands and she moves toward my front pocket. I dance backward, and she tosses the money at me. It flutters.

"I'm not a charity case. I'm not a damsel. Don't look at me like that." She glances at her watch. "Call me when you can take down Cyman."

She stalks to the parking lot, unlocks and enters a clean Mustang with that wretched 1998 design. I read somewhere that Ford actually executed the guy who designed it. The engine has a little gumption, though. She burps tires turning on Happy Valley.

Amanda is like me, and rightfully torqued at my six-hundred-dollar gesture. Nothing is worse than being understood. The understanding person deems himself on some lofty perch. People who seek to understand me invariably piss me off. I cede nothing—like Amanda ceded nothing.

I tried to convert an autonomous woman into a kept woman by waving a few C-notes after a night of snuggling.

I get it. I'm a dork.

Surely that's important enough to tell Amanda...

I rush to the Jeep. Swerve onto Happy Valley, pedal to the floor. I see Amanda ahead and I hang back, turn on 67th and follow her south.

I'll catch her and give her a breathless mea culpa.

But given how every instinct I've had with Amanda, except my first, which was to listen and comfort her, has provoked her ire, and given how I like her, am drawn to her, and want to spend eternity rubbing piña colada scented oil into her feet, surprising her every day with roses, dishing her chocolate gelato, and discussing Plato with her, and I don't want to dick things up even worse...

I'll just hang back.

Surveil her.

She swings into a driveway and noses into a garage. The door closes. I wait at the curb a block away. Can't be too conspicuous: neighbors tend to note strange vehicles idling in the heat. I'll give her a few minutes.

No sooner do I complete the thought than the garage door opens and the Mustang emerges blowing smoke rings. Amanda takes off again, faster than before.

I slip into drive and follow. In three minutes we're on 101 heading east. On and on she goes until after fifty minutes, she takes the exit lane for University Drive. I hang back. In four minutes she's at an Arizona State University auxiliary parking lot, catching a bus. I follow it into Tempe. She exits and I swing into a metered parking space. She enters a building. I'm a hundred feet back. I arrive at the door as she angles a hall corner. A moment later she ducks into room 117. A young Barry Goldwater with glasses and a crew cut heads to the same room.

"Excuse me, what class is this?" I say.

"I.T.—Indeterminate Tripe."

"What?"

"Indigenous Theory."

"What's that? What level class?"

"Seven thirty. Gender studies. Indigenous epistemologies. Postcolonial theory. Globalization. Colonial discourse analysis. Multisyllabic Wastes of Time."

"Thanks."

Amanda Cherubini works toward a PhD in political science.

TWO DAYS 'til RACE DAY

> How does it become a man to behave toward this
> American government today? I answer that he can-
> not without disgrace be associated with it. I cannot
> for an instant recognize that political organization
> as my government which is the slave's government
> also.
>
> Henry David Thoreau

I watch the news. Hock and Cyman have announced an alliance against the politics of indiscriminate dirt. The two have pledged to focus on the issues. They have agreed that their characters, moral-ity, indiscretions and ethical breaches, in short, how they have behaved with real live human beings in the past—should in no way inform vot-ers seeking to decide who will best represent their interests.

From my first prank, Hock has attempted to negate my attacks on his adversary. What is the old saying, the enemy of my enemy is my friend? Why am I not Mr. Hock's friend?

By the algebra of the equation, Hock and Cyman are not enemies.

Rachel be damned; I have my own reason to visit Barrett.

By the time I've decided what to do the temperature outside is a hundred thirteen. I fill my Camelbak bladder with ice and the gaps with water.

I slip into a pair of running shoes. Toss the pack on my shoulder and clip my iPod to my tank top. Skip forward to the Braveheart sound-track and imagine clans of hale Scotsmen breaking bread with a tribe of Blackfoot. I see Blackfoot on horses, drawing from quivers and aim-ing to the peal and rhyme of a dozen bagpipes.

I keep my eye on the rearview for a black Suburban. If Géraud and his silly mustache shows up, I'll execute him. I park, glance out my bro-ken side window and commit to getting the Jeep to the shop today. Later—as soon as I exhaust myself against the rocks and trail. I stretch quickly and set out.

What happened in the last few days to my unflappable desire to win Desert Dog? Sidetracked by women? My puerile bet to derail Cyman has morphed into saving a prostitute and a Navajo boy who may not be in Arizona any more. My feet beat dust from the trail sand. In twenty minutes I feel a unique sensation: intellectually faint and physically dazed. Heat exhaustion threatens.

I ease my pace and drink ice water. From this point forward, finish-ing the run alive necessitates controlling body temperature. I accom-plish this by adjusting speed and hydration.

Somewhere out here, Rachel has TFI agents at listening posts. Treasury probably recruits operatives from the same places everyone else does, Special Forces, Seals, Delta. It is a testament to their skill— as much time as I've spent near Barrett's—that I have yet to spot them.

No matter how good these agents are, though, they can't hear what goes on inside the compound, and that's why they need me.

I finish a five-mile loop and catch my breath at the Jeep. Sitting in the vehicle's shade, I stretch over shattered glass. Sweat drips from my brow to the inside of my sunglass lenses. My hair sticks to my back. The sun is hot on my skin. Though exercise is supposed to be good for stress, my focus and anger have swollen over the last hour.

I drive to Barrett's. Reading the gate, I'm no farther than "the congress shall make no law abridging" when it swings open, exposing a dirt lawn that stretches thirty yards before arriving at a long ranch house. On the left is a four-story tower, with windows overlooking the desert, and whose lighthouse-like balcony must be a fine place to sip Gentleman Jack in the evening.

I drive inside the compound.

To my right is a small motorpool of Jeep Wranglers, Nissan Titan trucks, and a series of Triumph Tiger go-anywhere-motorcycles.

The porch spans twenty yards across the façade and is decorated with rough pine furniture. I motor down the window and kill the A/C. Silence, save my crunching tires. I press the brake; slip it in park.

Iron bars protect the windows and looking close I see hinged boards beside them that will fold over, as if boarding up a home could stop an Abrams tank. Like the folks at Waco, Barrett seems to have mistaken the Constitution as having actual staying force against the might of the central state.

Or maybe he's decided if it doesn't, he has nothing to lose.

I kill the engine, glance at the glove box and castigate myself for having forgotten my .45, which lay in pieces, back at the apartment. Maybe someone here could teach me how to reassemble it. Upside down. Under water. In fifteen seconds.

I get out.

The front door opens and a Mexican woman of baffling girth waves me forward. On my approach her hair turns grayer and irregular gaps punctuate her toothy smile. I can't help but to like her genuineness. She wears an apron. As my shoe hits the porch step I smell the tempting aroma of seared beef.

She smiles in the manner of one who is fluent but pretends *she no hablo*. She gestures to a leather sofa in a room off the entryway, and disappears into a kitchen tiled with Sedona-red rocks and cabineted with knotty hickory.

I look to the plank floor. Boot footfalls approach. Cal Barrett looms in the entryway to the hall, looking as cowboy as the weathered shutters outside.

His boots are snake or lizard, I can't tell. Blue jeans and a white shirt. He wears a silver belt buckle big enough to have tools built into the backside. He wears a bolo but the cord isn't leather—it's braided steel. His hair flows like John Brown's and if he had a beard, I sense it would point to the rifle.

"C'mon into the inner sanctum."

The hallway stretches almost to a vanishing point. We come upon an open door. Barrett glances and continues without slowing. I look inside to a bank of blade servers. The modules stack one on top of the other and a geek in blue jeans, boots, and a white jacket grins over a clipboard at me. Barrett tramps down the hall. The geek swings the door closed.

Farther along, another door is open, this one on the right. As I near, bars resolve and it looks like a jail cell. Instead it is an armory. Inside... AR-15s in metal wall racks. I halt. A ceiling fan slowly whirs. Looks like twenty per rack, which are stacked close and tight and ceiling high, maybe thirty of them. Six hundred automatic rifles.

I am taken by how cool Barrett keeps his compound. At the entrance, the walls were thick—like adobe. But are they packed mud or reinforced concrete?

We pass another room, again with an open door. Security. A wall of television monitors and a pair of men watching them from wooden chairs.

What is the purpose of this display by Cal Barrett?

He turns with a military flanking move and continues without breaking speed. I turn the corner and ahead is a door. He opens it and steps aside, revealing the back "yard."

It is an obstacle course—sand pits covered in barbed wire mesh, balance beams over mud pits, rope ladders stretching up four-story log frameworks, with rappelling lines hanging from the other side.

Beyond is a barn and stable—with steel lines swooping ground-ward from the upper loft. I imagine it simulates a paratrooper's drop and roll. Before the outer cement block wall is a series of man-sized popup rifle targets.

And last, the crowning achievement: a putt-putt green on the right flank.

Barrett flips a switch and in a moment, mist falls from overhead PVC pipes. He drops into an Adirondack chair and motions to another. I take a place beside him, immediately disliking the off-balance cant. A man in an Adirondack is vulnerable, unless he's Cal Barrett in Cal Barrett's compound.

Barrett looks ahead, as if trying to make the face on a man-target a hundred and fifty yards away.

"I need your help," I say.

"The senator?"

"How did you know?"

"You don't have to worry about Cyman, son."

He speaks the way a president might say, "I'll have eggs Benedict this morning."

"He's done bad things," I say.

Barrett snorts.

"He burns women. Rapes boys."

Barrett shifts his weight.

"I'm going to end his career,"

"Why don't you end his life?"

"I promised I wouldn't."

"Ah," he faces me. "That's a promise a man shouldn't make."

We are still while mist falls from white PVC. It cools the skin. Barrett says, "Why'd you come to me?"

"I've read your interviews. Training for Desert Dog."

"So."

"So I think Desert Dog is a recruiting scheme. I think it's like the old days. You're the man who gets things done."

"Things."

"Things," I agree.

"You don't know what you think you know," he says. "But suppose I'm wrong. What do you want?"

"I want to take down Cyman."

"What the hell's that mean? A bullet in the head? Loss of the election? Fifty years in prison? What is it?"

"Publicity. I want video of him in the act, and I want every man and woman in the country to see it."

"I've noticed," he says, "that you've met with a certain Treasury agent."

"She wants me to infiltrate your group."

He nods. Waits.

"She says you're a terrorist."

"Your Treasury girl could swoop in on an Apache helicopter right now, and she'd still be too late for what's about to go down."

"Well, that's your business, not mine. I want your help with Cyman."

"That's what I'm telling you. You don't need it." He leans and though he barely shifts his weight I sense it is his attempt at intimacy. "I had a wife and son during the Gulf war. We lived at Bragg; I was with the Fifth Special Forces. Deployed eleven months. I come home and everything is gone. Took me two years to find out my wife moved my son to the People's Republic of California, and a hundred thousand dollars to have a court tell me I wasn't a fit father."

I sit in silence as his voice goes bowstring taut.

"The night before the deployment, she bared her soul. Told me couldn't stand the thought of being without me. She packed up the next day."

I nod.

"Why am I telling you this?"

"People lie. What happened with your son?"

"You've met Bernard."

"How's your wife?"

"Dead."

"If Bernard's your son, you know about the signs in Sedona?"

"You're wasting your time. Voters are happy because Cyman's *their* crook."

"Can you help me bring him down?"

"Waste of time. There's no such thing as a clean politician. No sense replacing one with another." He stands with surprising speed. Interview is over. "Be seeing you at the race."

"One thing," I say, standing. "Every stunt I pull, Hock bumbles his message so bad it's like he wants to lose."

"He's a real estate developer."

"Right."

"Cyman's son is on the Water bureau." He slaps my back. "I'll be interested to see how you do in the race."

He leads me around the outside of the compound, past a swimming pool, to my Jeep. Thumps my back again.

The vehicle's interior is hot enough to melt lead. Sweat breaks on my forehead as I wait for the cool air. Barrett's already turned back to the house. The gate opens and I drive through, and I'm thinking about Bernard Barrett, wondering if Rachel knows the family linkage.

A state police patrol car sits on the drive adjacent the pool by my apartment. The uniform inside watches tanned, dimpled asses glisten on white lounges. I swing into my parking space. Slam the door. Sling the Camelbak, half-full of ice water, to my shoulder.

The officer steps out of his vehicle and vectors toward the steps, apparently seeking a collision. He's the size of a eucalyptus tree but moves with the fluidity of a leaping greyhound. I slow and he slows. I face him while he's still ten feet away.

"What?"

"You Solomon?"

Do I want to explain I don't recognize his authority? That I resent living in a police state, of which he is the most obvious symbol? Declare his uniform means he is my employee, and I'm not happy with his performance?

"Yes I'm Solomon. How can I help you, officer?"

"I need you to answer a few questions."

"Sure." I stop on the step, keeping him in direct sunlight. It is a hundred and fifteen, last count.

"Let's go inside," he says.

"Got a warrant?"

"No."

"Let's not." I drink ice water from my pack, smack my lips. "What's going on?"

"Where were you on the evening of the eleventh?"

"I don't know. What day was that?"

"Two nights ago."

"Here, watching television." A ridiculous flood of guilt bubbles through me. It offends me that I cannot tell the truth, as if by lying I am forced to admit I did something wrong, instead of forced to choose the greatest expediency, which is entirely different.

"Anyone with you?"

"Is there a point to this?"

"A witness placed you at the scene of a crime, Mr. Solomon. I'm going to need to talk to your alibi."

"That's going to be difficult."

He shades his eyes with his hand. "Who is your alibi?"

"Am I under arrest?"

"Not yet."

"Have a pleasant day, officer."

I turn. He swipes my arm. Mistake. I drop him with a jab to the neck. He hits the stairs. Head on the rail. It is unfortunate that things escalated so quickly. Was I supposed to surrender to manhandling by an agent of the ubiquitous state government merely because he was in uniform? Of course I know how this will play out. He says he was reaching for the rail and bumped my arm, and I got the jump on him.

He's crumpled on the stairs. I glance around. No one pays us any mind. He's breathing, but out cold.

This was unlucky.

I look across the lawn. At the chicks at the pool. The shrubs.

What kind of sentence do they give for defending yourself against a cop? It's my word against his, and cops are deemed to tell the truth, and citizens are deemed to be liars. It's whatever he wants to say. I've got a few seconds while he's groaning on the stairs.

I grab my cell phone and record him there, prostrate, weapon holstered but available. I swing in front to get his face and badge. He rubs his head and regains awareness. Lurches to a seated position and I dance back a few steps, holding him at bay with the camera.

"What?" he says.

"You attacked me, officer. I subdued you. I'm making a citizen's arrest and I'm recording it on my camera. Get up; let's go to your car."

"You can't arrest me." He kneads his neck, glares. "Man, that hurts."

"I witnessed a crime and I'm holding the criminal. Let's go to your vehicle, so I can call in backup."

He reaches for his gun. Draws it and points at me. "Put that phone down."

I press a couple of keys. "I just sent the video of your quick draw to my attorney."

"You what?"

"You committed a felony. Assault. I have the right—the duty as a free citizen—to detain you."

"A felony!"

"Assault. You assaulted me."

"Did you get that on your video?"

"I did not. The courts can decide. I'm pressing charges. Let's go."

"The gall. You're not calling for backup on my radio."

"Is this a standoff, officer? I didn't mean to drop you, but you attacked me without warning. I'm a free citizen."

"I'm an officer of the law. Uniformed." He flicks the gun barrel toward his car. "I'm taking you in."

"No, officer; I'm taking you in." My phone rings. It is Keith. I answer.

"What's going on?" Keith says.

"Did you see the video?" I say.

"Yeah. Are you still there?"

"He's still pointing his gun at me." I smile at the officer.

"Do whatever he wants," Keith says.

"I agree. We'll own the bastard. Won't even get to court."

"No," Keith says. "Can you hear me? Stand down."

"Yeah, Rodney King. I get it."

"What? Are you listening—"

"Precedent for jail time? Oh—for him? I get it."

The officer isn't quite cognizant of his surroundings, by his face.

"Yeah, good point. Like Ferguson. Hands up, right. I'm taking him in. I'll see you at the station. Oh yeah, see if you can get Jesse Jackson on a plane. Tell him I'm part black, too." I close the phone. "You don't understand the mess you're in, do you?"

He squints.

"You assaulted a plugged-in law student. My father is a federal judge. My mentors grind chumps like you into their breakfast smoothies. And I've got you waving your gun around and stating you don't have to respect my rights because you're in uniform. The best thing for you is if you go back to the station and confess I never came home."

"But you did," he says. "That wouldn't be right." He lowers his pistol. Super trooper has a pang of conscience.

"What's your name?" I say.

He thinks for a moment. "Jack Stoner."

"Well, Jack. I appreciate what you're doing. It's a tough job and you've got to be prepared for anything. Keeps you keyed up and tense, all the time. Like you could just choke somebody. Boy, I understand. You got these punks running around, no respect for the law. No respect for the uniform. The country. Hoodlums—I know how you feel."

He nods. Swoops down and sits on the steps.

I sit beside him. "But examine your heart. You thought you were justified when you jumped me back there. You tried to take me by force—and I had to protect myself. I'm a *citizen*, see?"

His lip trembles. "But I'm an officer of the law."

"Sure. But I'm a *citizen*. All respect; you're doing yeoman's work. But the citizen is the boss. Especially citizens who are rich and the sons of federal judges. Especially those citizens."

He nods, his eyes dumb like a cow's.

"Shame that we're such a litigious society. That means we're a society that sues a lot. You're doing a good job." I wrap an arm around his shoulder for a press-and-release man hug. "I appreciate you. Look. Here's what I'm going to do. Look." I open the cell phone, navigate to the video, show him the start frame with him crouched unconscious on the stair. "I'm deleting it. See, Jack?"

He sniffles.

"Jack? Are you okay? Tell me what's going on," I point to my heart, "in here."

Jack has gone back to the cop shop. I have a few minutes to clear out. I stuff my laptop in a leather satchel, grab a double paper bag of canned groceries, a five-gallon jug of water. I put all the springs and pieces of the .45 into a paper lunch bag. I maintain a backpack with clothes, tent, sleeping bag, rock climbing gear, and other supplies in the Jeep. I'll be good for a week. Slam the door, twist the key.

But where?

Amanda.

Seventy-third and Union Hills. I'm there in fifteen minutes, rapping on her door. I hear muffled footsteps come down the stairs and in a few seconds, the lock slides and the door opens to the chains. She peeks through the aperture.

"Solomon? What are you doing here?"

"I looked you up. I've got to run. I'll be out of contact a few days. I'm going to bring Cyman down, and I wanted you to know."

The door closes. Chain slides. Door opens. She's holding glasses and a yellow highlighter. Studying in her jammies. "How?"

"I'll figure it out. And my offer stands. The other one. I'll be in touch."

I back away before she can say anything, before she can come out and kick my ass for being a nice guy, for caring about her, for offering kindness when she expects exploitation. In the Jeep I pick up Highway 101 and then northbound 17.

Miles pass in silence and I ramble over a mental desert with as many poison animals and barbed plants as the real. My buddy Stu—the Sedona cop I taunted in school—must have sold me out.

Amanda is on my mind as I strike a match to pine needles in a fire circle a hundred yards from an obscure forest road just south of Flagstaff. The orange tongues lick dried pinecones, which soon become grenades of fire. Heavier logs ignite. The sun falls and blue wavering wicks emerge from log butts. Ants flee cracks and fall into flames.

Pointless violence... Terrorism, from the ant's view.

Amanda. Such a doe-faced prize. Thin, but rigid. Like a reed.

Clouds blot stars here and there. The night is cold compared to Phoenix, where the heat radiates from the ground at night and doesn't dissipate until sun rises to heat things up again.

Up here, we is stoned, Jim Morrison said. But I'm sober as a pile of elk pellets.

Amanda.

The fire twists and cavorts, curls around logs with insightful precision. Embers glow at the pit bottom. Heat radiates to my face and I wonder how it must feel to buy milk and bread with dollars earned by having a masochist place embers on my back—while thrusting inside me. While I'm weak, exposed, humiliated, servile and broken.

How strong must a woman be to withstand such abuse? How strong to prefer that life over charity?

How vain?

Or is Amanda, once again, not what she seems?

I pitch a two-man tent; unfurl a self-inflating mattress. Heat a can of ravioli.

Amanda.

ONE DAY to RACE DAY

I think that we should be men first, and subjects afterward. It is not desirable to cultivate a respect for the law, so much as for the right. The only obligation which I have a right to assume, is to do at any time what I think right.

Henry David Thoreau

I wake to a bull elk call. He's close enough that my nylon sleeping bag vibrates. His footfalls thud the earth as he walks. I smell him through the tent.

Elk, simplified, are horse-sized deer. He presses against the tent, blasting breath like a hot air balloon furnace.

I dig out my Jeep keys and press the panic button. After twenty seconds of cacophony, the forest is silent.

What would a real Blackfoot have done? Slip out from the underside, gut the elk standing, and break fast on elk heart.

My cell phone rings. Rachel.

"What?"

"You can't run from me. I just wanted to share the news. Your roll-over IRA with all the CDs, and the account nicknamed 'Taxes' on the Gunslinger Day Trader brokerage website—no longer exist."

I imagine little green digits, computerized book entries fluttering away like a horde of butterflies erupting from a grassy field. My money. I open my laptop. The battery light flashes and I rush to jack the cord into the Jeep auxiliary outlet.

"I was in to see your guy yesterday," I say, stalling.

"My guy."

"Barrett. At his compound." I clear the screen on my cell phone and log into my day trading app. "Interesting man."

"I see you just logged on. Go ahead. Verify you are eighty thousand dollars poorer."

"That was tax money. My only question is which line on the 1040 allows me to say the government already stole this money?"

"Funny. Will you laugh when your trading account disappears in two days? Two million bucks dissipating into ether?"

"I have account statements."

"You'd be pressing your case in a U.S. court, right? Who cuts the checks for government employees?"

"Like I said, I went and saw your boy."

"Report."

"He's a good guy. Not too talkative. It takes time, you know. Trust."

"Check your account list."

I hit the drop down menu. My 'Tax' account is back. I click it and go to the balances tab. My money has re-condensed from the ether into green digits. "Am I supposed to thank you?"

"You are supposed to fear me."

I look around the woods. Smell air without exhaust. Register the feel of bona fide earth beneath my feet, instead of concrete. "I don't."

"Get into Barrett's. We don't have time to waste. Something big is going down, and if you are a patriot, you'll do your part."

"If I'm a patriot. Somehow the centers of power and the people on the fringe always disagree—"

"You're more white than red, Solomon Bull. If you don't want to find yourself living in the Stone Age, you'd better climb aboard. How many times do I have to say this? Barrett is deep into an operation. We don't know his objective. We don't know if he's going to tear down a building, a bridge, or a city. He might have a suitcase nuke. He's got the resources to surprise us, and we don't like surprises."

"Maybe you should focus on making Barrett fear you instead of making me fear you. Why don't you disappear his accounts?"

"He's off the grid."

"How?"

"We don't know. He has his own grid. Other operators across the country. We have hackers trying to bust into his network, but their technology is bought on the open market. We can't keep up. We have to fill out sixteen forms to buy a telephone headset."

"So get a Dell catalogue and buy something."

"This isn't a game!"

"Goodbye, Rachel."

"Two days," she says. "And you're dead broke."

I close the phone. Dig a can of black beans and a packet of peanut butter from my back pack. Breakfast on both, and muse they are elk.

Looking across the grove I consider how the landscape evokes cultural personality. Volcanic rubble covers the meadow in barbeque grill lava rocks. Twenty miles away, Cinder Lake attests the explosion that blanketed a hundred square miles with the porous rocks.

The people of the north take their personalities from the terrain. Tough. Dry. Silent, except for the natural sounds that seep from aloofness. The sound of a rock shifting under a boot. A fire crackling. A knife whittling a sprig of pine.

Phoenix creates an entirely different kind of human being. Or results from a different kind. Plants adapt to low moisture and the landscape both capitalizes on them and provides for them. The symbiotic competitiveness rubs off on people inhabiting an environment of scarcity, tightening their personalities. The interdependence that coheres often disintegrates the moment one group senses advantage, or that they are being taken advantage of.

I follow the forest road several miles back into civilization. I'd like to park in the ditch, grab my pack and flit over the rocks. Cook gopher snake and drink white pine tea. Watch the impending meltdown from a considerable height. But Barrett's operation, wondrous at it sounds, may or may not affect Cyman, and I can't leave it to chance.

And enticing as gopher snake and white pine tea sounds, there's also merit in stopping by the grocery store for pizza and frozen cheesecake.

This very night Cyman may again choose to burn the woman who's dazzled my heart.

Interstate 17 north. The San Francisco Peaks loom ahead. They used to be sixteen thousand feet, until they burped the top four thousand all over the surrounding miles. Twenty minutes pass like twenty seconds as I meditate on the contours of Amanda's side and stomach, recalling each separate moment she spent pressed against me. I pull into Bernard's auto body parking lot and back up to the open garage door to hide my license plate.

Bernard is inside. He wears jeans and walks with a shuffle. His ankle is still dicked up. He glances up from a fender. "What's going on?"

"I stopped by and said hello to your father."

He grins. "The secret's out."

"Why didn't you say something?"

"It didn't come up."

"Did you earn the Desert Dog tee? Or steal it from an open box when your pop wasn't looking?"

"Pop's always looking, and don't joke about the tee. Almost died getting it."

"You almost die a lot."

"What you here for?"

"I gotta hide the Jeep."

He glances across his shoulder to an open bay at the end of the building, piled thick with junk, two scrap motorcycles, an engine lying on its side, spilling hoses like entrails and bleeding oil to the cement; a parts-washer; a welder.

"Move stuff around. Make room," he says.

A half hour passes in banter and sweat. Bernard works on an El Camino and I clear the stall. I park the Jeep inside, close the bay door. "All right if I hang out here a little while? I've got to research Cyman and Hock. Something your dad said."

He shrugs. "What's your beef with Cyman?"

"Started out as a bet. Now it's personal."

"I can't talk details," he says, and looks up from the fender. "But you're wasting energy."

"Do either of these bikes run?"

"Junk."

"Wasting my energy? Your pap said the same thing."

"Trust me."

"Says the white man to the Indian. Oh, hey. Put this thing back together for me." I dig the paper sack holding the .45 parts from my pack and carry it to him.

He takes the pistol by the grip, looks it over, and assembles the pieces.

"Cyman has to pay, specifically. It doesn't matter if he loses the election, or if some catastrophe befalls his return flight to Washington. He has to pay for...what he has done."

Bernard hands me the .45. I snap the receiver, check the chamber, dry fire. Slam a full mag home.

"My father hunts big game every year in Colorado," Bernard says. "I go too. We stay at a friend's camp. Buddies come from all over. Different times of the year, different camps. Colorado. Utah. Montana. Michigan. Pennsylvania. New York. Georgia. We got people all over. You know how I mean? We show off our rifles. Catch up on technology. Tell lies and share concerns about politics."

A fleeting, but heartwarming thought: how many former Green Berets and Rangers and Seals and Delta are out there, keeping up with their buddies? And consider their charters. Their skills. Special Forces is all about training indigenous forces into warriors. Rangers are shock troops. Seals? Delta?

Anything they want.

"What's your father do for a living?"

"Nothing. He did security consulting in Washington a few years, then New York. Fortune 500 companies sending people to Latin America, mostly. He used his New York contacts to make money in stocks. Now he sits on gold."

"So why you live in Flag doing auto body?"

"It's my bliss."

"Right."

"I love sanding putty. The smell of dust in the air, and the way the sunlight catches it in the morning. Running my fingers across metal and putty and not feeling the difference from one to the other. The first coat of primer. What?"

"You bench four hundred and talk about bliss."

"My father taught me this, and if you want to understand him, listen. Two things worth doing: your bliss, and defending your bliss."

"My bliss," I say, "is going to be hanging Cyman by his nuts from a saguaro."

I open my laptop and sit in the jeep, launch an odyssey of research. A news story from a year ago mentions Hock's crowning achievement, a fifty million dollar development pushing the eastern boundaries of Phoenix.

Hock wagered high growth rates and cheap credit would turn his investment into a quarter billion. He leveraged his entire personal fortune and bought hundreds of acres of desert. He's got a hundred units going up right now, and plans for two thousand more.

The sticky part is getting the water. His plans were to tap the lower of a two-layer aquifer. The ground is broken. A hundred acres are flattened. Concrete pads are being poured by the dozens. Septic lines. Streets paved.

Mid-project, he runs for senate against Cyman. And then a baseball bat catches his blind side: the state's water supply company, SRP, "is concerned Duane Hock's development will tax the already overextended Verde River's underground water flows, and do so illegally." Nearby Yavapai Nation is supplied by the Verde, and is "exceedingly worried," said Jane Arcosanti, tribal government relations director.

I follow a few links, read a few articles. Then another doozie: Cyman's son Henry, a.k.a. Hank Cyman, is the director of the Arizona Department of Water Resources.

How lucky for Senator Cyman that the Yavapai tribe felt threatened by his opponent's development. *Fortuitous* luck.

Hock could take Hank Cyman to court, but Hock has houses contracted to deliver, and can't spend years litigating against the state. Nor does he want to be the candidate who is unfriendly to the Indians.

All that is readily available through the Internet. Speculation, from this point forward is simple: Senator Cyman makes Hock an offer. Lose the campaign. Drag your heels. Don't be too obvious, but don't campaign too hard, and you'll get all the water you need. For Hock, it is either lose millions of personal dollars and bankrupt his company, or take the deal.

I close the laptop. Think. The lesser of two evils is still evil.

It's hotter than the hubs of Hades in the garage. Bernard cleans his hands at the corner sink. The soap smells like oranges. We cross the street to Schlotzsky's. His ankle is improving; he barely limps. I buy the subs and a newspaper from the dispenser. We sit at a table by a window. I flip to the classifieds. The first ad is the one I want. '05 Honda Valkyrie, Black, clean, new tires and battery, low miles, $6,500 obo.

I've got a mouthful of roast beef and I get mayo on the phone's keypad. "I'll give you five grand, cash, today."

"Six."

"Done." I close the phone. "I'm getting a bike. Got to keep the Jeep in your garage 'til this blows over."

"Whatever. Thanks for the sub."

I slip a pen from my pocket and trace an inspiration on a napkin. The drawing starts with a meandering curved line. Of all things, it resembles the back of an elephant, and with a few arcing strokes, the beast is outlined. An oval for a head with a tubular trunk. Slap a striped hat on him and put an R on the crown. I erase the front shoulder, and replace with meatier lines.

I am not an artist.

Elephant complete, true inspiration strikes, and beside his head, I pen the long ears and noggin of a donkey. Its snout extends under the elephant's trunk, where its passionate mouth meets the elephant's. I erase half of one ear and bend it over, like a kissing woman bends her knee.

With bold strokes I flesh the jackass within the legs of the elephant. Skinny donkey legs complete the embrace.

In a moment of quiet audacity, I cross a Rubicon. I redraw the donkey's rear legs spread wide and locked around a now thrusting elephant, consumed in the passion of missionary-style love.

It would make one hell of a campaign button for a third-party candidate.

"What you got, there?" Bernard says.

I spin the napkin. He chokes. "Found your bliss, eh?"

I give it some thought. Though I've spent a fair amount of my life doing useless things, I can think of none within the last few days.

"You got to drive me to pick up a motorcycle."

"You carry six thousand, cash?" he says.

"Not on me. In the Jeep."

He shakes his head.

"What?"

"I should have sold you the .45 for a grand."

I take my trash to the bin. Before I dump the tray Bernard says, "You should keep that drawing."

I'm at some old guy's house on Hemlock Street. Bernard inspected the Valkyrie and gave it a thumbs-up. I snap sixty benjamins into the man's hand. His brow tightens and I can tell he loses count at forty something.

"Go ahead and count it again," I offer.

Bernard climbs into his truck and leaves. The old man takes another five minutes losing count before he gives up. "You say there's sixty?"

"That's right. You want we should go to the bank and they can count it there?"

"No, no. I trust you." He tosses the keys, hands me a signed title.

I've already heard the bike, driven it up and back the street. The machine consists of a car-sized engine, two wheels and a seat. I suspect the old man spent more time waxing it than riding it.

"Take good care of her," he says. "Change the oil every three thousand miles. Get in the habit of breaking the clutch before you start the engine."

"Thought that was just on the old bikes."

"Mebbe. Hell. I don't know," he says. He combs his fingers through grey hair, leaving absurd tousles. He takes small steps. Looks like a father giving his daughter to a gorilla.

"I'll take good care of her." I climb aboard. Fire the engine. Give the throttle a quick snap. He winces. Waves his hand to detain me, waddles to the garage and emerges with a full-face helmet. "Take this!" he yells. "Put it on."

This is like when your host offers a glass of water. It is easier to accept. I take the helmet. Glance inside, then at the old man's greasy head. I rest the helmet on the sissy bar and secure it with the chinstrap. Release the clutch with morbid care and the engine barely notices it is engaged.

Onward. I have a senator to destroy.

Less'n ONE DAY 'til RACE DAY

Let the consequences be what they will, I am care-
less, no man can suffer too much, and no man can
fall too soon, if he suffer or if he fall, in the defense of the liberties and Constitution of his country.

Daniel Webster

I cruise to the apartment complex in Phoenix, wearing the helmet, hair tucked under my shirt collar. Circle the lot. There's a black Suburban over by the pool freaking out the sunbathing chicks. I tool close. Géraud and his gay moustache sit inside. On the other side of the parking lot is an unmarked Chevy Caprice police car.

Passing the Caprice I see the officer isn't the young guy I ministered to yesterday. I stop alongside and flip my visor. The window motors down.

"Officer, I don't know if you've noticed, but there's a creepy guy in a black Suburban over there, looks like he's filming the girls. Maybe you could check it out?"

I circle the Valkyrie to the back lot and park beside a new Corvette. Red enough to make Prince break into song.

At the building I rap the door.

Keith answers. I step inside.

"Whoa, who—"

"It's me." I slip the helmet off and close the door. "Cyman's got a guy following me. Plus there's a cop waiting."

"Why?"

"Speech ain't free."

"Why are you here?"

"Who is Amanda Cherubini? You know more than you told me."

Keith steps away. He's decorated the place. He sits on a leather sofa, turns on a lamp made of copper and cowhide, and lifts a new pair of cowboy boots to a coffee table made of hewn pine logs and half-inch glass.

"Come into some money?" I say.

He shakes his head. "Katrina won the lottery. A hundred grand. You parked next to her first purchase. She blew ninety-five thousand dollars yesterday. All day, sun up to sundown."

"Where is she now?"

"Buying five thousand lottery tickets."

"She's ruined. You want to argue about the lottery system now?"

"She'll figure it out."

"No. They let people win every now and again to keep them addicted. They're just like the tobacco companies. They hire behavioral psychologists to figure out how to hook people. Which reminds me... Who is Amanda Cherubini?"

He sighs. "You like her, don't you?"

"Don't change the subject."

"I should have known better. Someday I'll take your advice and butt out."

"Keith! C'mon! Who the hell is she?"

"Amanda Cherubini is not Amanda Cherubini. That's her... alias."

"I followed her the other day. She's a grad student. Political science."

"She is that."

"What are you hiding?"

"I knew her as an undergrad. Dated her."

I run through the faces and names. I met most of the girls he dated. Even stole a few. But there is one he kept at a distance.

My brain starts to feel like air at twelve thousand feet.

I beat her door, not having bothered to pry her real name from Keith. The lock slides and the door opens. She's yawning and wiping swollen eyes and there's an afghan on the couch. Her cheeks are flushed. She's been crying. I close the door. Lock it. Take her arm and spin her. Yank her shirt up to the burn marks.

"What!"

She fights me but I pin her against the wall. "These fake or what? Made the whole thing up?" I press a burn. She squeals. Twists. I shove her shoulder to the wall. Face to face. "You lied to me. Who burned you?"

Her brow looks like some wayward farmer dragged a harrow over it with his Allis-Chalmers.

"Cyman."

"Oh, *your father* did this to you?"

She looks away.

"Don't lie to me again."

"Géraud." She sniffles and the whole thing ain't workin.

"Bodyguard Géraud?"

"My father doesn't know what I do. Géraud does. It's the price of his silence."

My mind reels. Who is this deceptive little snit in my arms? The one I'm bound to love forever— Why would she set up her father? "What about the Indian boy? Did you make up that, too?"

"Géraud told me about it while he was getting off." She wrenches her arm away. "Is that any better? Are you happy?"

"What?"

"You know everything. I take money from rich guys to sleep with them. My father's a senator who rapes boys. His bodyguard burns me? Get it the picture?"

I release her arm and step back. The air-conditioning unit kicks on and a draft chills my forehead. The front of my brain is blank. The neurons are a battlefield; my intellect runs futile calculations trying to understand new facts that don't jibe with the old. How can you love someone who deceives you? Not white lies, but whole cloth?

And then the inevitable memory. The night she stayed on my couch and we did angel kisses. Eye to eye, fluttering lashes against each other, her soul open.

"I'm through with you."

"Not so quick," she says. "Géraud knows about you. I denied it, but he knows. And Géraud is nobody to mess with. He's from the French Foreign Legion. That's why Cyman uses him. Total loyalty, and total lack of morals. Ruthless. He thinks you're going after Cyman about the boy, now. He's been on your tail since the first billboard, but now he thinks you're going to try something big."

"So what?"

"Géraud said if I don't talk you out of whatever it is you've got planned, he'll kill the boy."

She turns away, pulls her top to her shoulders and says, "You see yesterday's burns? You see what he did last night? If you want that boy to live, you've got to go on with what you were doing before. You've got to do another prank. It's the only way Géraud will believe you're not really trying to bring Cyman down."

"Why don't you call him 'Dad'?"

"Screw you."

"So I have to go on being a nuisance so Géraud doesn't think I'm actually trying to expose... your father."

She nods.

"Why you been crying?"

"Duh."

I lean on the stair banister, then circle to the steps and sit. "What's your name?"

She faces away. Launches herself on her heels to the kitchen and returns with a glass of water.

"My name is Ash."

"Ashley?"

"Right.

"You broke my heart, Ash."

"No," she says. "You did."

Miles pass. The six-cylinder motorcycle engine purrs and the fat tires eat road. The wind is steady and the noise becomes bland as boiled corn husks. I think of a war movie.

Toward the end of *We Were Soldiers*, Colonel Hal Moore knows the North Vietnamese are about to overrun his battalion. His only advantage is audacity.

Waiting invites his enemy to use its superior size and condition to overwhelm him. Cataloguing his resources, he counts his men not for their number but for their bravery. He counts his well-dug defenses not for the minutes they will delay death, but for the surprise the bulwarks will afford when he abandons them.

Outnumbered, surrounded, Colonel Hal Moore arrives at an elegant strategy. He attacks on all fronts.

I sit on a boulder beside the Valkyrie. Behind me, a never-ending stream of cars files past Bell Rock, Sedona's giant welcome sign. It is the first truly magnificent spectacle to greet travelers approaching from the east on 89A. Shaped roughly like a bell, it is six hundred feet tall and a shade of red any traveler recognizes from a thousand old westerns. The color satisfies, and you know God had a good thirty seconds when he put this sweep of stones on the map.

The sun sets and Bell Rock becomes a burgundy outline against an indigo sky. I rest my eyes by leaving my gaze there, and remind myself that as I sit here in judgment of Cyman, and plot to damage him in recompense for the evil he has perpetrated, that there is one who sits above who judges my actions as well.

Soon I can only discern the rock's outline by the stars it blocks. Traffic reverses as cars file out of town. By nine, traffic is thin. At ten, the roads are almost deserted. Midnight, lights extinguish. The village of Oak Creek sleeps. I share the parking lot with two cars, presumably belonging to backpackers who camp in the wilderness.

I get up from my boulder and walk around. I am near a picnic shelter and though the trashcan is yards away, the smell of corn syrup finds me. It must be maddening for the animals of the high desert... breathing dry air perfumed with the intoxicating excesses of the species that would drive them ever farther from their habitats.

A police car pulls to the second of Oak Creek's red stoplights. The occupant's head turns toward the coffee shop. The car sits, then drives away. I note the time and his exit direction and wonder what became of Stu.

This is the inglorious part of revolution. The legwork that spells the difference between success and failure, the boring time spent on homework. It is good to have a clear mind, a single purpose, and the resources to complete it.

Surprise, and the sun at your back.

My father, a leader in the American Indian Movement until he disappeared in my early childhood, spent hours doing the same. I wonder if he would approve of my participating in the American political system instead of bearing arms against it. For no matter how I would portray my actions to grandchildren clumped about my feet, I am a participant. Assimilated.

The scribbled lines on my notebook might, in court of law, be presented by an overzealous prosecutor as a component of a larger revolutionary narrative. But for all their originality and fun, they are not. I'm still in the box.

Again, I think of Camus—my good, dark, friend Albert Camus. Rebellion occurs when a person decides any future is superior to the continuation of the present. It is not a moment of bravery so much as profound frustration. I am not there. I won't accept *any* outcome. I want one specific outcome.

The essence of war is that one rejects another's authority as rule-dispenser. I have not yet walked to the cliff, felt wind lift my hair as I stared into the abyss. I fight the men who made the rules, but I pay them the courtesy of playing *by* their rules. And I allow them to judge me by those same rules.

Not so, my father.

Before the U.S. Government came to agreement with the Lakota in 1868, the Bozeman trail ran through the heart of Lakota territory. The government established military posts along the trail in the 1860's, pav-

ing safer passage for white expansion into the West. Red Cloud, re-
nowned from his youth for bravery and leadership, had seen the expul-
sion of the Eastern Lakota from Minnesota in 1862 and 1863. Between
1866 and the signing of the Treaty of 1868, Red Cloud waged the most
successful war against the United States by an Indian nation.

In 1865 the Congress, weary of perennial conflict, short on funds
from the Civil War, and mired in a post-war economic depression,
studied the reasons for continued aggression between the U.S. and var-
ious Indian Nations. Red Cloud's attacks kept the garrison soldiers
along the Bozeman Trail in a constant state of unrest. In December of
1866, Red Cloud handed the Army a crushing defeat of an eighty-sol-
dier column near Fort Phil Kearny, Wyoming. The U.S. government's
desire to wage a war it was losing, suffered. Congress released a report
in 1867 on the Condition of the Indian Tribes. This study led to an act
to establish an Indian Peace Commission to end the conflict.

Representatives from the U.S. and the Sioux Nation signed *The
Treaty of 1868* at Fort Laramie, Wyoming. The Treaty provided victory,
in a sense, for the Lakota, who agreed to stop hostilities toward whites,
stop opposition to railroads that didn't cross the reserved land, never
capture, or carry off from the settlements, white women or children,
and never kill or scalp white men, nor attempt to do them harm.

I've read the words so many times I remember them unbidden.

*In return, the government of the United States desires peace, and its honor is
hereby pledged to keep it.*

The treaty was a contract between two nations. It didn't create for
the Lakota an obligation to sever ties with their way of life, suffer tres-
passers, or assume American culture. The treaty set aside 22 million
acres including the Black Hills, exclusively, forever, for the absolute
and undisturbed use and occupation of the Lakota.

The Treaty began the process of assimilation by promising monies
for building a residence for an agent who would act as a liaison between
the two governments, a residence for a physician, carpenter, farmer,

blacksmith, miller, and engineer, and a school. Total monies set aside for these buildings: $23,500. The U.S. Government also agreed to provide the physician, teachers, carpenter, miller, engineer, farmer, and blacksmith to live in the buildings, and pay for their services.

Government promised to provide a pound of meat and a pound of flour per day per adult, a set of clothes for every man, woman and child on the reservation every year, and for every Indian who took up farming, a good American cow, and one good well-broken pair of American oxen.

Further, any Indian-turned-farmer would also be a citizen of the United States, while reserving all the rights of the Indian under the accord.

The treaty was ratified on February 16, 1869.

Even as it was being signed, rumors circulated that the Black Hills were filled with gold. In 1874, under the guise of seeking sites for a military post to allow so called "works of necessity," the U.S. Government sent Colonel George Custer and 1,200 soldiers on a 60-day reconnaissance of the Black Hills. They found gold in the roots of the grass.

Soldiers attempted to stop whites from entering the Indian lands, but few were prosecuted. Cities such as Sioux City, Iowa, dreaming of commercial gain should a gold boom occur nearby, promoted stripping the Indians of the land. An indication of the land's value was the Homestake gold mine, which produced more than a thousand tons of gold, worth more than a billion dollars today.

The Sioux refused to renegotiate. President Ulysses S. Grant decided that instead of rescinding the orders forbidding miners entry, no further resistance by the military should be made to the miners going in. By the end of 1876 over ten thousand whites occupied boomtown Custer City.

The next tactic to wrest the land away came in the form of a purchase offer for $400,000 per year or a one-time payment of $6 million for absolute relinquishment of the Black Hills. The Sioux refused to sell. General Crook and Colonel Custer were separately dispatched to round up dissenters Red Cloud, Crazy Horse and Sitting Bull, and their followers. Given the U.S. Government's heavy-handed and faithless dealings, over the summer of 1876 the chiefs and their bands, joined by Arapaho and Cheyenne, defeated General Crook at Little Big Horn and "massacred" Colonel Custer.

Because the chiefs defended the land they owned from armed thieves and military aggression, the U.S. Government declared void the treaty of 1868 signed at Fort Laramie. While the warriors were away with Crazy Horse and Sitting Bull, the U.S. sent soldiers to gather, disarm, and confine the women, children and elder Sioux who remained. In August, another emissary was sent with another round of documents to legalize the theft of the Black Hills.

Meanwhile, buffalo stampeded toward extinction. Between 1870 and 1875, two and a half million animals were slaughtered annually, and the last large herd of ten thousand was killed in 1883. Once numbering sixty-five million, appearing in herds up to twenty-five miles long, buffalo by 1890 numbered less than one thousand.

Their capacity to sustain their way of life decimated with the buffalo herds, government agents threatened to withhold promised food from the Sioux, forcing Sitting Bull to sign the Black Hills Act, also known as the "Sell or Starve Bill," in 1877. The act appropriated 23 million acres in exchange for subsistence rations.

It took until 1923 for the Sioux to convince Congress to waive the U.S. Government's sovereign immunity in order that the Court of Claims could hear the case of the theft of the Black Hills. In 1942 the Court of Claims said it didn't have jurisdiction and dismissed the case. In 1946 Congress established the Indian Claims Commission, but limited the Sioux to the right to sue for compensation, not a return of the stolen land.

In 1974, the Indian Claims Commission decided the Sioux were owed $17.1 million, representing the value of the Hills in 1877, and another $89 million, calculated at five per cent simple interest.

In 1980 the U.S. Supreme Court in an 8-1 ruling decided the U.S. Government violated the Fifth Amendment by taking the land without paying for it, and upheld the earlier award totaling $106 million dollars.

The same original principal of $17.55 million, however, invested at actual stock market returns over the 103-year period, would have accumulated well over $500 billion.

In 1968, headed by a group of activist ex-cons, more than two hundred Indians joined in Minneapolis to discuss issues critical to the Native American community. From this original group, Concerned Indians of America formed, then quickly renamed itself the American Indian Movement. AIM took as its symbol the upside-down U.S. Flag.

My father was one of that group.

My father spent his short Blackfoot life engaging the enemy. He participated in the takeover of Alcatraz, the occupation of the Bureau of Indian Affairs building, and the shootout at Wounded Knee that put Leonard Peltier behind bars. The FBI pursued him with a decided lack of humor until he disappeared in 1980.

I have a different perspective on the U.S. Government than Rachel or Cal Barrett.

Authors and activists cite the Treaty of 1868 when making the case for land restitution and sovereignty. But while government wrongdoing is obvious, how does a government atone for evil? What is stolen land or massacred ancestors compared to the theft of economic responsibility? I refer of course to the subsistence economy.

The Treaty of 1868 preserved a large enough block of land to enable a hunting-based economy. While the Treaty overtly attempted to turn Native Americans into white men by providing tools, schools, doctors, blacksmiths, and an offer to leave the reservation and join American society, it also left the Lakota sovereign.

This was not good enough.

Subsequent to the Treaty, the U.S. Government served a blow to the Lakota that its armies could not. It destroyed their hunting economy while creating a dependence on the government for "subsistence." The government promised food to eat—without producing the food. It promised clothing to wear—without killing the animal for the hide, or planting the cotton, or shearing the sheep. It provided a blacksmith without a mine for the ore.

The U.S. Government conditioned the Lakota, Cherokee, Navajo, Arapaho, Blackfoot, and all the rest to believe poverty was their destiny. It replaced the economic livelihood they understood with one that makes no sense, one that cannot exist, without government stupidity.

In a nation that views economic success a moral obligation, and poverty evidence of depravity, stacking the deck so that an entire race is dependent upon government subsistence is an outrage a just man cannot tolerate. Subsistence alone causes Native American alcoholism, suicide, poverty, teen births. Heir to rugged genes and generations of survival knowledge, the Indian today inherits an apparent choice between a way of life that is no longer possible, versus subsistence.

No one advocates a third choice.

A conquered man cannot look to his enemy for solace.

So half-white Solomon Bull lives in the city and participates in the white economy. But half-red Solomon Bull understands the thinking that animates men like Cal Barrett.

And the savage in Solomon Bull will not retreat from Senator Cyman.

I watch for police cars until two a.m., counting eleven occurrences of what are probably the same car. I rub my eyes, fill my tank at the gas station a hundred yards down the road. Buy coffee. Drive to Flag and park at Wal-Mart's lot.

Wake some friends.

RACE EVE

Each indecision brings its own delay and days are lost lamenting over lost days... What you can do or think you can do, begin it. For boldness has magic, power, and genius in it.

Johann Wolfgang Von Goethe

The keypad glows and I tap numbers. I'm at the old train depot, opposite downtown Flagstaff.

"Dude," Paolo says.

"I need you to make a video," I say. "Where you at?"

"Outside O'Fallon's. Waiting for a chick in a black Lexus."

"Wait—"

I'm on the bike, racing. I pull in front of O'Fallon's in three minutes and he's on the bench outside sitting beside a very ravishing Rachel. She's wearing prosti-boots like Julia Roberts in Pretty Woman, but her legs aren't chicken bone skinny. They're toned and tanned, and Paolo rests a paw above her knee.

I kill the bike's engine, kick the stand, swing my leg. Rachel smiles like a schoolgirl holding a tray of brownies.

"What are you doing here?" I say.

"Talking with Paolo. He's very sweet."

"He's drunk. He can't help you."

"You don't know what I want."

"I know you're bad news for my friends." I take her hand and lift. She remains seated.

"Dude, uncool." Paolo says.

"You don't want her. Trust me."

Trust me means I know something carnal that he doesn't want to know. The implication is she's a jungle of STDs. Paolo lifts his hand from her knee.

"Let's get some coffee, Paolo."

"Tick tock," she says. "Time's running out."

Paolo steps ahead a few paces and I swoop beside her on the bench. Lean close. "You dick with my friends, count me out of your games." I stand. "I can make more money."

I catch up to Paolo and Rachel's voice arrives like a knife in the back.

"Does Amanda Cherubini mean anything to you?"

I spin. March. She's sitting with a leg crossed on top of the other.

"Or did she tell you her real name... Ash Cyman."

"Who are you people? Is nothing below you?"

"Barrett, Solomon. Barrett. There is nothing in your world more important than Barrett. Instead of infiltrating a group of terrorists, you're up here playing games with a senator's reelection campaign. For what? A hooker."

"You have no right."

"No. I have power. And I'm using it to make the country safer. Is freedom a game to you? Some high-minded theme to argue about on an Internet chat room?" She hushes; continues in a whisper. "Because you don't have freedom without me doing my job."

"Funny, I don't have it *with* you doing your job."

"The world has moved beyond your pathetic antiquated notions of individualism. We're interdependent. You have to cede authority to others, or the bad guys win."

"No. You win by changing the bad guys' lives, not mine. Throw them in jail, not me."

"You're not in jail."

"A police state is a prison without bars."

"You said we should change their lives. That's what we're doing. If you'll just climb on board."

"What do you want? I've been in Barrett's house. I'm making progress."

"You haven't told me anything worthwhile. Your effort has been lackluster."

"Lackluster? You people! You think the knife has something to do with it? Or threatening my livelihood? Maybe some people lock up when an unelected power-suited government aristocracy backroom bitch barks orders."

"That's harsh, Solomon. Good, but harsh."

"You protect freedom? You march over bodies."

"I can't believe he won you over so quickly."

Paolo traipses back. "Hey Rach. Want some coffee?"

"Back off. You said three days."

She leans and in a voice that sounds like wind through bare November trees says, "We're running out of time. Something big is afoot. We've intercepted communications that we can't decipher, but we know we're dealing with a national organization. This guy has gotten the drop on us. So you're right I'm going to push hard. A nuke goes off in New York, it's on your head. Compare that to your notion of personal freedom, and tell me which is more important."

A good question. The knee-jerk response is that three million lives are worth more than liberty. But three hundred millions' liberty? Any state's most basic charter is to protect its citizens from foreign invasion. If the state fails, it wasn't worth having. But if in succeeding it destroys the freedom it was instituted to protect, its citizens have merely guaranteed their masters speak the same language. The question is how much government can a free society suffer, and remain free? Any more than that is death by a thousand cuts. A thousand taxes. A thousand laws. Regulations. Policies. Provisos. Caveats. Gotchas.

"You were doing better when you were just a naked chick in my shower."

Rachel exhales through her nose.

"I've got two days. You touch Ash, kiss my ass goodbye."

"What about me?" Paolo says.

"Dope. Come on."

Paolo and I leave her on the bench, her intractable lips frozen slightly upward, and her eyes straight ahead.

We enter a coffee shop with three dozen drunk or stoned Flaggies. I buy two grandes and two double shot espressos. Dump the shots like boilermakers.

"Drink. You have a long night ahead of you."

"What's her trip?"

"She's an undercover Treasury agent. TFI or some crazy sub-agency. She's bad news."

"She's hot."

"She'll leave a mark. I need you to make a video. Stick figures are fine... Avoid libel. Surprise me."

Layne is my graphic design buddy. He's spent his life working spare jobs he calls "gigs"—dish washer, fry cook, table busser. He followed his Nietzschean Will to Power to the veritable heights of night manager at a pancake house in Williams, but they shut down the shift and he walked rather than accept a demotion to cook. He's on the opposite side of the liberal spectrum from Keith. Layne has no cash, and just as there are people like Keith floating around trying to save people, there are people like Layne floating around, trying to be saved.

They bitch about "The Man" in one breath, and say, "there ought to be a program" in the next. They never grok that the sum of the programs is The Man.

Despite that, we're tight. He's a party animal, a daredevil rock climber, and for some obscure reason no doubt stemming from some traumatic childhood experience, he knows every species of tree in North America. He harnesses this encyclopedic knowledge to design radical outdoors graphics, and hopes to make his millions from graphic novels that feature trees. His comic heroes are granola eating, Birkenstock wearing, communal transgendered backpackers.

He's going to have a problem with what I do to Bell Rock, but that's down the road. I beat on his door. It is three, ante meridian.

A cat somewhere down the apartment complex erupts in a meow that, combined with a bank of fog, puts me in the mind of PBS's Mystery theme. I'm looking for Olive Oyl wailing on a headstone. The light flashes on and Paolo grumbles.

"Who's there?"

"Solomon. Open up. We got work to do."

"I don't work."

"Open up."

"Go away."

"I love you too. Come on. We got to save some trees."

"What?"

"Open the door and I'll explain." He opens the door and I step inside. "Dude, put some clothes on."

He's naked. I turn. He sleepwalks to the bedroom and sits at the computer bleary eyed and grousing that he's not going to brush his teeth for anydamnbody. He mutters through a wilderness of obscenity and emerges with, "What about the trees?"

"There's a senator who is cosigner of a bill to clear-cut the rainforests in Oregon. Almost the whole state, or something. We got to bring him down."

"I'm with like a dozen organizations. I didn't get an email alert yet."

"It was just on C Span. Did I say he's a Republican?"

"What do you want?"

"I want you to design a postcard. Just a slogan."

"A postcard?"

I could explain the logic of wasting my resources to attack not Cyman, but his constituency. But explaining myself will invite discussion, and in this modern democratic age where every opinion is valid, and every voice must be heard, I'll find myself debating with a man whose highest achievement in life has been saving enough money to buy a Mac off Craigslist.

"I'm going to buy a list of Republican donors. You get to call them names."

"What's going to be on the postcard?"

I utter words.

He nods. "That won't take five minutes. Watch this," he says, waking. He opens Gimp graphic design program. "I don't even need this. I could use Word and save it as a PDF."

"But then you wouldn't get to use Gimp."

"Right." He scratches something below the desk as the program loads. His fingers roam the keyboard with a musicality that approaches the sublime. Seconds pass and he hits the enter key with a grand stroke, signaling the completion of a masterpiece. I look. He's built a plain card with a black border. Thick, red letters, in a gothic font.

EXAMINE YOUR HEART, ASSHOLE.
VOTE HOCK

Not bad, since the goal is not to win hearts and minds, but to piss them off. Get them calling the press.

He says, "You think a postcard company is going to mail something with 'asshole' on it? Should you change it to 'schmuck'?"

"Do you know what a schmuck is? In Yiddish?"

"No."

"The same as a schlong. Or, in your case, a schlort."

He reddens.

"You shouldn't have answered the door naked. Change it to 'schmuck.'"

EXAMINE YOUR HEART, SCHMUCK.
VOTE HOCK

"All right. Can you save it and let me surf a bit?"

"Can I save it?" He shakes his head, insulted.

"File a grievance with the union."

"I wish I had a union. Here. If you want to really impress them." His fingers rattle the keys. I look over his shoulder.

VOTE HOCK
☺ OR WE WILL KILL YOU ☺

"I like it, but I'll take the other. You got anything in the kitchen? I haven't eaten in a year."

"There's fresh bologna. Oscar Meyer."

"Wow. Fresh Oscar Meyer."

Layne saves the art, lurches from chair to bed and he's snoring by the time I reach the kitchen. I return with a mouthful of bologna.

There's an icon of my file on the desktop. I open a browser window and search for a list broker.

Life is good for 159,000 people. Go to your computer and Google "America's richest Republicans mailing list." I note the address in case my postcard company can't find their own list, then upload Layne's art to a free online storage facility: I email it to my yahoo address. I can retrieve the file from anywhere with a computer—or have someone else retrieve it.

"You want to lock the door after me?"

Layne stumbles to the door, slams it behind me. I'm on the bike. Time to check up on my good drunk friend Paolo. He should be just about peaking, between the booze and the caffeine. I'm on the road. The air is cold and the ride is fast. Paolo greets me at the door like he's hard wired to a defibrillator. He pulls me inside and his computer screen is an incoherent mess.

"What's this?" I say.

"Don't get your panties in a wad." He minimizes a screen and clicks through a few PowerPoint screens. "You like?"

I watch.

"Add something like this: Cyman's son Hank is on the Arizona Department of Water Resources. Hock's development has run out of water. Now Hock kisses Cyman's ass in the campaign. Google a couple of sources and run with it."

"You got it," he says.

"Once you get it uploaded, how are you going to get anybody to see it?"

"Buzz, man. You'll be viral by noon."

By the time I hit Phoenix, get a shower at the swimming pool and dry off with a towel forgotten on a wooden bench, it is O-dawn thirty.

I'm hungry enough to eat a burlap bag of coyote carcass, but I opt for a pair of breakfast burritos from Stinky Pancho's.

I go to the park across from Cal Barrett's ranch, stretch across the bench, doze.

When I open my eyes the sun has climbed into hot territory and my watch reads nine. I've missed vital minutes, and tear-ass into Phoenix on Interstate Seventeen. Since the postcard will take more processing time, I head to an old friend's Scottsdale company first. Postcards from Hell. It's supposed to be a play on a chick flick movie title, kind of an avante-guard, in-your-face advertising stroke of genius. It looks like it's going well, because Bruce meets me accidentally in the lot, and steps out of a Mercedes CL500—about ninety grand worth of leather interior snobbery.

"Bruce, my friend."

"Solomon. Must be business, here this early."

"Everything is business to you. That's why you'll have a heart attack by the time you're fifty."

"This type-A has the best insurance money can buy, and lives on tofu." He slaps my back, smiles like Joe Biden, holding my eyes, but vacant.

"I need a rush job."

"Ugh. We've got all we can handle this week."

"I'll pay you more."

"Tell me your needs."

A sprinkler pops up and catches our legs in a spray. We hustle to the sidewalk. I follow him to the door. He jingles keys and in a moment we're in his office. He launches into a leather chair and rolls behind his cherry desk.

"Can you log on your computer and go to Yahoo.com?"

His brow wrinkles but he humors me. I tap in my login id and password. It's a dump account for junk. I open the email I sent a few hours ago from Layne's place.

"The attached file is my postcard. Just send it out to the richest ten thousand Republicans in Arizona. What's the rate?"

"To get it in the mail today? Triple standard."

"What are friends for, right?"

"That hurts. I'm in business, here."

"Triple is fine. You still have my card on file?"

He pulls up my client account.

"Bill the card. But the postcards must go out today. Nothing gets in the way."

"Nothing," he says. "You should get some sleep."

"I'll sleep when I die."

Ferdinand Vasquez, proprietor of "LPC Advertising," runs his oper-ation out of a full-size Chevy van parked in his driveway. A retired Army first sergeant, Vasquez years ago discovered a business need not being met by other entrepreneurs. He also noticed a yeasty slop of busi-ness ingredients: cheap illegal labor, endless housing developments, de-pendable sunshine, and businesses dying to get their word out. He mixed them together with a flash of lightning and like Miller and Urey's abiogenesis experiment, created something not quite what he expected, but interesting. He cornered the market, then drove his labor costs down by hiring indigent children, illegals.

The "LPC" in his company's name stems from the Army acronym, Leather Personnel Carrier. When an NCO says the troops are taking their LPC's, they know they're walking.

The first time I worked with Vasquez, he scrambled twenty kids with a single message from his iPhone. "Indigents have cell phones?" I said. He smirked. "Indigents got everything." I never minded buying his service, figuring if the people he hired worked for him, they must have found some economic advantage in doing so.

I rap the door and open it. Sit in the passenger side. He looks like a Mexican Arnold Schwarzenegger, sixty years old and built like a horse taking steroids.

"I need a job done. What's it cost to have five thousand flyers spread all over?"

"All over where?"

"Every car in the Phoenix Times parking lot. Every car within a five-block radius of the Capitol. Any leftovers on cars at the mall."

"Five block radius got a lot of cars, man. You got the convention center garage, Citi garage, you got a laaaaaata cars."

"Then skip the malls. Five thousand."

"When?"

"Today."

"I don't got the manpower."

"I could scare up a dozen illegals from the junipers by Circle K." My cell phone rings. I glance at the number. Bruce. Probably upping the price for the postcards or coming up with some reason he can't get the job done today. I silence the ringer.

"It'll cost extra. Thirty cents per," Vasquez says. "Fifteen-hundred dollar. Cash."

"You're a thief, Vasquez."

"A capitalist pig," he snorts gleefully. "You got the flier?"

"No."

"I build it. Twenty-dollars." He climbs to the back of the van, a mobile tech room. Computers, printer, copier, and reams of colored paper. He wakens a laptop and looks expectantly.

I lean. "Make it say..."

I've got a third cousin who looks like Magua from *Last of the Mohicans*. His name is Russell T. Wolfchild. He goes by the trendy Russ T, making him the only Indian in the world named Rusty. He's a hoodlum in the best sense. A hoodlum on everybody's good side—but he runs with some real knot heads who might be up for some beer money. I don't see him much, but we embrace like long lost—cousins.

"Sol my man. Tu loco, *loco*." He gesticulates, jabs my arm and I brush his fist aside. He's playful like a puppy, but the wrong person says the wrong thing in earshot of his crew, they're a pack of wolves. I've seen bands of teenage punks like this jump guys older, bigger, and stronger, and beat them down in front of their women.

"Russ T. Wanna earn some scratch tonight?"

"What kind?"

"Hundred each."

"A hundred? You want us to wash your car?"

"Nah, I want artistry. I want graffiti all over this city, saying one thing." I pull him aside. "Can I trust you? Can you lead these boys and make sure they don't get caught, and make sure they get the job done?"

He nods gravely.

"One message only. You guys start painting gang colors, or Joanie loves Chachi, it's over. One message only. Can you keep your crew in line?"

Senator Cyman lives in Payson, but likes the city life. He's a regular guest of the Grand Mason Hotel, outside of Scottsdale. Maybe they have a comfortable arrangement of looking the other way in exchange for patronage. The right vote on a special tax waver, or some such. He's got two more days in Phoenix, Amanda said.

I can't think of her as Ash. If I do, I have to admit she lied, and more, I have to admit I fell for it. I'm tired.

I hope two days provides enough time, because this flurry of stunts is only the diversion.

In the back of my head I wonder if I should be looking for the boy. But how? Even if I could rescue him, there's no sense in doing so until Cyman has had one more round with him. Vulgar as it sounds, I'm taking the utilitarian view on this one. Until I've got proof in my hands that will make it impossible for Cyman to torture any more children, I must refrain from interfering with this one. And rather than contort myself into some self-hating pretzel of doubt, I choose to hate the sick bastard who has caused the situation, the predator senator.

Desert Dog is tomorrow and I stockpile calories. I get butterflies thinking about it. I'm in razor blade shape, but if I don't get rest, I'm in trouble. I stop at a pizza joint and power through two thirds of a sixteen-inch garbage pie topped with everything but rotten fish. I'm bloated on soda and carbs and sleepy as savannah lion that just filled its guts with water buffalo.

Hauling ass to Flagstaff again. Heat dissipates as I climb toward Bumble Bee; the bike is built for these roads. The engine generates music like it generates torque. The fat round tires sound like pulling masking tape from glass. Pizza sits like a sack of iron in my belly, but the seat is wide and soft, and the wind just cool enough to make this moment something I'd like to etch in stone and look at later. I'm glad to be here now. The grassland to my right flank looks like the stuff Rumpelstiltskin spun into gold.

Onward.

Past the Sedona exit, uphill, then the San Francisco Peaks welcome me to Flagstaff. On the motorcycle, incognito with a helmet, I'm comfortable. Cyman's goon Géraud has drifted from my thoughts. But now that a few operations are in place, it is time to focus my thinking on the Grand Mason Hotel.

I want video evidence. I want the world to see what happens when the elite remain in position so long they lose grounding, and see themselves as entitled like lords over mice. I lean into the parking lot at Bernard's garage. Park. Pinch the bridge of my nose and close my eyes a moment. Yellow lines flash vertically through my mind.

3, 2, 1, wake.

"Hey," Bernard calls from the stall.

"How's your bliss?"

"Blissful." He stoops, looks across the hood of an old Trans Am, judges it with the critical eye of Michelangelo scraping a layer of fresco from God's fingertip.

"I need your help," I say. "If you can't help me, you know someone who can."

He is silent.

"I want to break into a hotel room, install video equipment, and catch a pedophile in the act."

He stands with hands on hips. Looks like a bulldog.

"You should wait," he finally says. "If you still want my help in a week, you got it."

"Whatever you guys have planned isn't going to punish Cyman the way he's earned. His actions can't stand. I need your help, or I'll do it myself and probably get busted."

"You should talk to my father. See if..." His voice trails off and his face is pinched. "You should talk to my father."

"I have."

"Again. We have a group. Maybe he was waiting for Desert Dog... Giving a few people a chance to get on the right side of things."

"Why are you so *frustratingly* cryptic?"

"You're a good guy. You got your mind right. My father's aware of that. He has someone who might help. I can't say more."

I open my mouth and he shakes his head. "You look stupid tired. How long since you slept?"

"Couple hours this morning."

"Crash today or crash race day."

"Tell your dad I'm coming to see him."

"I don't got to tell him."

I drive to Barrett's. My helmet is on and before I dismount, the motor drawing the gate opens. Either Cal Barrett is friendly to bikers or he knows I'm on a black Valkyrie. I glance at the video monitor. That's right; I'm coming to see you.

I motor forward and as I stop at the deck the gate closes behind me.

Cal Barrett opens the front door. He wears khaki shorts and his hair is in a ponytail. He's got a Wilford Brimley twinkle in his eye. "Still trying to bring your senator to his knees," he says.

"You know what Yoda said about trying, right?" I pull off my helmet; hang it from a mirror. "Do or do not. There is no—"

"Who the fuck's Yoda?" He studies my face with a subtle expression of pity. "You running my race tomorrow?"

"I'm running. But we got other business to talk about."

"Treasury girl send you back in?"

"Haven't seen her in, dunno. Hours. Dunno. She doesn't know anything."

He nods.

"I need your help. I know you're anti-government. Hell, that's obvious enough. Why can't you help me bring one evil bastard down? One who's been raping Indian boys?"

Barrett is slow to respond. Slow to lean against the deck post. Slow to adjust his nuts. "'Cause I have an operation going on, Solomon. Because there's serious history about to be forged. And going after some two-bit punk like Cyman puts the whole thing in jeopardy. He'll rot in hell for what he's done, if your facts are right. Why should I jeopardize everything to play God?"

"When's the last time God struck down a child molester, you can think of?"

Barrett goes inside and leaves the door open, which I take as an invitation. I follow, and note the thickness of the walls—about a yard. How much concrete and steel is behind that spackle?

The place is abuzz. Either he's got a crew of helpers for Desert Dog or the compound is the command center for another operation. I'm leaning toward the latter, though it makes no sense to run the race and launch a clandestine operation at the same time. Three men in the kitchen mumble beside a coffee pot. One sees me and shushes the rest.

Barrett continues down the same hall as before and pivots into the tech room. I follow. A man who puts me in the mind of the Muppet named Beaker swivels on a stool, then stands with hands behind his back, at ease, when he sees Barrett. Behind him, a bank of television monitors displays the compound from every imaginable angle. The outlying row shows external shots of the desert, aqueduct, the driveway. One camera is focused on the lot where I park the Jeep when practicing for Desert Dog.

The hi-tech components seem out of place in the middle of a hacienda. The door arches and the hallway floor is timber. But inside the tech room, the floors are speckled white linoleum; the lights are fluorescent, and a bank of computers to the side look like a backup to Mission Control, Houston. A nearby computer monitor has a spreadsheet titled Operation Guillotine.

"Carry on, Mike." Barrett says. "This is Solomon Bull. I want you to work with him today. What do you need, Solomon?"

"Video surveillance. Two feeds. Disguised. Something to fit a trendy hotel room. I don't know. You're the pro."

Mike bounces a look from Barrett to me. Opens a closet and pulls a clock radio from a shelf. "The camera's behind the numbers. See the grey spot? It's invisible when it's plugged in. The device is programmable, so the signal won't interfere with the second camera. It's also motion sensitive—it'll only run when your subject is hot. Two point four gigahertz and self-correcting digital transmission. I've got a lighthouse painting, a tower fan, a telephone. What do you want?"

The senator would notice a painting changing overnight. Still, I study it for the camera and come up blank.

"Inside the lighthouse. The light," Mike says.

I peer close and a tiny glass bead resolves. "Crafty, but I don't think so." The tower fan grabs my eye. "That thing swivel back and forth?"

"Right. Good for making sure you get coverage of a wide area, but intermittent. What is the target?"

"A pedophile."

Mike glances at Barrett.

"A senator," Barrett says.

Almost RACE DAY

We will find a way or make one.

Hannibal

Mike drives a black Nissan Titan to the Grand Mason Hotel and parks under a canopy of palm fronds. My temple bounces from the window the whole ride; my mind roams through sleepy-foggy bogs; computations like two plus two equals four are tantalizing but out of reach.

The lawn is golf-course green and the only American-made vehicles in the parking lot are Hummers. We pull overnight bags stuffed with random clothing—props—and a sizable suitcase with the fan, clock, receivers and VCRs, from the Titan's bed.

Inside, a suited bellhop reaches for the case. Mike declines, checks in at the desk. I park on a sofa and stare at the atrium and mezzanine. A pair of elevators rise from a marble floor and ascend six stories inside a glass cylinder.

Mike returns with a pair of plastic door keys. One of those profound two plus two thoughts has stationed itself front and center of my cerebellum. I've taken a deceitful woman's word about a senator. I don't know with certainty the Indian boy exists. *But the burns on her back did...* Am I so hungry to believe the worst about public officials that I'll accept any charge of disrepute on face value?

I follow Mike into the elevator. We exit on the third floor and in a minute he's unpacking in the room.

"I'll get you set up, and then I'm out of here," he says.

"Sure. You got the other operation going on. I understand."

Mike squints. Smiles. "Yeah, Desert Dog."

"Nah, the other operation. Guillotine."

He's uncoiling a power cord. He stops then continues. "What do you know about that?"

"Just that it's a big deal. Ten states."

"You might want to refrain from talking about that, before I refrain you." Mike connects the receiver, VCR, and television. Plugs in the alarm clock and aims it at me.

I watch my mug on the television. "Why black and white?"

"Best resolution in the dark. Where were you when all the detective shows were on?"

"Reading Nietzsche."

He shakes his head. Looks at his wristwatch. "Where's your girl?"

On cue, there's a knock at the door. I check the peephole. It is Ash. I open the door and Mike catches his breath. She ignores him.

"You ready?" she says.

"You have a key, or what?"

She holds it up.

"How did you get that?"

"I have a key to Géraud's room. He has a key to the senator's room. I swiped it last night."

"Won't he know it's missing?"

"He'll blame a maid. He hates Mexicans. He hates maids."

"I hate Géraud," Mike says.

I'm doing two plus two math and getting five. "Excuse us, Mike." I take Amanda's arm and lead her to the bathroom. She trudges behind me like a teenage girl being dragged to the grocery store or some other like totally un-chill place with her parents.

I close the door. Release her arm. "Amanda, I need to know who the boy is."

"I don't know. I only heard Géraud talking about him. You want to find the boy, you have to follow Géraud."

"Forgive me, but why do you keep coming to Géraud knowing he's just going to burn you? I'm tired. I can't remember. What was it?"

She snarls. Reaches for the doorknob. I block her.

"We've been through this. He knows too much about me. And a night of snuggling on the couch doesn't entitle you to every secret."

I take both her wrists and our faces are close. She smells so good I could cry. She heaves against me, brushes a breast against my ribs. "I'm about to hang my ass on the line for you! I have to know!"

I release her arms. Shrink from her. From myself.

"I'm not a hooker," she says.

"That's a splash of wake up." I sit on the sink. She sits on the commode lid. I touch her shoulder, and though she doesn't shy away, she doesn't press the contact.

"Why'd you pretend?" I say.

"To make you think Cy—my father—abused me."

"Why didn't you just tell me about the boy?"

"I didn't have any proof."

"But you had the burns. May as well get some mileage out of them. Where'd they come from? Hot wax at a frat party?"

"Screw you. I told you. Géraud."

"Why would a senator's daughter, taking her PhD in political science, be humping her senator father's security man?"

I see her left hand coming and let it connect. Feels like a Styrofoam two by four. Cute.

"What's Géraud got on you? Selling crack?"

"It's none of your business!"

"What? Did you join the Democratic Underground? Do you head the local Moveon dot org?"

She looks away. Her chin dimples and her eyes narrow. The look says I couldn't pull the truth out of her with a dozen Clydesdales, but it's written on her face. The senator's daughter has switched teams, and to keep it from him, she's taking abuse at the hands of his bodyguard.

Nah.

I weigh a reasonable father's anger over his politically wayward daughter versus his anger at having her body mutilated with cigarette cherries. This dog is so far from hunting, it's dead under the doorstep.

"That's it," I say. "You hate him enough to debase your body and join his enemies. Whatever. Just tell me one thing."

She stares straight ahead. Her cheeks are flush; her chin is pulled up and trembling.

"Is the Indian boy real?" I say.

"I swear I didn't make him up. Can't you see he's what this is all about to me?"

"Give me the key."

She offers it.

"You're going to be a great politician." I leave her.

Mike taps the senator's door and there is no response. I'm at the elevator, listening for the approaching car, the telltale whir of the cables, the ding! Mike slips into the room and I enter the elevator. I ride to the top, then the ground floor, and wait. Pace inside the glass-walled booth, watching the atrium floor for Senator Cyman or Géraud. I check my watch. I've got Mike's cell number in my speed dial so if I need to, I can send him a text and get him out of there. Instead, inside of three minutes, he chirps my phone and I rejoin him in our room on the third floor.

"Go okay?" I say.

He nods. Turns the television on. The fan oscillates, and the camera is always on. It feeds a shot of the bed and the periphery on each side to the television.

"I'm surprised it transmits this far," I say.

"Has a range of fifteen hundred feet, but only through three walls," he says. "I put the radio on the desk facing the bed, and the fan across the room, as a backup in case the action moves around. The clock only sends a signal when there's motion, and the first VCR is rigged to only record when it receives a signal. The second is continuous, so you'll have to check the tape every six hours."

"Isn't this kind of low-tech? Why not just record it into a laptop?"

"Oh we've got that kind—" He censors himself.

"Guillotine," I say.

I'm tempted to crash in the hotel, but Mike's leaving and my Valkyrie is at Barrett's compound.

"Got your key?" Mike says.

I pat my pocket.

"I'd love to change out the video tape for you every six hours, but I've got work to do. So set your stopwatch, if you've got one, for about five and three quarters hours."

"Couldn't you set the VCR to record everything from seven to one a.m.?"

"If you're certain your senator won't be getting his rocks off at six or two."

"I'll change the tape."

"All right. Let's get out of here."

I follow him to the elevator. Sleepy—like my consciousness floats in castor oil. We cross the lobby and step into the smelter of midday Phoenix summer.

Words and images take extra time to register importance, and as Mike unlocks the truck cab and enters, a man stands at the bumper of the Hummer beside us, blocking my way to the door. It takes me three seconds to realize I'm looking into the face of French Foreign Legionnaire, cigarette cherry woman-burning Géraud. His eyes crinkle at the sides and we're slow, like two cave men parsing a quadratic equation charcoaled onto the cave wall.

He lunges; I shuffle past and he latches my arm. I swing and it's like I'm in a dream fight. No skills. No timing. No strength.

The senator is at a fundraiser and it would make sense for Géraud to be with him. Instead, Géraud lands a pair of punches to my jaw and for an effete Frenchie, he packs some torque behind his knuckles. Stunned to wakefulness and pressed against the Hummer, I retort with a series of jabs to neck, plexus, armpit, groin.

Géraud wheezes. Crumples forward and with a violent twist, stabs my right arm with a blade I don't see until it comes out red. Tricky wicked. It's the kind of wound you know is bad before you look.

I dispatch a knee to Géraud's chin. His head snaps back. The Titan door swings open from the inside and Mike is leaning across the seat. He pulls me inside, slams the shifter south and peals tires out of the lot and onto Third Avenue. A couple quick turns and we're on the highway headed for the compound.

"Operation's blown," Mike says. "How bad did he get you?"

"Why blown?"

"All he has to do is get the hotel clerk to tell him which room we were in."

I grab my phone and dial with red sticky fingers.

"Grand Mason," the man says.

"This is Luke S. Walker, United States Department of the Treasury, room three oh one. Within a few minutes, Senator Cyman's head security man will ask you for information about me. I understand the senator is a special guest of the hotel. However, if you provide information such as my name or room number, you will find the Department of Justice investigation which is currently housed in room three oh one, which my agency at the Treasury is supporting, will expand its scope to include the Grand Mason Hotel, and not just the dirty politician who likes to stay there. Am I clear?"

"Uh—"

"Good." I close phone. Look at Mike, prepared for approbation.

"Luke Skywalker?" he says.

Mike exits the highway and turns north on Seventh Street. He pulls over at a gas station. "Let me see your wound."

I'm holding my arm and the blood has trickled to my fingers. My arm reminds me of an old painting of a Normandy invasion soldier staggering forward while half his body is soaked in red.

"No artery has been hit. Simple puncture. We'll get you patched up at the compound."

"Barrett keeps a doctor?"

Mike shakes his head. "Barrett is a doctor."

I wake at the compound gate. In a moment Mike holds the front door open. Barrett leads me to the kitchen and seats me at the table where a basin of steaming water, bandages, ointments await, along with stainless steel devices that could be for healing wounds or making them, depending on the disposition of their user.

Barrett twists my arm, studies the entry wound.

"He's had training," Barrett says. "He was going for the brachial artery, and sliced you on the way out."

Barrett wipes blood with a cloth, rinses it in the basin, and daubs the area with alcohol. He stands. "Lay on the table so I can work on you."

I comply. The table is something straight out of an old English mead hall, the kind Gawain might have taken a beer wench on after the party died.

"This might sting," Barrett says, and swabs the slice with hydrogen peroxide. I wince. After watching a cotton ball fizz for a few minutes, Barrett stitches my arm closed.

"You gonna try to race with that?" he says.

"Damn straight."

He nods and his head bounces a few times with what appears to be step-fatherly appreciation. "Here." He goes to the glass cabinet, returns with a tube of mercurochrome looking stuff, and wipes it all over my arm. Then he coats it with a layer of antibacterial ointment. Finally, he applies a water-resistant bandage that seals to my flesh all the way around the puncture.

"How long since your last tetanus shot?"

"Three years."

"This'll hold till the race is over. But we'll have to shoot you full of antibiotics tomorrow morning. You get in the aqueduct, God knows what's going to be swimming in your veins."

"How many times will I be in the aqueduct?"

He smirks. "Enough you could lose your arm from the infection. You want the t-shirt that bad?"

RACE DAY

The American Indian is of the soil, whether it be
the region of forests, plains, pueblos, or mesas. He
fits into the landscape, for the hand that fashioned
the continent also fashioned the man for his surroundings. He once grew as naturally as the wild
sunflowers, he belongs just as the buffalo be-
longed...

Luther Standing Bear

I stand in a group of forty guys. Five chicks that look like professional assassins loiter on the fringe. They've got bodies of rock and
faces like Amazons bringing down the kill. War paint. I bet they'll
be the toughest competition. Not from some heightened p.c. sense of
emasculation—just that challenges usually originate where we don't
expect them.

And these women are not merely athletic. They're beefy.

My arm swelled overnight. Flexing my biceps is torture, as is fully extending my elbow. I tell myself the human body is designed for contingencies. The mountain bike portion of Desert Dog is on a trail with only a few treacherous geographies. The aqueduct swim may be a challenge, as will climbing the rock face. I don't know if there are many other surprises, but I am well hydrated. I slept thirteen hours, broke fast on eggs, pancakes, sausage, and a quart of coffee.

Mike slipped over to my apartment to fetch my mountain bike and Camelbak this morning. He forgot my iPod, but other than that, I'm golden. He was in a hurry to return to the hotel and replace the VHS tape. I suspect Barrett has relieved me of the chore.

Cal Barrett climbs to the bed of a black Nissan Titan with an opened tailgate. He wears a Desert Dog t-shirt, faded jeans and boots. "You can leave your bikes for now," he says. "Park them over there."

Confusion. Grumbles. Whelps push bikes to a clearing while they glance back and forth. The event has always started with a long bike ride. Men sit on the dirt and swap bike shoes for trail shoes.

"I'm mixin' things up," Barrett says. He glances at his watch. "As you know, there are no rules. You enter this race at your own risk. You die out there, it means you shoulda had more sense than to start. Don't expect anybody else to help you negotiate an obstacle. The only disqualifications are from you not completing the course, or dying. Am I missing anything?"

I look for Mike. I'd hoped for an update before the race. I don't know if Géraud has tracked him down and left him in a gulley, or buried him in the desert.

My arm throbs. I close my eyes to pull my mind together. Open them.

"You will find the route well marked," Barrett says. "I'd tell you what to expect, but that would defeat the point." He turns sideways, and almost as an afterthought, points west and hollers, "GO!"

We're off on foot. Electricity jolts through me and I understand how God might have felt on day eight, thinking everything's fine so far, but I got a hunch these people ain't right...

The contestants stretch into a line with small clumps of competitiveness here and there. Most whelps seem to realize the race is less about beating the other folks than beating yourself. We're packed close enough the air is thick with dust from our feet. After the first few miles, each contestant will sense his place in the hierarchy. We'll see who the alphas are. Until then, it's best to take it easy and monitor body temperature.

I ease into a lazy stride and enjoy the sounds of the race. The percussive plodding of running shoes mixes with the sizzle of breathing and asynchronous gasps when a long stride ends with a twisted ankle or the trail suddenly turns steep. It is human music. Elemental. Primordial. An atavistic strain in every man harmonizes with the ancient survival tune.

Behind the human symphony is the concurrent buzz of bees. I see one of the little Africanized evil ones now and again, nearly invisible against the vegetation. These are the bees they scared us with in elementary school. You remember the maps, predicting the bees would take over Mexico and then Texas and Arizona, and conquer the contiguous U.S.A. by 2030. Well, they're here. They're like other bees, except with tempers.

The group behind me is as large as the pack I follow. Mediocrity at the beginning of an enterprise is hardly worth getting exercised about. By the end, I will lead them.

A pebble works its way across the bottom of my foot and lodges in the toe of my shoe. With each stride, it jiggles side to side. I wriggle phalanges to no avail. I jump aside, avoid a pod of Cholla, whose fluorescent yellow, pulse-seeking needles burrow deeper into the skin with each heartbeat, and strip my shoe, shake it, and look up to see the squad of Amazons trotting by. I balance on one foot, not so ungainly as to fail to offer a solicitous grin. The last Amazon, the only one of the crew with a gymnast's quads (the kind of girl you worry would break your thing off if you ever had the nerve to stick it in her) reaches outward and shoves me.

I lurch from ten-thousand Cholla needles, land in the pushup position on rocks that tinkle like glass. My injured arm gives way and I collapse. I look up. Scramble to my feet.

I'm in last place. Leg over leg. Easy does it. The enemy isn't the forty-four folks ahead, it is the sun above. It'll bake every one of us eventually. The temperature started at parity with our body temperatures, but quickly rises. The high is projected to be one sixteen by noon. If Cal doesn't have us in the aqueduct by then, we'll die. Two guys on four wheelers follow a comfortable distance behind me. I suppose to pick up the heat stroke victims.

As the trail winds around a hill, I catch occasional snippets of the foreground. The Amazons advance steadily through racers. A quick count puts them in ninth through thirteenth places.

The trail cuts right around a boulder and I stumble on a man crouched over his leg.

"Dude!" I roll and he curses. "What the hell?" My injured arm screams but the pain is more flash than bang. I spring to my feet and wobble to a stop.

"That bitch!" he says.

"What?"

"She blew out my knee. With a kick."

He must think he's walking back to the starting line, not realizing he's running a loop. "You got water?" I say.

"I'm fine."

"You're within a couple miles of the start line. We're running a loop. You should turn around. Or wait on the four wheelers."

"Anybody behind you?"

"I'm dead last," I say.

"Pay attention to the short chick. The power lifter. She'll take you out."

I emerge from the encounter with a brief surge of energy. I suspect, from my pace and lightheadedness, that I've covered five miles. Though my Camelbak is packed with ice water, and drawn tight to my body it cools my core, I am nonetheless cognizant that today is brutally hot. The sky looks like a painting, blue and rich. The terrain melts under the wavering air. Sweat lays on my skin. I approach the lap-one line. The trail diverges to the left, toward a series of eighty-foot crags, a mile or more in the distance. From the height of a small dome I see the string of contestants stretches about a half-mile. I look over my shoulder. The aqueduct is the other way. Barrett wants us to bake before blanching.

The path to the rocks is straight. A two hundred yard flat drops into an arroyo ahead, but before that, this is as close to track-running as we'll get. It is terrain built for speed. Many of the folks who have cooked their internal thermostats for the last five miles will be suscep-tible here.

Time to make my first move.

I gulp ice water, splash a small amount to my face and hair, and open my stride.

This is the pace I recognize instantly.

Runners have a sense akin to a musician's perfect pitch. There are bands of speeds where we know exactly how fast we are running with-out appealing to a stopwatch or a mile marker. I'm on a six minute, fif-teen second pace. I know its face like my mother's. I lock to the sound of my soles like a percussionist locks onto a beat. My hair blows. My stomach is tight and the men in front lift their paces as if aware insur-rection mounts behind them. It is futile. I pass one after another. They are uniformly thin. Rib cages peek under hairy armpits through tank tops. They are not Van Dammes, like Katrina worried. They are regular men pushing themselves farther than they ever thought they might push. Some look ready to collapse. Flushed faces. Wobbling steps. I read surprise at the brutality of the heat and terrain. Delirium. Several run with a limp, presumably after meeting the squat Amazon.

My temperature approaches the red line: I'm dizzy and an obscene pressure builds behind my eyes. This is the line. Like the six minute, fifteen second stride, I recognize this place from having been here before. I've been down with heat stroke. You never forget how you felt the moment you blacked out. You never forget how you felt the next half hour under a tarp your buddies rigged while freaking that you were going to die, while they stuck IV needles into your arms that they would have preferred to save for getting over a bender night of drinking. I back off my pace, but there's a welcome sight ahead to congratulate me for my latest burst of effort. A pair of shorts, roundly filled, and labeled, EAT ME.

She vanishes on the downslope of a knoll.

The Blackfoot were not a desert tribe, but a high plains tribe. Still, I'm closer to the earth below my feet than the men I pass.

As a teenager I grew my hair out and my mother told me something she intended to shatter the part of me that identified with my Blackfoot blood.

The American Indian Movement had splintered into factions, and for my father, the fight was too important to sit out with a white wife in Phoenix. My father's disappearance held ramifications for how my mother raised me. The last thing she wanted was to have her half-white son wear an eagle feather in his eighteen-inch hair, and wage war against the government.

She'd fallen in love with an Indian, but not his war. And she certainly hadn't forsaken the white culture that informed every facet of her existence, from how to bake a ham to how to celebrate the winter season by hacking down a tree. One Saturday when I was asleep on a sofa, age fourteen, she slipped behind me and cut off my hair. Pulled me out of the public school where a small tribe of Apache, Navaho, and Pueblo found common cause against the Mexicans and whites, and dropped me into Saint Xavier, the Catholic school on Indian Bend Road. *Indian Bend*—the honest, break your heart truth. Sent me to learn about YHWH.

I woke with my hair gone. Bobbed, like some chick in saddle shoes. I guess she thought I'd ask her to buzz cut the rest of it, after seeing what a mess she'd made of it with the shears.

—No.

And then it was about preserving my mind, preserving my will. I wondered if someday when I climbed a mountain, fasted for days, and was visited by my sacred animal, it would turn out to be a mule. You see them standing oblivious to their masters, resolute in their oblivion, imperturbable and grand. I tried to be a mule, but it takes a lot of focus to emerge from a Catholic school with your mind right. No matter what you do, they get inside. They rap your knuckles until your ears are open, and the words have their own magic because in some fantastic way they are true. There was a man who lived and died and convinced a lot of people he lived again. He wasn't Blackfoot, but he spoke to a Samaritan. Good stuff.

No Indian may avoid assimilation, in a certain sense; the world is wider than we knew five hundred years ago. But we can avoid licking deceitful conquerors' boots, I reasoned, and fought to keep my mind sanctified by the trees and the wind. Yet greedy nuns pried open my mind, and ignited a thirst for information about Western ideas.

In college I learned Aquinas and Kierkegaard and Kant; and balanced them with Yellow Feather, Red Cloud, and Pontiac. Different kinds of wisdom. Different approximations of facts.

Sweat leaks into my left eye and burns; the salt concentration is high. The Amazons follow the trail into a wash that points toward the crag ahead.

From training here I recognize an opportunity. A switchback leads out of the arroyo and up on the level desert again. I scramble up, face the hills and sprint. My temperature is still obscenely high, but if I don't get ahead of the Amazons before they reach the rocks... then what? If they are slow climbers, the guys ahead of them will expand their lead, while those of us stuck behind will languish, unable to pass for fear of getting shoved off the façade, or stoned.

In a few seconds I see them in the wash below. Their strategy must be to keep the same strong pace throughout the race, while disabling as many men as possible along the way. The girl in the lead is a tall, beastly red head. Her skin is flushed, burned. Her thighs are wide on the top, meaty. There isn't a cellulite dimple on any of their asses, and every now and again one mutters something encouraging to the rest. They command more respect now than when they started, I imagine, since they have twenty-some of the toughest guys around reading their shorts and eating shame instead.

The second girl in the line swoops to the ground and lifts a rock. In a quick underhand swing that designates her a ladies' softball pitcher, she whips the stone at me at about sixty miles per hour, best guess. It zips a few feet from my head and she smirks.

"You should know one thing," I call.

"Oh yeah?"

"I hit girls."

I add a burst of speed and complete the pass where the upper trail joins the lower. I'm ahead of the Amazons.

I do hit girls. Did hit girls. When I rode a school bus to Saint Xavier's, I'd curl my rail-thin self into a seat and try to ignore the raucous play around me. Maria Morales was a big, big girl. Three grades ahead and corn fed. I had less muscle than a deer carcass after a pack of wolves worked it for a day. Maria and her sister, a gratuitously plump girl two grades ahead, were de-facto queens of the bus.

I don't know if it was me or them that started it, but I ended up pinned on the bus seat under both while they alternated pinto bean farts on my back and head.

They compounded the insult by tickling me.

I writhed and wiggled free, then attacked with fists and feet fueled by ancient humiliation. I earned a three-day suspension—and was never farted upon again.

Years later at the dojo, I re-learned that a woman is as big a threat as a man. Don't discount her because of her sex. She won't discount you because of your stupidity.

This last mile has passed too quickly. My thermostat—my light-headedness—tells me I'm in dangerous territory. The sprint past the other whelps and then the final burst to clear the Amazons has left me wobbly. The more I wipe the sweat from my eyes, the more salt gets in. The treacherous trail includes talus from the slope approaching the rock face. Orange highway cones channel the men ahead of me to a narrow segment of the rock face. One has crawled over the top, that I can see, and four climb the wall. Thirty yards behind, the lead Amazon charges closer. By passing her I have become her target.

Three men catch their breath at the foot of the climb, hands on hips, heads back and looking at the wall. I run to the rock face, leap and negotiate the first three holds, lifting me five feet from the ground. My arm shrieks where Géraud planted his knife. I feel muscle tear. The rock is griddle-hot and though the sting goes away after a few seconds, the radiating heat roasts skin that is already burned from sun. Above all, I'm surprised my arm has retained most of its strength. Géraud stabbed with the grain, and though the surrounding muscles grumble, they do their job.

I climb like I've been here before. In a moment I've got Elvis leg; everything shakes from thigh to ankle. It's the adrenaline, the sugar in the muscles saying let's go to war, and the leg saying stand by until we get orders. It is cellular rebellion.

To my right, a vertical fissure extends twenty feet. My next few moves take me closer, but the wall is too flat. My running shoes slip over smallish pocks climbing shoes would needle into. A good climber relies on his legs for force, and upper body for finesse. Without appropriate shoes, all I've got is upper body strength to get me through the rough patches—and this is a hell of a free climb in sneakers. My bet—forty feet. The likelihood of a free climber dying here is good, especially with slippery hands and rubber legs. Cramps. Wounds. Resting, I become mindful of the burden of ice water on my back, which reminds me to drink. I suck from the hose until I get a brain-freeze headache, which I pause to enjoy with the now-steady burning in my arm.

They always say you're never supposed to look down. I say, look down all you want. It's how you know how high you are. The Amazons are at the base. The girls drop to their eat-me asses and sitting between Cholla and saguaro and creosote, cram their feet into climbing shoes.

I glance above and the climbers wear climbing shoes. I'm the only without, and it's because I spent the day before gathering evidence against a senator to impress a girl. A lying girl.

Rocks are jealous. If you want to live, think about the rocks. I'm fifteen feet from the ground. That fissure to the right would allow me to layback to the midway mark and retain my lead over the girls. I've got to get to it—but can I with a wounded arm? I smell my blood and a shadow flashes across the rock from a vulture circling in the sky.

The Amazons march up the rock with the same metronomic cadence.

Three points of contact always, no matter what, except if it can only be done with two. That's the rule, except when I break it. I have to reach too far to retain my left toehold, but my other two contacts are bomber so I lunge.

We go through most of our lives not needing to do anything specific to stay alive—but get into a situation where you must act now, and it doesn't matter if the action is finding a finger nub, or flipping a Bic six times in a row. You focus.

Muscle up. That's the problem about not having climbing shoes. It's all fingers and forearms, and that sux. A couple finger moves and I'm there, but not before a terrifying in-between moment where gravity begins its inevitable work and my synapses and muscles must shoulder true responsibility for remaining alive. My wounded arm performs but not without warning it might fail the next test.

With hands planted on the near side of the split, and feet braced against the far, I begin to move upward. It's like climbing a skinny tree by holding the top and walking up it. Kids can do it.

I reach the top of the fissure in short order and rest on a ledge. There are loose rocks and I wonder if the Amazons will accidentally dislodge them upon the men who have been chasing them for the last five miles. I stoop to the nearest stone and chuck it into a nest of Cholla. Not as many points as walking an old lady across the street, but hey, this is Desert Dog.

I glance up the rock face; two men climb above me. I mumble a brief thanks that they're not directly above. If one were to fall, he'd take me thirty feet.

I pat my hands dry on my shorts and shake them loose.

The Amazons climb vertically, in a line. If they're smart—and they seem as cunning as they are committed—they've got their best climber in the lead. She'll show the others the holds, and the others will expend less energy.

I resume the wall.

The Amazons must realize that alone they are weaker than the men they face, but together, both smarter and stronger. They've thought this out, and beating them will either be a matter of flat-out putting serious distance between us, or splitting them up and breaking their strength. If I do neither, they'll spit me out the bung side, like the guys behind us, clutching blown-out knees and ankles. I glance downward and the one in front looks like she's climbing a ladder.

Nothing marks the crux, but one look and you know this is where fate is decided. The guys at the bottom look like dwarves. The guys above me have climbed over the edge. Here, three quarters through the climb, I wait. Each second frozen on the rock face wastes strength, but there is no feeling worse than reaching for a hold and missing, or worse, finding the hole shallow or the knob slippery or the ledge crumbly. I'm at a disadvantage, not having climbing shoes. The others will probably push through this section, the toes of their shoes rubber points that tease support from the tiniest of pockets. I lean from the wall as far as I can, and scope for pockets and fissures, tiny ledges.

One feature is key.

Ever see that show on National Geographic where the African tribesmen outwit baboons with a hole in a rock?

The tribesmen hollow a pocket that allows an open hand to enter, but traps a closed one. They fill the hole with grain. A baboon grabs a fistful of corn, but can't get the rock to release his hand before the tribesmen arrive and club him to death.

There's a pocket at the crux. If I swing a hand into it, I'm strong enough to hang until I discover the holds to climb to the ledge above. I scout the route to the top; the best texture is on the left. My right hand will go in the hole. With luck, there won't be anything inside, and my stab wound won't rip farther.

My current handholds are strong. Way to my right is a hip-high crevice, and there's another near my knees.

First, my left foot fills the fissure by my knees. Transfer weight and extend my leg. Reach... inches short of the pocket. I probe with my right foot, stretch... find the hole. Canvass above with my right hand. Nothing. Glass. Next best is finding a hold below that will do the same work. I resume my old hold with my right hand and with my left, scan below my chest, out as far as I can reach, everywhere, until my fingers alight on a tiny sill. Too tiny—maybe.

The Amazons are getting close, a dozen feet below me. The lead girl's eyes are like glass. Her jaw is set and there isn't a thing I could do short of falling on her that would stall her progress. She has the confidence of a cat.

I press my left thumb into the ledge and reinforce the hold with my index and middle fingers. The rock is sharp. I shift and my thumb bears most of my weight. Feels like Nurse Ratched buries a razor into my flesh. My left leg dangles; the right protrudes for stability. I throw my right hand, press into the baboon hole, unite my fingers into a fist and hang.

The weight on my wrist tears skin and my biceps scream bloody murder. I pant a few quick breaths, close my eyes and find myself. Blackfoot. This ain't gonna last. I swing my right leg down and in a single, pendulum motion, swipe a hold of the ledge above with my left hand. My shoulder grinds half out of socket. I open my fist but my hand is stuck in the hole.

Open, but stuck.

I'm too hot to think. Jaded like comes from heat stroke. There's a bunch of Amazons coming to club me; what the hell's gone wrong?

Finally I get it. I twist my hand and slip free. Mantle to the ledge, get a foot on it, a second, and the rest of the rock is corrugated. The holds are big and rough; the sweatiest hand won't slip. My running shoes fit the slots and the last ten feet are more a test of repelling the blackness at the edges of my consciousness than finding the strength to go on.

I throw an Elvis leg over the top and roll. My lungs heave. Last I saw, Amazon was at the crux. No time for rest, but I've got to breathe just a little. I drink water. Hold the valve open and slap icy spray to my face.

The mountain continues up a boulder-strewn slope steeper than the sheerest-pitched chapel roof in Salem. Rocks look like pebbles in the distance, but are the size of Smartcars, and appear as likely to dislodge as stay put. If the downside on the other half of the mountain is the same, people are going to break legs.

RACING

When it comes time to die, be not like those whose hearts are filled with fear of death, so when their time comes they weep and pray for a little more time to live their lives over again in a different way. Sing your death song, and die like a hero going home.

Chief Aupumut, Mohican

I scramble over boulders, sometimes on hands and knees, sometimes leaping from one rock to the next. Rhythm is impossible. The terrain demands exertion in one second but not the next. By getting off the beaten path, I've seen more lizards than usual. I wonder which is Jim Morrison, reincarnated and demoted several steps down the Linnaean hierarchy, ironically to the rung he chose while stoned immaculate.

The girls slow, either tiring or exercising great care to avoid ankle sprains. I muse about how to deal with them, should they overtake me and force me to reclaim the lead late in the race. One nagging thought comes back, hydra-like, each time I sever its ugly head: Not saying I'd ever do something like this, unless in self-defense, but if I take out one of the Amazons—blast her knee, pop her in the solar plexus, ram a shoe up her ass—what will the others do? They rely on each other for group strength, but does their loyalty extend far enough to carry their wounded across the finish line?

Army Rangers know their mates will never leave them behind. But have the Amazons made a similar pact to carry out their wounded, or would they become a team of three, fiercer because of it?

The gap has expanded between me and the scorched Amazon leading the troupe. A pair of guys flank to the right, giving wide berth but trying to overtake the girls while they seem disadvantaged. I glance back every few steps. The Amazons fan to the right and the guys fall in line behind, but avoid coming close enough to receive one of the roundhouse kicks that has crippled at least two other contestants.

I crest the top. The girls are fifty yards below me, but there's no sense wasting time gandering over the valley. I do, anyway. The route circles the mountain another three or four miles to the aqueduct. We'll climb the chain-link fence and dunk through however many crossings Barrett has decided upon, and then however many laps on the mountain bikes it takes to satisfy him that anyone who finishes would be willing to go on and on, no matter what obstacles arise, until he's wearing either a Desert Dog tee or a casket.

I race along a narrow trail across the crown of the mountain, a flat about two hundred yards wide. Rocks dislodge under foot and the saguaro, century plants, and juniper give way to a thickening grove of Cholla. Cholla is the satan of cacti. It grows chest-high and appears to be a series of interconnected fingers and pill-bottle sized lobes. Each brandishes a thousand fluorescent green spines, strong as steel and sharp as a 33-gauge hypodermic. And the little bastards have barbs. Your heartbeat is enough to drive them deeper. Little demons. A lobe of a thousand needles will snap free when an unlucky animal brushes it, earning Cholla the name Jumping Cactus. Cholla is so good at hitching rides, it has lost the ability to sexually reproduce.

I think I know what's going to lie over the edge of the mountain: a Cholla grove so thick, there's no passing without filling shoes and legs with needles. As a happy bonus, the rocks will slip and roll. It won't take the force of a falling body to sink one of those needles two inches deep.

When Barrett said there were no rules, did he mean we could circumvent his obstacles? Is my objective to get down the mountain, or to get down the mountain through a bed of Cholla?

Ahead the other eight whelps wade through needles. The living Cholla plants are like a division of neon pincushions in formation over the entire six-hundred-foot slope. Carpeting the ground are the brown needles of broken lobes that failed to sprout roots. They lay everywhere, like thousand-pointed caltrops.

I follow what becomes an obvious path forged by the men ahead, obvious in that a lot of the easy needles have been picked up, and what remain are decayed brown ones that are as likely to snap as penetrate a running shoe. To my left I spot a seam of black rocks above the bed of needles, almost like a bridge of stones across a stream. I shift direction. Glance rearward. The girls are making what we men call good time.

Uncanny time. They cross the Cholla like they have nothing to fear; they are Shadrach, Meshach, and Abednego, and there is a fourth one with them. They march without care, protected from the glowing green needles. They cover downhill distance at a crazy pace; they'll be on me in thirty seconds. It's like they glissade, or ski—and a sickening sense rises in me that I understand the source of their advantage. They're using their climbing shoes—the hard rubber resists the needles, and covers the sides and top of the foot. Low down, conniving—clever. Very smart.

I leap, dodge a pumpkin-sized barrel cactus, and I'm on the seam of black rocks. It isn't quite a path, for there are still Cholla, living and dead, all around. I leap from one stone to the next and maintain my lead over the Amazons while overtaking men ahead of me. The steepest part of the mountainside past, I anticipate the open trail. I'll gain another half minute, as the Amazons switch shoes. Best guess is a three-mile run to the aqueduct...

I hear breathing, loud like Maria Morales on the school bus, stalking from behind, and before I can spin or leap aside, a stiff-arm to my back sends me off the vein of black rocks into the air toward a granddaddy Cholla.

"I hit girls too," she says, passing me.

I get one foot down and kick hard; I miss most of the Cholla but four bulbs of needles are all through my hand and arm. I know they're there, but it takes a second for the pain to register, and I'm hurtling toward a blanket of needles that would scare a heroin junkie straight.

I land in the push up position, hands on rocks. Catch myself just above a bed of old and new needles, and the pain in my stab wound is like a mini-drawing and quartering. My arm fails and I drop to my elbow.

Stagger to my feet. Assess the damage. The needles don't hurt—yet—for now it's my arm. I reach to knead it, but there's a fistful of needles preventing me. Nothing quite registers except another human being did this to me on purpose. I stumble a couple steps and my eyes and brain and muscles begin communicating again. I've got at least eighty needles in each hand, and as many as a hundred on the right side of my chest. Most are attached to Cholla fingers, and there is a simple excruciating trick to remove them.

All at once.

Back on the seam of black rocks, I whip my right arm and snap my wrist, launching a pair of Cholla lobes. I repeat with the left, already beginning to resume my path down the rock seam. The girls are only twenty yards ahead and I'll be damned if the wages of their sin will be advantage. After whipping both hands, I pull needles with great speed and severe disdain. What is pain at this point? Everything is pain. This is what Siddhartha must have been contemplating. I'm yanking needles and increasing my pace as I get the hang of using two parts of my brain for simultaneous projects.

I clear the Cholla field well ahead of five more guys, but have lost five places to the Amazons.

They uniformly drop, replace their climbing shoes with runners, and wrestle to their feet. They are methodical and reserved. I'm still pulling cactus needles. Blood dots my hands and Cholla lobes bounce on my chest with each stride, like the Dr. Kevorkian of acupuncturists has treated me.

The girls are clear now and I stand amid the shoes they've left and perform surgery on my chest: in a single sweeping motion, I rip my shirt over my head and eject a hundred needles from my skin.

I suck a jet of ice water from the tube, douse my head and swoop into a mile-destroying stride. I'm loose now, warmed up. White-hot metabolism. *Pissed.* The brief respite of running down a grade ends shortly, leaving a sprint to the fence, barely visible across the valley floor, between scrub juniper and cacti. We follow a four-wheeler path. I debate forging a route around the girls, but I'm not so fast that I can manage an obstacle course with the same speed as they are handling this dusty trail.

I'll overtake them in the aqueduct. Maybe drown one or two.

I've been in a state of heat exhaustion for a while, now. The danger is that I no longer sense a clear demarcation between I'm fine and I'm dead. And if heaven is a desert, how will I know? The threshold becomes vaguer the longer I flirt with it: skin alternately dry and burning or sweaty and clammy, head hazy and hot. Where am I, on the spectrum? I stumble. Tumble forward. See the squat Amazon's nostrum embossed on her derriere: EAT ME.

I reorganize awareness and it's like coming to. I'm on all fours.

I have a sensation of having slept. My pulse races and my thoughts are like undercooked eggs. Scrambled, poached, soft boiled; runny.

There's a man ahead of me who just passed... left me here to die, maybe, without splashing any water on my face.

I stagger to my feet and lurch forward. Spray ice water on my head.

I don't know how many places I've lost. I was ninth, but could now be last. My arm wound stings with leached-in sweat. I step forward, spin, gather my bearings and see that most of the whelps are still behind me and indeed, I've only given up one place in the rankings: the sportsman who passed me for dead.

My mother saw my hair growing and flowing and worried that despite living in the white world I would reject it. She saw the way I watched *Dances with Wolves*, not yet knowing the disdain with which my Indian brothers regarded the flick. She saw me spend my allowance on *Man Called Horse*, *Geronimo*, *Last of the Mohicans*. She saw me put down my New Testament and read *In the Spirit of Crazy Horse*.

She drove me to the reservations east of Phoenix: Squalor. Trailers and houses made of unpainted cement blocks, dust for lawns, old men wearing flannel shirts in the dead of summer, riding horses while tumbleweeds blew across dirt streets, and kids played in their underwear.

"Do you want to live like that?" mother says.

"Yes."

And she smacks my cheek and says, "You are less like them than you know."

The Amazons reach the aqueduct fence almost simultaneously and begin the grasping climb to the triple strand of barbed wire at the top. It isn't even at an angle, or electrified. The girls throw their legs over in scattered sequence and the short-legged girl tears her blue shorts. I'm on the fence beside the fellow who left me for dead, and we're both watching the gymnast's black panties.

"Hot enough for you?" I query.

"You were breathing," he says.

I pass him on the fence, maybe from my experience as a juvenile climbing such fences to get to the coolest places to play. I treat the top of the fence like a rock mantle, swing one leg then the other over the barbed wire and flip over, pole vault style, without a cut. I flop to the other side, cross a ten-foot section of dirt and I'm on the concrete chute. The current is rapid—faster than a running man, and I look to the opposite side for a target. The girls splash into the water like a line of synchronized swimmers. The current rushes them away and though they swim, they move sideways faster than forward.

Footsteps rush me and I pivot.

"Get in, loser!" The man who left me for dead pushes my back, but I'm in motion, spinning, and use his force to catapult him into the aqueduct. I cling to his hand an extra second, and he raps his chin on the concrete chute.

I'm losing time. I take three steps back, run and leap. Splash. The water is electric and my sanity returns with the shock of coolness. Even underwater I feel the current tugging, sweeping. I surface halfway across with no idea how far the water has carried me from my origin.

Arm over arm. Hurts like hell, but the water energizes me, as does my newly birthed fear of drowning. I've lost sense of time, competitiveness, everything. I'm all about one thing: getting to the other side. I touch the concrete; the current drives me too fast to grip any crevices in the wall.

I see the girls have worked this out as well. They've managed to slip a piece of rock-climbing protection in a fault between concrete slabs, and four of them cling like a human chain while the redhead fishes them out. They're dead ahead. One watches me with fury in her eyes. Passing them, I latch onto the spear chucker who threw the rock at me.

"Hey Babe!" I call.

She wriggles, all elbows. The redhead on the bank is engaged fishing out the next in line, so the one I've grabbed deigns conversation.

"Let me go, jackwad!"

"*Cun—.*"

"Oh No You Didn't."

A pocket of crumbled concrete above makes a good hand hold. I get a grip and release the Amazon. I'm half out of the water, hair in my face, and see from below and coming up to my chin a woman's pink running shoe.

Head-snapping contact.

I keep my hold, but the rest of me is limp as lasagna and back in the current. The Amazon I'd latched onto raises a leg and kicks at my arm, while the red beast above tramps my fingers. I hold fast. First, a quick jab with my left hand to the one beside me, catching her below the armpit. She screams and thrashes with her knees about my rib cage. I chop her neck. She loses her grip on the one in front of her and the current pulls her to me; she grasps my side, then my arm, then my fingers, and the red head above scrambles to her knees and clutches for the other but they're apart now.

We'll see how the team fares as individuals. Or teams of two.

"You're gonna die," the one ahead of me says, as the redhead sprints alongside the girl the current rushes away.

I climb out. On my knees, catching my breath, I see the other two push off and swim after their colleague. Team above all else.

They're going to make some really great wives.

They've left the piece of climbing equipment in the concrete crevice. Laying on my belly and reaching, my fingertips are an inch away. I worm forward until gravity seems moments from pulling me back to the water, and release the protection from the crack, back up, and gain my weary legs. The girls have found purchase upon another seam in the aqueduct, a hundred yards downstream.

Cal Barrett designed the course to punish those who stay in the water too long: every inch the current carries you must be retraced on foot. Spray-painted arrows on the concrete point upstream. I set off at a sprint. Ragged men who look as close to dead as I felt a moment ago splash into the aqueduct on the other side. I'm refreshed and running, probably an eight-minute mile at this point.

I race until a giant orange X marks the spot, along with an arrow, to jump back in the water. As if I'd miss it, a few feet ahead the graffiti says "Jump now!"

I leap from a dead run, still holding the rock climbing gear. I swim and at the other side, drag the hook along until it catches, and use it for an anchor to climb out. My running shoes leak water and squish with each stride, and it doesn't take but a few minutes until I'm hot and dazed again. And then find another orange X. In the water and out. Run and find another. Five times until the last X is red and points to the fence, and the trail beyond. I scramble up the chain link, over the barbed wire, and from here, it is an easy two miles to the ranch.

An easy two miles, but two miles just the same. At this point I've probably run ten, along with the extracurricular fun Barrett's thrown in. My wounded arm hangs at my side; it isn't worth the trouble of holding up. For all my labor, I've only gained a hundred yards on the girls, and I suspect they're emerging stronger from the water than I did. Angrier.

I plod forward. The sun is merciless and my shoes are waterlogged. My hair drips a steady river down my back, keeping at least that part of me cool, but in minutes I'm back to dizzy and wondering where the exact threshold of death by heat stroke lies.

If I fall, will the girls nurse me? My feet stumble along, unsure who to take commands from. And my field of vision presses in from the sides. A child has his finger on the dial and the chandelier is dimming. Setting the mood. My stomach, of all things, is in revolt, turning over as if I'd taken a mouthful of effluence. I spray ice water on my face, slap my cheeks, carry on.

Four guys are ahead, somewhere, but their lead is so great I can't spot them. Now I see a group of men and trucks: the finish line. Cal

Barrett waits there to hurry us to our bicycles. I've dreamed of this moment, the first time I come to the finish line, prepared to be cussed forward. I'm not surprised when he slaps my shoulder and wordlessly points to the mountain bikes.

I climb aboard and wobble upright.

"They've got ninety seconds on you! Two circuits," he yells.

I unzip the fanny pack I have looped around my handlebars and extract my secret weapon, a packet of xXx energy gel. I carry a half dozen. I tear it open and squirt the lime sugar ginseng corn syrup ephedrine into my mouth. I feel more energetic just tasting it, and within seconds my legs are stronger and my mind issues coherent thoughts. Just in time for the final surge. If I'm to win, it'll be within the next thirty minutes.

Systems check: My hands and chest no longer sting from the Cholla, though my shoes are ruined with broken-off needles. The bandage on my arm swells. I press it and purple menstrual clumps spill down my arm. My temperature is high, dizzyingly high, but the wind on the bicycle is a gift from God. Or maybe Cal Barrett planned it this way to save lives.

The sun is high and the temperature is at its apogee. The number, whether it is one hundred twelve or twenty, is meaningless. The bike ride is an opportunity to cool down.

I've barely settled into a routine; my thighs are hardly warmed to the new exercise, when I come upon the man in third place. I wait for the trail to diverge into two parallel paths for a short distance, and make my move. The other is too exhausted to rally, and I assume third place.

The trail becomes rocky and an uphill segment looms ahead that requires either downshifting and horsepower, or speed and balance. I pedal fast and furious until a thigh cramp surprises me and I bounce over the rocks trying to keep my legs loose and the pedals moving. At the crest, I look across an expanse.

The two leaders have me by a hundred yards. I dodge rocks and swerve and jump until at the bottom the trail flattens. I stay on the hard pack: less drag. They bob into and out of sight with each obstacle, gulley, turn. I peddle harder, fearing they are losing me, yet each time they appear, they are closer.

Their energy flags.

I take advantage of a smooth trail to unzip my handlebar fanny pack and rip into another pouch of energy gel. Salt in my eyes. My shoulders burn from the sun and my fingertips are swollen. But the leaders are within reach. I glance over my shoulder and there's no one in sight behind me.

The pedals turn endlessly, chain, derailleur, whir, clack, twang as I shift and grind up the next hill. Headway. The loop nears completion. We near the compound, the start line, and the leaders pass and then I do and half of the bicycles are gone. The remaining machines lean on trees or capsized where they were thrown, like M-16s bayoneted into the ground.

But the Amazons' pink Cannondales are gone.

The two men ahead of me begin the final lap to cheers from a group of bystanders. I've closed to within thirty yards, but can't close the gap before the parallel trail I used to pass the last time.

"Move over!"

I look right rear. A guy on a black Diamondback challenges me. Madness glints in his eye, as if he'll die of torment if he doesn't overtake me. I want him to suffer. I downshift and stand, pound the pedals, jump on the damn things to fend off my challenger. The trails converge. He angles closer and closer, rams my side, bounces away. Hits a row of rocks bordering the trail and wipes out. He's on his side.

A bend in the trail lets me look back without risking death. He can't walk—his legs are spent, just as I know mine would be if I tried to use them for anything other than pushing pedals.

The fight has brought me closer to the leading pair.

The end approaches: a time for all-out effort, impassioned risk-taking, calculated moves. This is when every alpha seizes the madness of greatness and asserts himself, or realizes he isn't what he hoped, and tucks tail.

I down another energy packet—enough sugar to buzz a brontosaurus. My heart flutters and my thoughts race to my mother explaining why she won't return the Indian books she stole from my room. "You'll wind up ignorant. Useless. Or you'll try to get even for three hundred years of evil. You have to forget your ancestors. You have to forsake your blood."

"Forsake my blood?" I massage the words as if to coax a reluctant meaning, one that isn't so brazen as the obvious. "That's like telling a woman to forsake her snatch because it's a man's world."

"You! Where did you get that mouth—" and she belts me. So the fourteen year old Indian boy grimaces and turns inward while his mother unknowingly tells lies—innocent lies that are the bastard product of her love for me and her cultural brainwash—about how there is only one path for an Indian boy, a half breed. And when she's talked herself calm, she drops the Daisycutter she presumes will shatter me. She thinks she'll pick up the pieces and put together a little white boy.

She says, "You know, I met your father's mother. Did you know she was white? White as snow."

One slice. I'm reduced from fifty percent to twenty-five.

My world is destroyed until I look in the mirror at my shiny black hair, cheekbones. The dark skin, crooked nose, thin lips. The spatial intellect and rhythmic sense of language. I got everything from my father, and he got everything from his, and that sustains me through the rigors of living in two worlds. All the genes that matter came from the right place. I heal, but below the pink scar is a puss-filled abscess called assimilation. It is filled with fast food, television, stock accounts, the

English language. When I hear of Desert Dog, I see the race is an opportunity to lance the wound and clean out all that rotten flesh, and remember who I am and where I come from.

A real Blackfoot would win Dessert Dog.

The down slope is wide enough for one bike to pass another. I'm more than half way through the six-mile loop and the remainder is narrow enough that the only way to pass is by hook or crook. This, then, is my moment of truth. I crest the next hill and though my thighs yell they need rest, just a couple strokes, I push them. I stand. Jerk the bike with my arms to add force to my down-leg. Rock the bike. Up shift and fly like a madman over the rough, bouncing and banging, into the air. Swoop through the gulley and catapult around, above, through a turn, and pass the man in second place.

But the man in first is made of steel and fueled by diesel. He's fighting, and I have nothing left to propel me past him. It is all I can do to keep my legs moving. As the leader reaches the narrow path, he slows.

My front tire is inches from his rear. He kept his speed until the path is so narrow there's now path around him. I could wreck him and ride over him, but not for a t-shirt.

He grunts like an exhausted steer. A rock wobbles his tire and he overcompensates. I smell sweat and Right Guard.

"Yield," I say, "Or pick up the pace."

He stands, presses into it for a few strokes, and then coasts.

"Get over!" screams the man on the black Diamondback. "Or I'll take you both out!"

The leader pulls a water bottle from his bike frame and drinks.

A few yards ahead the trail drops into a wash. The sand at the bottom is a bog, ground up from the other feet and wheels. But to the side of the descending trail, the bank ramps to an edge.

I hang back. Give the leader his space. The jackass behind me rubs tires.

I downshift. Squeeze both breaks hard and slide on the dirt. The guy behind me collides, falls forward. Curses as he goes down.

I glance back and he's holding his nuts, and the leader has opened a small gap. I hit the pedals hard. Leg-cramping hard. Everything. Men would rebel against orders like these, but my muscles are Blackfoot, and my synapses are Blackfoot, and every nerve is Blackfoot. The wind rushes through my hair. A hawk shadow crosses before me and a coyote paces my right. The leader pedals into the basin of sand and lurches, loses balance and struggles to waddle his bike forward.

I hit the edge and sail two thirds across the gulch. The bike smashes to the upslope and bounces on its shocks. I pump like mad.

I lead.

The wind is strong and every rotation is torture to my thighs and calves and mind but I am what I know I am. And though the man who rubbed tires gives chase, and the Amazons fight closer to him, and twenty follow them, none can sustain my pace because I am propelled by the roaring wind of identity.

A yellow crime scene tape marks the finish line.

I glance behind and there's no one for yards and yards. I coast. My eyes crest with water and though I tell myself it is sweat, the water refreshes my delirious dried eyes and I'm happy to have the world know I weep. I pump a few more strokes, spit ice water into the air and drive through the spatter.

I tear through the yellow tape Barrett has stretched between two saguaros, and coast to the shade of a tarp tent with a fan and swamp cooler inside. I stumble from the bike on Jello legs and Barrett catches me, lowers me to the canvas floor.

"There you go, son," he says. He presses a white t-shirt to my chest and then takes it back and opens it for me. The pit bull's face is severe, and the medallion that dangles from his spiked collar bears my place.

#1.

Barrett returns to the finish line and I prop my head on a duffel bag. Outside the tarp, among the groupies, I see a familiar backside. Legs like the chick on the *For Your Eyes Only* Bond poster.

She twists to me and smiles coyly, sans machine gun.

Rachel.

DOES CYMAN BONE ANIMALS?

The mass of mankind has not been born with saddles on their backs, nor a favored few booted and spurred, ready to ride them legitimately, by the grace of God.

Thomas Jefferson

The sly little wench has infiltrated Desert Dog. She wears a blonde wig, but the grin—and the rest of her—is unmistakable. She turns from me as contestants cross the line. The Amazons come in second through sixth, then the guy who crushed his onions on his crossbar. The guy who lost the lead in the sandy gulch follows. Barrett slaps a t-shirt into the belly of each and they file into the tent. As I lie on the canvas and do nothing but breath, a contingent of nurses, most of them named Ursula, blitz the tarp. My Ursula kneels beside me and swabs my arm with an alcohol soaked cotton ball. She plants a needle and leaves me with an IV dripping cool Gatorade into my bloodstream.

Even in the center of this triumphant scene I am not at rest. The Amazons have finished in fine form. They cluck at each other and I feel the weight of their alternate gazes as they study shirts the sum of whose digits is five higher than they anticipated.

Rachel stands adjacent, kind of beside but apart from the Desert Dog groupies. She talks to the compound guards, anybody that looks like he has brass. She's infiltrated the race, and her deadline for me was—today?

Do I have any money left? If she bankrupts me I'll join Barrett's team out of spite.

The swamp cooler blows tacky cold air and the IV chills the vein in my arm. I slip out the needle. Crawl to my knees, gain my feet. Blood abandons my brain; the little girl dims the chandelier and darkness presses the edge of my mind. I step toward my bike.

"Hey asshole!" I look at the red headed Amazon's auburn legs, leathered cleavage, freckled face.

"You forgot something," she says.

My t-shirt is on the tarp. The gymnast stone-chucker tosses it to me. "Good race," she says.

"You ladies be well," I say.

Outside the tarp, the blast from the swamp cooler dies and it's nothing but early afternoon sun. Brutal. The compound sits to the right of the tent. The gate opens as I near, pushing my mountain bike by the seat. I open the front door without knocking. The Mexican cook smiles and I follow the hall to the tech room. The door is open and Mike sits at a desk, his head and torso silhouetted by a bank of television monitors.

"Did we get him?" I say.

"His bodyguard was on to us. Check this out."

He presses a button and the monitor shows Cyman's room. The picture sweeps to the right, stops, wobbles on bundled drapes, and moves left, across the bed, and completes its journey at the inside wall.

A torso and legs enter the picture, holding an electronic device. From the man's size, it is Géraud.

"That's a frequency scanner," Mike says.

Géraud faces the fan, holds the scanner closer, and then steps to the side. The picture goes blank.

"He unplugged it."

"What about the clock?"

"When he was standing by the fan, he wasn't within the clock's camera angle. It wasn't on." Mike presses a button on a second VCR and the monitor flashes to a static view of the bed. Senator Cyman sits at the corner.

"Did we get anything?"

"Stuff you don't want to see." He makes a jerking off motion, turns the VCR off.

"We've still got the camera in the room, right?"

He nods.

"We'll get him tonight."

"If he doesn't return to Washington. Somebody's been giving him a hard time."

"What do you mean?"

"Check this out." He pushes the chair and coasts to a computer monitor; pulls up a window with the Rudge Report.

YOU TUBE VIDEO BLASTS CYMAN
SENATOR RESPONDS
VIDEO GONE VIRAL: #1 THREE HOURS AFTER LAUNCH
VIDEO (Adult Themes)
REFRESH FOR UPDATES

"There's a video out that links Cyman, his son at the water bureau, an Indian land management babe, and get this, Duane Hock—the guy running against him."

"No kidding," I say.

"Right. But you wouldn't know anything about that. Then there's all the flyers distributed around the Capitol building, the Times building, and the state police Headquarters. Someone has it in for Cyman. You know what the flyers say?"

"I'm guessing here. 'DO YOUR JOB. TAKE CYMAN OUT.'"

Mike glances past me. Slaps his hands to his knees. "That's all the time I have."

Barrett is at the door. "Looks like you were busy, yesterday," he says. I shrug.

"They've got a good idea who you are. Picked up an APB for Solomon Bull off the scanner about an hour ago. You ought to stay here."

"Is that how you see it panning out?"

"What else are you going to do?"

"Take my pack to the woods. Say to hell with all of it."

"You might sleep on that. There's an empty rack in the billet at the end of the hall. You're welcome to it. I'll have Ursula come by and hook another IV into you."

I open my eyes convinced I'm dead, from a dream that I can't remember, and sit on the edge of the cot. My arm bandage has been changed and I recall one of the Ursulas mumbling to me, trying to keep those giant strudel-fed boobs out of her way while debriding and repacking my knife wound.

The compound is quiet. From the ambient light, maybe seven in the evening. I exit through the back—without risking a conversation with Barrett or any of his crew—but my Valkyrie is within the gates and I might as well be in a prison. Inside, I find Mike's replacement in the tech room.

"Can you open the gate for me?"

"Good race. See Barrett in the kitchen."

The house is still, like a hibernating computer. Great potential, urgency, passion—bridled by silence. A ticking wall clock. But toggle a mouse and the compound will waken.

I find Barrett in the kitchen eating chocolate cheesecake at the long, plank table. His face is consternated, but changes as he looks up. He drops his fork on the plate and the sharp report lingers.

"Damn cheesecake," he says. "I could eat it out a dead monkey's skullcap."

"Sounds delicious."

"Get some—it's in the freezer." He waves. "You did some quick research on your boy."

"Hock?" I pull a chair. "You said where to look."

"I didn't know about his son and that Indian woman."

"I don't follow."

"Your video on YouTube lays it out pretty clear."

"I had a friend put that together."

"Give him a bonus. You haven't seen it yet?"

"No."

"Cyman's son Hank runs the Arizona Department of Water Resources. Hock applied to drill to a second level aquifer for his fifty million dollar development, and after being promised the rights, he runs for Senate. The Indians raise hell, saying it'll suck the Verde River dry. Verde supplies the rez. Suddenly, Hock is playing nice with Senator Cyman."

"Right. I got that."

"Your buddy who put the video together found the connection between Hank Cyman and the Indians."

I lean forward.

"Jane Arcosanti—the one raised hell and shut down Hock—directs the government relations group at the Yavapai Nation."

"Right…"

"She and Hank Cyman are co-owners of Saguaro Silver Spa and Bistro."

"Spa and Bistro."

He shrugs. "They're big back East, I take it. The water company has Hock by the balls, and your video makes it clear—if anybody out there has eyes to see it."

"Not with reality television competing." I say.

"There's the lesson for you. Government is never by the many. The many can't figure out what to have for lunch, let alone what they want in their leaders. Government is by the few. Always has been, no matter what form you call it, or where or when. You deal with the select few holding the strings, you get the government you want."

When he says *deal with*, I don't think he means strike a bargain. "Guillotine," I whisper.

"What?"

"Nothing."

He studies me over an inbound fork of cheesecake. "The graffiti was a nice touch. 'SENATOR CYMAN DOES NOT BONE ANIMALS'. Fifty underpasses and retaining walls. Make a politician explain why he has doesn't sleep with animals. Genius."

I look at his cheesecake. Push away from the table. "I need you to let me out of the compound."

"You're a free man." He cranes toward the door. "Phil!"

The man from the tech room appears.

"This is Solomon," Barrett says. "He's a guest."

"I'll be leaving now," I say.

Phil nods. Vanishes.

"Come back real soon," Barrett says.

In three minutes I'm on the Valkyrie heading north. I've got heat exhaustion chills and I could have eaten six pounds of cheesecake. I cut into a McDonald's and buy a couple value meals. With my helmet on the sissy bar, I chow down on the highway, balancing the paper bag on my lap. The wind catches it after both Big Macs are in my gut. The crows can fight over the fries.

Miles melt as the sun drops and the sky changes from hazy orange to black. An hour from the city the lights fade and the air is cool. I lean close to the tank, slow to the speed limit and harvest heat radiating from the engine. At the Prescott exit I stop at a truck stop and buy a heroin hoodie and snuggle up for the next hour's ride. Flagstaff greets me with air cool enough to fog my breath.

Bernard isn't at the body shop. I cross the lot, navigate a couple backstreets and stop at his house. The light is on but there's no answer at the door. No vehicle in the driveway. No sounds from inside. He's big enough that the floorboards would broadcast his steps. I back the bike to the street and pull away.

Twenty yards along, my mirrors flash with headlights. A familiar car pulls into Bernard's drive.

I coast to the curb. Wait and watch—I'll give him a couple of minutes to settle in before rapping on his door.

The car is a sedan. Bernard exits the passenger side and as the car backs toward the street, a purple street lamp illuminates the driver's window.

Rachel.

She stops, accelerates away. I throttle up and begin a half-circle turn. I have to warn Bernard—but a thought strikes me. What if Bernard got Rachel into Desert Dog? What if he's jamming a shoe into his father's gears? Literally, from the French *sabot*, or wooden shoe.

Sabotage...

Didn't Rachel orchestrate me buying the gun from Bernard?

Bernard walks toward the house and looks my way as I approach. No way to pass without him recognizing me. I pull onto the drive. Kill the motor. Dismount. Stretch.

"You had a hell of a race today," Bernard says. He shoves my shoulder.

"Yeah, lot of fun."

He unlocks the door. "You want to come in? What's up?"

"I need to get into my Jeep."

He stares.

"In your garage," I say.

His eyes are still and his face tranquil, but the calm betrays a mutiny below the surface. "Oh, yeah. I wasn't thinking. Let's walk over." He closes the door, locks it.

We cross the lawn. My shoes grow damp with dew. Head through a copse unpenetrated by streetlamps. I look ahead and to the sides for escape avenues while I do calculus with human X's and Y's. Rachel gave me a deadline that I didn't meet. I haven't given her any information, but she knows I won Desert Dog, and probably that I rested afterward in Barrett's compound. She might imagine my victory will earn Barrett's trust. Maybe she thinks he's wooing me into the clandestine side of his operation. She might give me another day, if her bosses can wait.

Rachel, though, is one *proactive* female. She's not going to put all her eggs in one basket and entrust it to a guy like me. She's an "if you want it done right" girl. She's going to infiltrate the group to whatever degree she can. Thus she was at the Desert Dog finish line.

Rachel and Bernard didn't kiss in the car. As he walked away, he didn't look back at her like a love-struck hound—and if you're tagging Rachel, you look all you can.

So what is she doing with Bernard, other than business? Treasury business. And if anybody has the green to buy a man's fealty, it's the Treasury. They print green.

What's the old saying—keep your friends close...

Bernard walks like a board with legs. Maybe he was working out earlier. His fists are balled up.

"Why didn't you run Desert Dog," I say.

"No time. Things going on."

"Sounds mysterious."

If I say *guillotine* to him, I'll get a few answers. Will he bring me into his conspiracy against his father's conspiracy? As Frank Herbert said, the plan within the plan? Or will he perceive me a threat and seek to remove me?

Each step reminds me of my overworked thighs and abused back. Muscles are tight. Reluctant. The wound on my arm has begun to sting, maybe predicting foul weather like a rheumatoid senior's knuckles. Barrett never gave me an antibiotic—unless Ursula did—she must have.

Chatter in my head, when I need to watch Bernard.

We're in a dark grove under oak foliage between houses, lit by a glow from a curtained window. Bernard scratches his head and turns—looks like a pirouette. "What do you need in the Jeep?"

My fingertips tingle. I catch a whiff of mint, like from gum.

"Rock climbing gear."

"Tonight?"

He's walking again. I pace him. We near a streetlight. "I'm going rappelling."

"That's hairy in the dark. What's going on? Something like the cement blocks in Sedona?"

"Something like that."

"Need a hand?"

"I got it covered."

Bernard looks paranoid when he thinks hard; the brow comes in tight and low, lips pursed. Cro Magnon on the cusp of algebra. We're at the garage. He swings the door open and waits for me to enter.

"I'll tag along," He says. "Make sure you stay safe."

"I only have one harness," I say.

"I got equipment. What rock?"

"Bell."

"Sweet."

"But I'm not rappelling. I'm sinking a few bolts."

"For rings?"

"Right."

My jeep wears a coat of dust. I navigate around the Dodge Omni getting racing stripes, the junked motorcycles, the V-8 on the floor leaking oil.

"I guess I'll take the jeep. My stuff is inside. You want to open the door?"

"Cops are looking for that Jeep. We'll take this." He nods at the Omni.

"That?"

"Grab your gear."

Tied to my backpack is a separate, smaller pack containing rope, nylon webbing, figure eights, karabiners. Basics. And in a box behind the passenger seat is a battery-operated Hilti drill and bits.

I transfer everything to the hatchback. Bernard tosses me the keys and walks to the garage door opener. I start the engine, which sounds like a chainsaw motor, slip the automatic clutch into reverse and ease up on the brake. The Omni squirts out the bay. The garage door descends and Bernard locks the side door. I look left and right like a felon about to take his shot at freedom.

The passenger door opens. Dome light pops on and the car rocks as Bernard slips in shotgun. I tramp the gas and cut the wheel.

"You know anything about drilling bolts?" I say.

"Nah."

"Do much climbing?"

"Here and there."

What am I saying? He's done Desert Dog. "I'm drilling four bolts on the top of Bell Rock."

"I saw the Hilti. That'll make some noise," he says.

I turn onto 89A south, the drive through Oak Creek Canyon, past all the red rocks, from Flagstaff to Sedona.

"Shouldn't be too bad," I say. "Oak Creek houses are far enough, and I figure hitting it at ten, there's still a lot of ambient noise to confuse anyone that hears it."

"It could be a giant, rock-eating woodpecker."

"We'll risk the noise. I'm not going to use an auger."

He laughs but I search his every sound and motion for a surreptitious threat. Though I've shed my assimilated self, I'm not yet comfortable in my new skin. I'm used to being Solomon, not Bull. I want to trust, but a deep ancestral voice guides toward wariness.

We pass the miles in silence. I slow as we approach flakes of Quickwall reflecting headlights on both road shoulders. The cement blocks are gone.

Bernard says, "Tonight's operation about the senator?"

"Yeah."

"You got moxie," he says.

"I got a reason, so it's no big deal. Not like a virtue, or something."

"Nah, I think it is. The futility is beautiful. How's drilling a few bolt holes make a senator unelectable?"

"It's part of the package deal. You ever hear of a media blitz? Take a product. Take tampons. You put a story in the newspaper, run a radio ad, and slap a big-ass photo on a billboard, and maybe get one of those peppy morning show women to talk about it for thirty seconds, and people think Arizona's hemorrhaging tampons."

"Not likely. Think about it. They're tampons."

"You get the picture."

"All that for one senator."

I pull into the parking area by Bell Rock, off an untraveled side road. Exit. Bernard takes thirty seconds extracting himself from the low, tiny seat. I sling the pack and let him lug the Hilti.

The trail wends through undergrowth until ascending a rock plat-form that blooms onto the side of Bell Rock, then trail gradually circles and mounts the summit. From there in the daylight, Sedona and Oak Creek are a spatter of boxes, not much different than any other. With-out the rocks, Sedona is nothing.

If you've seen *Billy the Kid* or any of forty-three select westerns, you've seen Sedona. The rocks appear licked in flames, scorched; the vegetation at the base is like emeralds and the sky, cobalt. Hot or cold, the air is crisp like the breath of God. Slap a rainbow in there and hip-pies have naturgasms.

Of the rocks, Bell is the welcome sign on road 179, the grand an-nouncement to travelers that something is different about this place. Follow 179 into town, (ignore, if you can, the trinket vendors, blanket salesmen, aura readers, and greasy spoons masquerading as restau-rants) and then take 89A north through Oak Creek Canyon, and you'll find terrain that invigorates your sense that the Creator had a purpose, and it was at times purely artistic.

It is this marvel, Bell Rock, that I plan to desecrate, if only for a ge-ologically short time.

Two-thirds of the way to the top is a false summit. Bernard follows me on a trail bordered on the left by rock and on the right by four hun-dred feet of vertical drop. I am alert for the shuffle of footsteps that would signal Bernard ramming me over and protecting his conspiracy with Rachel against his father.

"It's beautiful up here," he says. "What's the plan?"

"I'm going to anchor off a couple hexes and drill four holes, then sink the bolts."

"Must take forever."

"Two minutes per hole. It would help if you'd keep a lookout over on that point, where you can see both directions on 179."

"Sure," he says. "You expect them to come flashing reds and blues?"

"I don't expect them to come at all, inside of twenty minutes. But since you've proven an aptitude for security—"

The hammer drill makes short work of the sandstone and I have the bolts sunk in minutes. Oak Creek, below, scarcely trembles. I wipe dust from my hands, gather the hexes, karabiners, webbing, and rejoin Bernard at the ledge twenty feet away.

"I was thinking," he says.

"Yeah?" I wait for him.

Bernard waves me forward. "I don't see in the dark too good," he says. "You go first."

"Is that what you were thinking?"

"Nah."

I watch the edge as we descend. His feet scuffle against the rock and every second I fight the expectation of feeling hands on my back, and mentally rehearse the throw I'll use to cast him over the edge when he attacks.

"Now that you've won Desert Dog, did my father have a conversation with you?"

"He said he noticed senator Cyman's public relations issues."

"Nothing else?"

We trek in silence for a minute and he says, "When he asks, you better spend a minute thinking."

"What's he going to ask, Bernard?"

"If he thinks he can trust you, he'll invite you to join his organization."

"You mean the guys that get together at hunting camps and talk politics?"

"That's the group."

"I'll spend a minute thinking."

BELL ROCK

I put my crew on notice. Layne and Marz will meet me at the train station in Flagstaff, a redbrick, 1920's style Amtrak depot that doubles as a welcome center. They sell maps, photo books, and eight-inch chocolate chip cookies. Public restrooms, and a big parking lot.

Paolo hasn't answered his phone for the last twenty minutes. I scarf hot wings and water at O'Fallons, directly below his apartment. The stairwell empties to the street. I open three lemon scented clean wipes, go outside and then inside, cleaning my fingers as I climb the stairs, and pause at his door. He mumbles inside; he's talking normal but bar noise and the door garble his words. He might be on the phone—but I didn't get a busy signal, or dumped into voice mail.

Every one of us is a sneak—usually when what we want is at odds with what others want for us. Stealth aids survival. We trust ourselves with trivial dirt: who picks his nose, who primps herself when no one is looking, who steals food from another's plate. We file in our minds a congressional library of slime because in all these oyster guts we know, someday, we'll find a pearl: information that can prevent a hassle. Avoid prison. Or maybe a quick heads' up that will save our lives. The promise of treasure keeps us spying. So I wait by Paolo's door and listen. Sounds. Sometimes they form into syllables. "eek.... woun.... graa..." None useful.

And then Paolo's voice is relieved by a woman's.

My forehead taps the door. She stops speaking. I rap several times with my knuckles, aiming for a crisp bark that will fill Paolo's drawers with waste—a knock that sounds like the law.

They are silent. I pound again. "Paolo, open up! It's Solomon."

A dead bolt cracks to the side and the door opens two inches, secured by a chain. Paolo's eyeball peers at me from a room illuminated by a pair of lava lamps. Incense wafts through the aperture. "What, man?"

I slip my fingers around the door. "I need your help tonight."

"I'm outta commission tonight."

"Who's with you?"

He hesitates. There's a subtle movement around his eye—not a blink, but narrowing around the orb. "No one."

"I heard her voice."

Through the crack, his face goes sheepish. Yeah, real cute, buddy. All's forgiven. Liar.

"Let me guess," I say. "Rachel."

"No, man. Who's Rachel?"

"Stand back from the door."

"Why?"

I step back.

"No! Don't kick it in. Just a sec." The door closes; the chain slides and Paolo stands before me in a wife-beater and shorts, sporting a half-chub. On the sofa, leg crossed over her knee, and chest swaddled so tight her jugs look like they're hanging upside down, is Rachel. The television is on with the volume off. Mood lighting to accent the lava lamps. Who hasn't?

"Hello, Solomon," she says. "Time's up."

"Paolo, you should probably see a doctor and have them screen for STD's. Rachel gets around."

"Rachel?" He turns to her. "Rachel?"

"I can be anyone you want."

"Paolo—you met her last week on the street," I say. "Her name was Rachel, then, too."

"Anyone you want," she says to Paolo.

I say, "What'd you tell him your name was? Sophie? He has a hardon for Sophies."

"Mary Lou. From Alaska."

"They don't name girls Mary Lou in Alaska," I say. "So, Rachel, has Paolo been of any help?"

"Some."

"I didn't say anything about you, man," Paolo says. "I was trying to get laid."

"Just lay down. That's all it takes with her."

I close the door. Paolo steps backward, decidedly not in my path to Rachel. My cell phone vibrates in my pocket, but I silence it. Rachel uncrosses her leg, does a Sharon Stone flash and adjusts her hips. I raise the stakes. Slip the dead bolt home.

"She wanted to know where you were. I didn't know, so I was ogling her a little before she left. You know. Look at her. I got to try. C'mon, Solomon. You know what I'm saying?"

"Mary Lou?" I say.

"He's relentless. I'm glad you're here. I probably would have slept with him out of pity. Lets' go outside and talk."

Paolo whimpers. "But..."

"You have a hotel nearby?"

"If I thought screwing you would do any good, I would. Most guys, give it to them once and they're like sick puppies. At your feet begging. But not you."

Paolo blinks.

"Not you," she says. "You leave a girl with cramps in her feet for three days, then pretend she doesn't exist."

"Oh, shut up."

"But that has nothing to do with why I'm here. That's personal, and I'm here for business. I've been instructed to wipe you out. My operations people are holding your accounts in a little bundle, dangling over an incinerator. We'll wipe out every trace of you."

I think of *Sinners in the Hands of an Angry God*. Not the best sales literature. "That wouldn't be such a bad thing," I say.

"I begged for one more chance to talk to you. Get you to come to your senses. I've flirted with everyone you know, trying to find you. You must come to grips with reality. You call it a police state, but I call it the only way to make sure the animals among us don't run rampant. It's the way things are. There's a big, big man holding a lot of strings. You don't have to be tied to him, but you damn sure better get out of his way when he comes at you. You must make amends. You must talk to him. You must talk to me, or else he's going to pull all those strings and your whole world is going to dance, and everything you think you know is going to be exposed as false. The people, the institutions, the rules. Nothing will be so innocuous as you thought, and it'll all be coming for you. That's scary, and you better think hard. You'll have nothing. You'll be a wanted man. Nowhere to go. Nothing to do. No one to turn to—"

"I get the feeling Barrett would take me in."

She shakes her head. Exhales. "Yeah. I bet he would."

"I came here to talk to Paolo," I say.

"Are you hearing me?" she says. "Everything you own will disappear unless I can tell my boss that you're willing to help. If you don't give me a reason to stop him, you no longer exist. Your money is gone. Your everything. IS THERE NOTHING YOU CAN TELL ME ABOUT BAR-RETT?"

"He likes Leroy Anderson. Aside from that, you're on your own."

Paolo says, "Whoa! That's you!"

I face the television. I've never seen the photo before. It looks recent, from the sunburn. Maybe taken with a telephoto lens. "Turn up the volume."

A midday-news anchorette named Dusty Corcoran smiles and announces there's a fifty-thousand-dollar reward for information leading to my capture and arrest for the defamation of Senator Cyman. Paid for by a political action committee, a 529 called *Arizonans for Integrity in Washington*.

Thank God Campaign Finance Reform got money out of politics.

"Fifty large," Paolo says, stoned by the count, looking about his apartment, as if imagining another twenty lava lamps, maybe a mirror on the ceiling, and strings of beads between kitchenette and living-roomette.

"Curious, Rachel. Can you call them off?"

"The local police? Probably not. But I can take you to a place where they won't matter. If you cooperate."

"What, exactly, does cooperate mean?"

"Barrett's a terrorist and he's going to attack the United States. When will it start? Who is involved? Where are they?"

"I don't know." My cell phone vibrates again. Distraction. I press the side button while the phone is in my pocket.

"But you must have an idea," Rachel says. "You spent a day in the compound with Barrett."

"Snoring on a cot after almost killing myself in the race. And what were you doing there?"

"You weren't getting any information to me." Her jaws tighten and I suddenly see she won't age well. "I'm going to hold off my boss one more day. I'm going to follow you to Phoenix and make sure you enter the compound. And I'm going to camp at your apartment until you call me on this number." She passes me a card. "Didn't I already give you one of these?"

"Not going to happen. I've got to work tonight. So what you're going to do is leave me to talk to my loyal friend, and I'll call you when I have something that can help you."

"I fought for you," she says through gritted teeth.

Paolo clears his throat. I'd forgotten about him, and the numbing drone on the news about the latest two babies that drowned today in Phoenix swimming pools.

Paolo faces Rachel. "We aren't going to have sex, are we?"

She stands in a single motion, struts to the door, runs her fingertips across my arm as she passes. Big Murtha yawns, stretches.

"Take it easy, Rachel."

I close the door behind her and my cell vibrates again. I fish it out. Keith.

"What the hell?" Paolo says.

I shush him with an open hand while I answer my phone.

"Yeah?"

"Katrina is gone. Vanished. I'm worried."

I'd like to groan but I present myself better. "She's a big girl with a new Corvette."

"She's depressed. Suicidal. And she never came home last night"

"I don't know where she is."

"She could be anywhere."

"You have to ask yourself how much you're willing to give to save a person who doesn't want saved."

"She isn't pregnant."

"She isn't?"

"She confessed her sins last night, like she was clearing the air. She made it up about the baby. She was desperate. She promised no one would ever have to trouble with her again. Then she gave me the copper and cowhide lamps."

"You let her out of the apartment after she said that?"

"She snuck out. I stayed up watching television."

I see a vision of Katrina lying face-down in a gutter, in a pool of thousand-island puke. "Keith, I can't just drop everything..."

"Is that it? She made her choice, and that's it?"

"What can I say? I can't get to Phoenix until maybe five a.m."

"Call me. The only way I won't be looking for her is if I find her."

"I'll get there sooner if I can."

I swipe off the phone and sit on the sofa.

"What's up," Paolo says. "Katrina missing?"

"Yeah." I slap my knees. Stand. "I need your help. One more job. Tonight."

He rolls his eyes.

"And one more thing. If you need money, don't get squirrely and turn me in. I've always been ready to help my friends."

His face shows that he has taken great offense, just like, I imagine, he wants it to.

Years ago Paolo and I closed a bar and Paolo spent the last ten minutes drinking the pair of beers we ordered at last call. Between gulps and belches he worried about not making it to McDonald's in time; he was jonesin' for a Big Mac. But first he had to drain the main vein, and by the time we had McDonald's in our sights, the pimpled kid working his way through Northern Arizona U. stood at the door with a set of prison warden keys, closing for the night.

"You got to let us in!" Paolo cries, and drags his sweaty, oily Italian face across the door glass. "I neeeeeeeed a Bic Mac!"

The kid, looking half-stoned, turns away and doesn't look back, though Paolo lays siege to the door, muttering, cursing, shaman-dancing for ten minutes while pimple-boy and his compadre work mops like inmates in their own store. When they turn, they keep their eyes on the ground.

"You're freaking them out," I say. "They're going to call the cops."

"I need a Big Mac."

The kid approaches the glass, brandishing his mop handle across his chest. "I'm going to call the cops," he says, enunciating each word with a wide mouth, as if drunks see better than they hear.

"Just get your Big Mac from the dumpster," I say. "They're still hot."

"Unh?"

"Go around back and fish through a trash bag."

This gale of reason corrects Paolo's course and he bids pimple-boy adieu with a flourish, marches to the cement block shanty with a wide-open gate that holds the dumpster. In seconds he's chowing on Big Macs, one in each hand.

If starving, I would eat the trashed burgers without second thought, and sneer at the man who judged me. But failing being homeless and hungry, with home and a box of raisin bran only a mile away, shame would prevent me from sampling.

But to Paolo, it didn't matter that he didn't pay. The sammiches were trash. It didn't matter that the sammiches were trash. They were only a few minutes old. It didn't matter what anyone would say. No one was there to see him.

No moral absolutes; all equivocation.

Paolo is the kind of guy who would hand over his friend for fifty grand.

Layne and Marz, so far as I know, haven't heard of the fifty-thousand-dollar reward on my head. Paolo has, and though he's been back to normal the last couple hours, I haven't let him out of my sight. And Bernard, down at the base of the rock preparing to sandbag a spotlight on the hood of a Jeep Wrangler, has troubles with his father that make me question his trustworthiness. Does he know I saw him with Rachel? Is he waiting for me to make a move?

So why put my nuts on the block? Why trust these men?

Because there's a senator out there who thinks constituents are livestock. Who thinks Indian boys are hot. Thinks no one is ever going to make him pay.

And he's campaigning against a guy who will say anything to lose.

Maybe Rachel has something to offer. I could tell her what I know about Barrett, the snippet I picked up from Bernard about good buddies all over the place who hunt and talk politics a few times a year. Mention an operation named Guillotine, the subtle way both Bernard and Cal Barrett implied bringing down Cyman wouldn't be worth my trouble because their much-larger operation would soon commence.

Or I could ask Barrett to make me a part of the show, and funnel information to Rachel as quickly as I get it. And then join her. Buy suits and Rockports. Praise be to the Machine.

Another route: I've got the dough to retire early. I could specialize in bringing down senators. Congressmen. Any politician that abuses the sacred trust, uses his office for personal gain. A guy could spend a lifetime bringing evil men to their knees. A thousand lifetimes.

I stretch. My hair piles at my shoulders and I remember the lesson of Desert Dog. I am Blackfoot. My friends are a narrow group and I love them. But the others—enemies or acquaintances, government agents or state police, my responsibility to them reflects only their expedience to my cause. Nothing more.

I slip my heroin junkie-jacket off. The rock surface will radiate heat long into the night. I extend my arm fully and stretch my wounded biceps; the burn is like from a killer workout, the heat as if from a flame.

Infection. Did Barrett tell me to come back for medical attention, or be-cause Guillotine would begin? As soon as this is done, I've got to get to Phoenix for a shot. I slip on my climbing shoes, cinch my harness, don my pack.

I set up my rappel line and my thumb glances over a nick in my rope. Too dark to judge the damage with conviction, I press the cut and hold the fray between thumb and forefinger. The rope is compromised. No way I can trust it with my life—but I have no back up. I debate for a moment and then tie a loop at the center of the rope. Slip a locking kar-abiner through it, and then another, in case my karabiners have had the same misfortune as my rope. I'll rappel from a tied double strand, and leave it when I'm done. There's no other way. Loop the line, open my Soloist belay device, and clip it to my harness.

"You boys ready?"

The four of us are positioned at the bolts I drilled yesterday, spaced about twenty-five feet apart, on the apex of the false summit of Bell Rock. Layne and Marz are ready. Paolo needs a second to tie his shoes.

I press the transmit button on my cell phone walkie-talkie. "You there?"

"I'm here." Bernard says, "Nothing going on."

"We're ready."

"Go," Bernard says, "and tell me when you need some light."

"Roger that."

"All right, boys. Let's go," I say. Four hundred feet high, at eleven p.m., I'm not worried about my voice drifting to the people gulping one last cappuccino a thousand yards away at the coffee shop. We wear black cotton ninja suits, knit caps and small black climbing packs, loaded with cans of white spray paint. Except a few homes in Oak Creek below and a row of streetlights, the landscape is black.

I lean against the static line, testing the steel loop I bolted last night. Hoping the rope holds. Of course it will hold. Of course.

"Paolo—you might want to be careful on that bolt. That was the last one I drilled, and it felt funny going in."

"Funny?"

"Yeah, so I only screwed it in half way."

I release my brake arm and kick out, bounding fifteen feet. I lock the Soloist and I'm free to use both hands. The ropes whir as the others descend and then, almost in unison, their feet scuff the rock face and their lines bounce. I fish over my shoulder for a can of paint. Find one and shake it twice. Two half-inch steel ball bearings clang into the darkness, but the echoes die quickly.

Into my walkie-talkie I say, "All right, Bernard, let there be light."

Seconds pass. Below, two hundred yards away, Bernard flips a switch. A two-million candle-power spotlight burns into a red lens, and then a black plate of Plexiglas, which filters the blaze into fine beams that form a glowing red outline on Bell Rock of an elephant and donkey, consummating love.

"The lines are too thick," I say into the walkie-talkie. Though I stenciled the outline into the painted Plexiglas with a razor, the light projects against the wall in a colossal dimension, each line three feet thick. Bernard is too far away. The outline spills over the flat, paintable surface by thirty feet.

Still, it is beautiful.

"Turn the spotlight off," I say, "and bring it in."

"Three minutes," Bernard says.

The light dies and after a second the black form of the Jeep crawls forward over rocks, shrubs, whatever. Bernard does a good job of keeping his vector to the rock consistent. The jeep stops and his shadow works at the hood.

"Ready?" he says.

"Light it up."

The lines are too wide, but moving closer will not fix them. "We'll paint the outside outline," I say.

"This thing is huge," Bernard says into his walkie-talkie. "Unbelievable."

I climb five feet, lock my Soloist, and bound to the right until the pendulum effect has me climbing rock. I plant my feet and spray the outline with white paint.

"This is rich," Layne says to my left.

Marz, situated below the others, works on the arch of the elephant's lower back, as it prepares to thrust its fifteen-foot pecker, which will not be illustrated, deep into the donkey.

"If Mum could see me now," Paolo observes.

The jokes fade and we work; each traverses the rock facade, painting as he goes. I get the feeling there are eyes down there watching. What must it look like from below, as four different places in a dim red outline become white, and reflect more brightly the outline of a Godzilla-sized elephant and donkey making sweet, sweet love...

We stow empty paint cans in our packs. Paolo sprays with gusto. He grunts enthusiastically and continually, like a child making the airplane noise as he pushes a model B-25 through the air over his head.

Suspended from a slightly frayed rope, the thought occurs that because I've never had a bounty on my head, I've never run a thought experiment on what it would take to buy one of my friends' treachery.

If I listed each in order of least like to fall to temptation, Keith would be on top, and Paolo at the bottom. Keith because nothing is more important than his ideals: not reality, nothing.

I've never minded Keith being my opposite in so many ways because I knew where he stood and that he would honor his convictions. But Paolo? He's a good-times buddy. We drink beer together and swap lies. I don't think there's much beneath, and that is why he scares me. Paolo at the bottom of the list because nothing is ideal to him. Nothing is worth dying—or living—for.

I ease the Soloist belay device and ease down a few feet. Shortly, the others follow.

I flip my walkie-talkie open. "We're going to drop a few feet now. You may want to turn the spotlight off. It has to be getting hot."

"It's burning," Bernard says, then the light goes out. I'm glad to hear he's still there, and not on his way up here to cut my rope.

"Shut it off every two minutes," I say. "Leave it on for a minute, and we'll trace the outline. Then we thicken our lines in the dark. Last thing we need is to blow a bulb when we're half-finished."

"Elephant'll be pumping the air," Layne says.

"Okay. Tell me when you're ready."

"Turn it on."

Again, we paint. The system works and we cut the lighted intervals more. We find a rhythm to our work, and looking across the rock, I find the others are waiting for light.

"What happened?" Marz says.

"What's going on down there?" I ask the walkie-talkie.

"Cop. Probably just a drive-through. He's parked at the gas station."

"I can't see him," I say. "Can he see this part of the rock?"

"Wait a sec. I'll ask."

"Let's wait," Marz says.

"Screw that," Paolo says. "Let's get this done while there's time to drink. Can any of you see him?"

—No's.

"Then he can't see us."

"Turn it on for five seconds," I say.

Bernard flips the switch. The cell phone in my pocket vibrates. I don't want to think about Keith and Katrina, but it would be nice to know he found her. I spray a quick slash along the rock to mark the light, and it disappears. I dig my phone out of my side cargo pocket. It is Ash Cyman.

"Ash?" I say, keeping my voice low.

I'm too late. She's probably talking to my voicemail right now. I slip the phone back into my pocket and paint a little more. When my line is done, I listen to the message.

"It's happening tonight," she says. "Are you going to get him, or not?" She sounds overwrought. "I'm going to get him. I'm going to. I know it's tonight because Géraud told me to be there for him tonight, and then said he'd be late because of my pervert father. So I know he's getting the boy for him. So you better call me right now if you're coming. If you're going to do what you said and bring him down. Because if not, I'm going to do it myself. I don't know how, but—"

The message ends, cut off. I dial her number and it rings. And rings. No answer.

I check the number against my memory and try again. No answer.

I call Bernard. "What's Mike's number?"

"Mike who?"

"Your father's tech guy."

"He—uh. He isn't going to be available."

"Give me the number."

I tap it into my cell as it comes through the walkie-talkie.

"Hello? Bull?" There's static.

"That's right. I need your help. About the hotel—"

"I'm not—I can't help. I'm not in Arizona."

"Not in Arizona."

"You'll have to follow up on your own, if you think it's worth the trouble."

"Where are you?"

"Touring the capital with some old friends. All the important landmarks, you know?"

Guillotine.

The word doesn't escape my lips.

I'm going to have to stop Ash and retrieve the film.

"Good luck." I close the phone.

What will Ash do? Confront her father? Would a man like Cyman have a moral issue disappearing his daughter?

Something in me still flutters for her, though not the part that suits up with a tux and diamond ring. The part of me that craves her is the part that smiles at puppies and sunsets. There's something fragile inside her. Some strain of her voice communicated with the part of my biology that is supposed to protect the vulnerable.

I try her phone again. No answer. She's probably on her way to the hotel.

I check the guys' progress and we're at the halfway point on the donkey. I estimate twenty minutes from completion. But that doesn't matter. I can't just levitate my ass back to Phoenix. I have to drive, and the fastest I've ever made the trip is ninety minutes, and I swore I'd never do it again because I was never sure what was the road and what was my life flashing before me.

What the hell was Ash thinking, leaving a message like that and not answering my call?

The police car Bernard warned us about passes below a street lamp and tools up the road, passing within a hundred yards of Bell Rock. Its taillights blink over the horizon.

Overhead, clouds roll in from the east and stars vanish. The new moon has risen and glows behind a formation not yet complete. A wall of warm air overtakes Oak Creek. My arm tires. I shake it out. Sweat grows cold and I lose myself in the work amid the sound of whirring ball bearings as the others intermittently mix their cans, and the sandpaper sound of feet slipping, and the harmonic hiss of spraying nozzles.

Long moments suspended on a rope. Will it break? Is the bolt secure? What about the integrity of the metal? Did someone at the factory have a bad day when he built my rope, my bolt, my rappel ring? My wounded arm presses to the forefront of my mind. Antibiotics. Katrina is missing. Ash has gone rogue. Cyman maybe buggers an Indian boy, now. Bernard is informing on his father. Rachel will have me destitute in hours. Paolo is going to turn me in.

And I'm painting an elephant laying pipe in a donkey.

"I'm done," Paolo says. He has painted the elephant's trunk, then after lowering himself three times, the donkey's snout, and then its front legs. He is fifty feet below me.

"Drop about twenty feet. You might be able to swing far enough to paint the legs below Marz."

I switch to my wounded arm when my left shoulder flags, but I can barely lift the spray can. Not that the strength isn't there—just that it hurts so much to use it.

The donkey's jaws are done and I start on his upside-down ears. To my left, Layne works on the donkey's front legs, wrapped in a passionate embrace around the elephant's torso. Marz, twenty feet away, paints the elephant's hips and groin.

"How close are you to the donkey's back?" I ask Marz.

"Two minutes."

I start the donkey's neck, spray a dozen elongated S's to signify a free-flowing mane.

As the minutes drag, my nervous excitement wanes. No one is dead. No helicopters. No snipers from the coffee shop. No bolt of lightning from an angry God.

My walkie-talkie sputters, "Cops!"

"What's happening?"

"Just came over the scanner," Bernard says. "Someone reported lights on bell rock. Cop gave an estimated time of arrival of eight minutes. Another said ten minutes. A third said ten. Maybe."

"That many cops?"

"I think they know it's you."

I yell across the rock to the boys, "Cops on the way. They saw light. Eight minutes ETA."

I tell the walkie-talkie, "Give me light one more time. I'll tell you when."

"Boys, we have ten minutes to get it done and get out of here. In thirty seconds, I'll have the light on one last time. Finish up and scramble."

Lines whir.

"Turn it on," I tell Bernard. "Just leave it on."

"I got to bug out, soon," Bernard says.

"We're tracing the outline. Just be a minute."

"Done with the outline!" Marz calls. The others follow.

"Kill the light and bug out," I bark into the walkie-talkie.

The light goes out. The sound of a Jeep engine, gunning over ruts, carries to the rock wall. Bernard emerges on the main road and parks at the crest of a small hill at a palm-reader's shop.

"I can see them," Bernard's says on the walkie-talkie. "Sedona... couple miles."

My boys paint furiously, cutting wide paths, bounding from side to side. Marz rappels down to link to Paolo and Layne's work.

"Done," Marz says. "Done," says another. "Done."

I'm higher than the rest. "We have a minute," I say. "They can't get up here right off, and they won't shoot us. I don't think."

"What do you want to do?" Marz says.

"Paint H-O-C-K in big letters. Fill that donkey up with HOCK."

I paint C-Y-M-A-N.

CHASE

Philosophy has to grant that revelation is possible.
But to grant that revelation is possible means to
grant that philosophy is perhaps something infi-
nitely unimportant.

Leo Strauss

Two patrol cars flash into view on the road from Sedona. They swerve into the tourist parking lot and car doors slam and voices carry. I open my cell phone one last time and try Ash. No answer.

A spotlight splashes on the rock. We're caught, all of us. "Let's go! Drop! Leave the ropes!"

I kick hard against Bell Rock and bound thirty-feet to the next ledge and thanks to the cops, my landing is illuminated and smooth and the boys find solid ground with no problem.

"It'll take them a half hour to get back here. Take your time," I say. "Be a shame to fall the last two hundred feet."

Karabiners tinkle. Ropes whir. All within the glare of spotlights.

"My feet are killing me," Marz says.

"New shoes?"

"Yeah."

"We'll switch to boots when we're on the ground. Let's bug out."

The path is wide; I jog and my posse follows around the side of Bell Rock, out of the spotlights. Northward, another pair of police cars approaches with red and blue lights flashing.

The slope flattens and I stretch into a run. My toes are crinkled tight in my climbing shoes but escape awaits in the small ravine at the base of the rock. Juniper scratches my face. The guys giggle and curse with glee. Hidden by brush and trees, heaving for breath, we stop at the bottom where we've cached daypacks with boots and beer.

Layne pops a can of Coors Light.

"My feet—O my poor dogs," Marz says, and unties his climbing shoes.

Paolo opens a pint of vodka, stops untying his climbing shoes and takes a gurgle.

"Let's not celebrate too much," I say. "We still have to hike two miles."

"They'll be all over this place soon," Layne says.

My arm feels like fire and is so swollen it barely fits in my heroin hoodie. I've got to get to Phoenix, beg Ursula for antibiotics. Will Bernard try to stop me from returning to his father's compound? Best not talk to Bernard before I go. I'll take the bike.

"Let's move!" I say. I dig my cell phone for another try at raising Ash.

"Solomon!" she says. "I'm so sorry. You've got to help. It's all going down right now!"

"Where are you?"

"I'm at the Grand Mason Hotel. The bar, watching the lobby for Géraud and the boy. I was going to call the cops."

"That won't work. You can't do that. Ash? Ash—" The phone is dead. Bad coverage.

It comes back. Ash says, "Can you hear me?"

"Yes. Don't call the cops. They'll never bust him. First, the hotel will warn the senator, and second, even if they catch him, they'll look the other way as soon as they recognize him. Then you've got to worry about Géraud burying you in the desert."

The screeching thwacking sound of a helicopter's rotors force me to raise my voice.

"Can you still hear me?"

"Barely," she says.

"The only way to guarantee he goes down is by making the whole world know, and you've got to let me do that! We've got cameras in there! We'll get him!"

"Can I trust you?" she says.

"You have to. I'll be there soon. I'll call in two hours. I'm tied up!"

"That sounds like a helicopter—"

"I love you!"

I close the phone wondering why I said that. I don't love her. I don't love anyone. But it's done said. I'm knee deep in berating myself and Layne grabs my shoulder.

Layne points. "I think that chopper's here for us."

Ahead, to the right, the chopper spotlights the ground where we came from. "Over the side!" I yell.

"What's down there?" Marz says.

"I don't know, but it's not a jail."

"Might be nothing at all," Layne says, and disappears over the side. The others follow. I'm last.

The cops aren't after me for painting Bell Rock. They've no doubt concluded that it is the same band of merry raiders who have done the billboards, the overpasses, the fliers, the You Tube video, the under-passes, the postcards. To them, we—I am not a good person who has slipped into criminality one time. A redeemable person. To them, I've gone serial. Worse, my crimes aren't against other citizens—something they could lose in a bureaucratic swamp of paper. My sins are against the State. Defiling state property for anti-state purposes. Defamation of the ruling elite. Usage of the national postal system for the conveyance of pernicious truths. I may be a gadfly, but the elite don't suffer bugs.

The boys make no sound after disappearing and though half-convinced I'm leaping into a chasm, I step forward.

The rock face rolls over, becomes steep, but by turning backwards I'm able to reverse walk down the slope. The helicopter light sweeps by and though I'm not exposed in the blast of white light, ambience reveals the grinning faces of Layne, Marz, and Paolo. They huddle twenty feet ahead in a copse of pine trees. The rotors roar. The spotlight flashes another direction and I leap the last few feet as the rock becomes truly steep.

I race to the boys on ground covered in crunchy-soft pine needles. I could be wearing tap shoes and running on cymbals and not hear it. The helicopter beats louder and lower; the thwack of the rotors combines with the steady low blare of the exhaust to rattle my guts. It hovers overhead and the spotlight casts a beam barely fifteen feet wide.

The light creeps along the ground, closer.

"Get against a tree! Up against a tree!" I scream, and lean into a pine. The others melt into vertical shadows and the ground is burning white and the glare makes me wince. 'Don't move!" I shout, "Don't look up!" But I know they can't hear me. I can't hear me. Layne hugs a tree ten feet to my side and the others are out of view, not yet exposed by the light. The rotor wash blows dried pine needles on the ground and I can feel my hair breezing against my back and lifting to my face. My silent prayer is that through the tree limbs, my hair is indecipherable from the rest of the forest being shredded and blown by the wash.

Layne smiles tightly, his eyes narrow. Any face would smile under stress like this, but his grin is deeper—he's enjoying it.

The spotlight shifts away and I am out of it, and then Layne is out. Marz and Paolo glide over rocks ahead, toward the edge of an expanse that leads to 179, the road to Sedona. The helicopter cuts toward Bell Rock and the spotlight scours the side, as if second guessing whether we made it to the ground yet, or not.

Our vehicles are in a community a mile on the other side of Bell Rock, parked under leafy maples along the road. Between here and there are no doubt a half dozen police officers on the ground.

The rotor noise echoes off Bell Rock. Layne and I find Marz and Paolo crouching beside a boulder under the last tree cover between us and the road.

"Isn't that Bernard's Wrangler at the coffee shop?" Marz says, and nods toward the knoll.

"Yeah. He went there when the cops came over the hill. He must be hanging loose, watching the action," I say.

"Have him pick us up," Marz says. "We can hoof it back to our cars, but if we get stopped, we'll have a hard time explaining all these empty spray cans."

Layne says, "A quarter mile downhill, the brush comes right up to the road. We can meet him there."

I dig my cell phone out and call Bernard. "Meet us up the road, a half mile from your location..."

I flip the phone. "Two minutes. Let's go."

They take off. I watch.

There's no way I'm getting in Bernard's vehicle until I know what he's doing with Rachel.

And Paolo? Maybe it's best to let that friendship fade.

Layne, Marz, and Paolo fly across the rocks and between bushes and cacti. I lose sight of them. At the coffee shop, the Wrangler's headlights come on and it crawls onto the road. Passes me, slows, stops. Three shadows jump inside. The vehicle waits, and waits. I imagine the argument, and call Bernard.

"Go ahead without me. I have some other work to attend."

The Jeep putts away and they've made their escape.

My arm throbs. Maybe this is what my ancestors felt. How many modern men look at the moonless night and invite the emptiness inside? How many feel like I do, that for all our progress, we can never protect ourselves from nature, from microbes or mountain lions? A billion people have never spent a night without a roof overhead. Have never heard a noise in the dark and wondered if it had teeth and was hungry.

We build cities to isolate us from perils outside the gates, but after generations of civilized living, known perils become unknown, and then forgotten. Three million people in Phoenix scarcely realize coyotes don't go home every night to a full dish of Purina and a stainless-steel bowl of filtered water.

The wild exists outside the city, so it doesn't exist at all.

Until frosty white Tinkerbell disappears, and in some deep, genetic-memory dream, you realize stomach enzymes are quickly converting Tinkerbell into coyote crap. Then you shudder and though a part of you mourns the Manx which is now so much chewed meat, so many calories waiting to be burned, the rest of you is happy to rest a DVD on the tray, press the button, and let technology substitute a fresh stream of made-up violence to take the place of the real violence just outside the gates.

Most won't have a clue until the electric goes out and the grocery stores run out and they find themselves alone and hungry, surrounded by others who are alone and hungry. The survivors will be those who never forgot life outside the gates.

I'll be in the mountains when the day comes.

Pain brings me back.

How many Blackfoot warriors felt this exact pain in their arm? How many had an arrow pushed all the way through, and had infection set in? Did they know, from experience, when a wound turned black, they were destined to greet their ancestors?

The fastest route to my Valkyrie crosses behind the rock on terrain I only assume is like the rest, rough in spots, but passable. The helicopter circles Bell Rock; it has climbed a couple hundred feet and the spotlight illuminates a fifty-foot circle. It wouldn't take much bad luck to wind up in the center of it.

I doubt my pursuers would expect me to head toward the cop cars on the other side of Bell Rock. I can see their revolving reds and blues flashing off the coffee shop glass, and the rock, and the sky. Last count, there were three squad cars. Maybe more have come. I breathe deep. Flex my aching arm. About to stand, I think of Ash. Beautiful Ash—

Retrieve my phone and press the digits.

"Solomon?" she says.

"I'm coming for you, baby," I say. "What's going on?"

"I must have missed him. I've been watching the lobby, but he never came."

"Don't worry," I say. "We'll get him. If anything happened, it'll be on the video. I'll be there in three hours. Two and a half, maybe. As fast as I can. I'll come for you. I won't let you down."

"I have to save the boy," she says. Her voice is flat. "And end my father's career."

"I own this," I say. "This problem. I own it. I may not be able to call again until I'm almost there. Stay safe. Get out of sight somewhere."

"I didn't want to let it happen one more time," she says. Her voice falters. "How much can a little boy take?"

What can I say? I'll kill her father? That would be justice, and part of me believes it is every person's duty to be the judge. But I'm not getting from this PhD student that she wants to debate Leo Strauss's take on Natural Right. She wants to know that in the end, things are going to come out all right, because she can't see a way through it. I know what that's like, and I know that's when people get desperate.

"I own this," I say.

"I'll wait if I can."

The line goes dead. I run. Ignore my arm. Ignore my feet and legs. Rather than put the phone in my cargo pocket where it will flap against my leg, I carry it in hand. After a quarter mile getting slapped in the face with brush and twisting my ankle in the dark, I tell myself the physical pain is squeezing tears from my eyes.

Rachel had said we must forego wreaking vengeance on the evil of the world to be protected against it. In so many words. But that's not true. It's bait and switch. We've ceded the right to crush evil to the men with badges, but most of the evil is too smart for them. Most of the evil is among them—not that crooks wear badges. No. The biggest crooks are their bosses. Like Cyman.

I run behind the coffee shop, the bike shop, the tarot reader's shop. Circle a gas station. Three police cars are parked at the scenic pullover where they sell twenty-five-dollar parking passes and never empty the trash barrels. A few more, red and blues flashing, tool along the road that cuts to the right side of Bell Rock. My Valkyrie is a mile and a half up that forbidden road.

I can't cross 179 under all these lights—I resume my former vector another two hundred yards, sprint across the four-lane and barely throttle back for the duration. My lungs burn and I press hard enough to get a side stitch, something I haven't felt for ten years. All out. Frenetic. Houses pass. Cars, trucks, parked on the side of the street.

Hang in there, Ash...

I'm on a street parallel to the one on which I parked, looking out for cops. Throwing glances alternately over each shoulder, and after a half mile of a pace that is beginning to feel like madness, fate rewards my diligence with headlights turning onto the street behind me. I slip behind the closest maple, a foot wide, before the lights catch me in their glare. I'm exposed.

I jump behind an ancient El Camino somebody must have unearthed doing an archeology dig.

I crouch, then stretch flat on the cement and roll partly under the vehicle, in shadows.

The horn blares. Headlights flash against the garage door and the red-and-blues go off. The cop car is only a couple feet away. No way I'm going to look. I low-crawl on cement around a pickup truck, snag my backpack on the front bumper. Car doors slam—officers on foot.

Shadows are my friends. I wiggle backward, forward, climb to all fours and ease around the house. Cop shoes squeak on polished cement. I turn the corner as a flashlight leaps behind me. Ahead, more houses. Lights and roofs, forever. I haul ass over shrubs, around walls, and make a giant arc toward the Valkyrie.

The flashlights are back there somewhere, but from the cops' slowing pace I bet they're thinking, the graffiti *is* kind of funny...

And Cyman *is* a dick.

There are empty spaces between the locals' cars where Paolo's and Layne's vehicles were parked. But ahead is Bernard's Wrangler, and standing at my Valkyrie, I'm within eyeshot of his rearview mirror. Dig my key from my pocket, and my sweaty brow is suddenly cold when I look beside me and a tree trunk has moved five feet closer.

Bernard stands with his arms crossed.

I slip the key in the ignition. Bernard steps to me. His eyes are plaintive, and somehow in a split second of silence he earns my trust...

I leave the key in the ignition and rest my hands on my thighs.

"Solomon," he says, steps closer. "Hold on a second."

"What's up?"

"You weren't with the guys, and I started wondering."

"Yeah..."

"You saw me with Rachel—the TFI agent?"

"You got out of her car."

"There's nothing going on between us," he says.

That's not the denial I expected. I was thinking you'd explain how getting friendly with the woman who's investigating your father doesn't add up to you betraying him. "What?"

"I'm not seeing her, or anything. She's all yours. If you want."

"All mine?"

"She... likes you."

"What are you talking about? She's investigating your father, and you're slinking around with her after dark. Have you blown the whole thing yet? Did you tell her about Guillotine?"

"It isn't what you think. I'm not... with her."

I turn the key and give the throttle a tiny blip. The motor turns and the sound is pretty, six cylinders in perfect agreement as to who's doing what and when. Harmony is always mechanical. Free will won't permit it.

"I gotta haul ass. Thanks for the help, Bernard. I don't have you figured yet, and that's the truth."

"I'm on the good team," he says. "You'll see soon enough. For now you've got to trust me."

I pull away. *No I don't.*

I take a circuitous route far around Bell Rock and arrive on 179 south, toward I-17, about two miles below the swarm of cops and lights. There's a pair of helicopters now, and the attention my little misdemeanor garners confirms again that you don't smite the State. It must appear unassailable. That's why it marshaled ten Bradleys and two Abrams tanks against David Koresh and his wives and kids. If the State appears the slightest bit vulnerable, regular citizens might take pitchforks in hand and demand a little natural selection among the ranks of the elite.

Can't have that.

I stop at the Prescott exit—a place I've become familiar with, lately, and change out of my ninja suit. Buy and slam a Red Bull. Take a leak behind the store because I forgot to ask for the key.

I don't call Ash. I imagine she stews in melancholy, and I have nothing new to say. Much as I want to step in and be her hero, I recall what happened the last time. I told her she broke my heart, and she said, you put it out there, dumbass.

So I slam down my visor, twist the throttle and navigate to the southbound interstate. Miles flash by and the air warms. I lean through the dicey thirteen-mile bobsled route after Sunset Point. When the road is flat and straight, I pick up speed and cruise at a cool eighty-five, with the logic that a cop wouldn't stop me for going exactly ten miles over the limit. Why? A stock broker lady in Asheville, North Carolina, once confessed that was her strategy, and I adopted it without parsing the logic. Now I'm not sure, but I'm making good time.

I take the Happy Valley exit, make a few turns, drive a few miles. When I arrive at Cal Barrett's, the gate swings open.

Bernard called ahead.

Barrett greets me at the door in boxer shorts. He's got a Stallone body—muscles taut in open defiance of wrinkles. His underwear is white with a funky Christmas tree pattern—but his face isn't Christmas at all.

"You trying to get yourself killed? For a stunt?" He grabs my good arm and ushers me to the kitchen. Ursula wipes sleep from her eyes beside the sink.

"Stunt?" I say.

"Painting a rock for kicks. Some clownish picture. The people are beyond that. The ones who get it are already boiling over. And the ones who don't, won't, no matter what you say or do. So you go up there with your arm rotting off, hoping not to break your neck."

"Aw shucks, Barrett. I didn't know you cared."

"Let me look at that wound."

I pull my heroin hoodie off; yank my shirt sleeve. He starts with the bandage at the corner and lifts it carefully away from my skin.

"We need to talk," he says. "Things are getting serious. I figured to let you cool down after the race—I always let the boys enjoy a little hospitality before I sit 'em down for the truth. But you launched a war against the senator, and by God, I understand why you did it, but time's running out."

Ursula stands beside him and wrinkles her nose at my arm. She daubs the purplish meat with alcohol, presses it from the bottom side and goopy gooz erupts through the puncture—like brown blood bubbles on a half-cooked hamburger. I smell it and my stomach turns.

Barrett says, "You see these streaks under your skin? You feel the heat coming off that thing?" He places his hand on my forehead. "You're burning up."

"Give me some antibiotics. I'm not done, yet."

"You're no longer a guest. You're a ward. You don't go anywhere until the fever breaks. Not if you want to keep your arm."

"Well, you better give me a dose of antibiotics that looks and sounds like shock and awe, because I'm walking out that door in ten minutes."

He hunkers and makes eye contact. "You don't get it, do you? I thought you'd have seen everything by now. You know what a guillotine is. You know I've got men all over. *All over.* And you know I hate corrupt government like damn I don't know what. And you've never put it together. Everything you're doing is vain. You're a free man, and I won't stand in the way of a man and his will. But you need to think for two minutes before you decide you're going to risk losing your arm to go after that stupid senator again."

"Three hours," I say.

"What?"

"I want three hours. Then we'll have this conversation. Until then, it doesn't matter. I know what you're going to tell me—but here's what you don't understand. You may hold Cyman accountable for his crimes against the people. Great. But I'm going to hold him accountable for his crimes against a person."

"An Indian," Barrett says.

"A boy." I squeeze the corners of the table and Ursula shrinks away. I've got enough caffeine and sugar and ginseng in me I'm about to come unglued. "There's a boy out there right now, Cal, who's bleeding from his ass. He doesn't think there's an innocent man on the planet. And there's a young woman who has cast aside all the privilege her senator father gave her, to give this boy a chance at justice. You deal with the big picture. That's fine. It's going to take men of vision to set things right. But there's a boy and a woman who might not make it to your better world, if I don't risk a little infection."

Barrett clasps his hands. Bows his head.

I nod at Ursula and she resumes cleaning my wound.

Barrett walks to the far side of the kitchen and stands with his back to me. "Clean him up good, Ursula, and give him a triple of Vancomycin." He glances at his watch. "I believe we have about eight minutes until he walks out that door."

I nod.

"Three hours," Barrett says.

END GAME,

My arm throbs like Ursula used a wire brush. I've got a new layer of ointment and a triple dose of antibiotics in my bloodstream. My nerves are shot. I look forward to the hundred hours of sleep my adrenals will require to find stasis. After everything is over, I'm going to get a hotel in Prescott overlooking the courthouse square, and I'm going to focus on breathing clean air and nothing else. If I continue breathing, I will be satisfied with my progress. I swear. Amen.

I dial Keith.

"News?"

"Nothing," he says. "I've been driving around town all night. I stopped at every club she's ever gone to. Every one she hasn't. And since everything closed, I've been driving the streets, looking like I'm prowling for hookers."

"Where else could she be?"

"I don't know. But this is the second night, and I'm scared."

"I know, buddy. I know."

"Are you near? Can you help?"

"This isn't a good time, Keith."

"Does this have to do with Ash Cyman?"

"More to do with a boy who isn't responsible for his situation yet."

"Someone young enough to save?" Keith says.

"Stay in touch. Let me know when you find her."

I press END and wait a second. Yeah, I'm trying to save someone. But it's different, I think. Saving the world isn't a responsibility; it's a narcissistic fantasy. But saving a kid in harm's way—that's a responsibility. The only thing to do, if you call yourself a human being. This isn't about politics. It's a boy.

I dial Ash. "Where you at?"

"I'm in the shrubs by the parking lot." She yawns into the phone. "He never passed by when I was in the lobby, so I'm watching his car. I'll get him when he leaves."

"Do you have your car there?"

"I do."

"If he comes out with the boy, follow him. You hear me? No confrontations."

"If he comes out with the boy..."

"No confrontations. Say it, Ash. Follow at a distance. Say it."

"I won't confront him. I'll follow him."

"And call me. I'm twenty minutes away."

"Hurry," she says.

I close the phone. The straight stretches on I-17 in the city are easy game for ninety mile an hour progress; visibility is a mile and there's nowhere for a cop to hide. On the curves after Peoria Avenue, I cut back to seventy. The air has turned dry again over the last few hours and my eyes burn. I blink them alert. Last thing I need is to wind up at a police station while Ash crouches beside a shrub and waits.

Exit, turn, drive, turn. In the parking lot I see Géraud's Suburban and, relieved, I look for Ash. She stands and I park in an open space. Get off the bike and squat to stretch my knees and back, and Ash stoops, wraps her arms around me. I stand and she buries her face in my chest. Her soft parts press me and I recognize her vulnerability.

This moment is why men exist.

There are bad things out there that justify the species keeping quick, smelly, violent bastards like me around. We're here to remove the threats that might prevent our women from making little people big people. Good big people. That's the simple view of Homo sapiens that comes to me, feeling Ash's breasts against my ribs.

"It's okay, baby," I say, and press the round of her back. She sniffles.

"He never came out."

"He probably used a back entrance, and the kid's already gone. So now we retrieve the video cassette."

"What about the boy?"

I nod at the black Suburban. "Géraud is here. He'll help."

She pulls from me. Grips my forearms. "Why do you care? I asked Keith for help and he brought me to you. Why do you care?"

"It started as a bet." I lead her a few feet and we sit on the curb. "We'd watched an election ad on television, and I said I could knock some points off your father's lead. Keith bet me I couldn't, and I started that night."

"Break the Cyman," she says. "You don't know how ruthless the boys were in school when they learned what a hymen was. But I'm glad for your wordplay on the billboard. Break the Hyman, vote Cock. My father actually believes he suffers for his constituents. Scorn really exposes the messiah complex."

"I intend more than satire. Have you been watching the news?"

"I'm surprised he didn't have a stroke after learning he doesn't sleep with animals."

"Postcards, fliers, YouTube. Wait until you see what my crew did tonight, in Sedona."

"What?"

"Just wait."

"What?" She pokes my ribs and her melancholy face fades for a moment behind cherry cheeks and curious eyes.

"I took the same group that did the roadblock, and we painted Bell Rock. It's an elephant and a donkey going at it, missionary style. The elephant says Cyman and the donkey says Hock."

"They're all the same?"

"Not exactly. They pander to different groups but behind closed doors, collude against us. Your brother runs the water department. He has a side business with a Yavapai woman who also is a tribal leader. When Hock runs for senate, she starts raising hell about Hock's land development stealing Indian water. Hock suddenly has fifty million dollars hanging in the breeze, at your brother's mercy. Hock suddenly plays nice with your father."

"I thought there had to be a reason for his sudden incompetence. So your illustration on Bell Rock—"

"The You Tube video supports Bell Rock. It documents all the links and references news stories."

"I don't understand why you went all-out. I mean, I pushed you. But you aren't the kind of man who gets pushed. Why'd you help?"

"First it was the bet. Then you. Then the boy."

"Me?"

"I told you that."

"But you don't know me."

"I knew enough to start."

"And now?"

I wait. I think of how I felt realizing she lied to me the second time.

"We'll work on that after we save the boy." I begin to rise, which takes a moment. My legs, back, and arm have suffered over the last few days, and rousing them from repose takes time. She touches my shoulder.

"Stay a minute longer," Ash says.

I sit.

"It's hard to grow up with a family in politics, and not believe they're doing useful work. Even though my dad was endlessly talking about limited government, I wanted to see government work."

"So that led you to being a Democrat?"

She silences me with her eyes. "No. It led me to want government to be effective. I wanted to understand politics, sure, but more than that. I wanted to understand government. They're different, you know?"

I shrug.

"Politics is the doing side of it. The labor. The strategy. Government is the architecture. The framework. Politics is dirty, back-slapping or back-stabbing, maybe both. But government is pristine. That's the way I've always seen it."

"Uh. Sure."

"I studied political science for my bachelor's and master's, and researching my thesis, I joined the Peace Corps. I worked in Kenya during the elections. Odinga—the challenger—was leading. The incumbent squeaked by him and was sworn in for another term before there was a recount, and Odinga's supporters rioted. Six hundred people died. I heard gunshots every night. And I thought, not that these people didn't deserve democracy—but that government itself was failing them. At that point, it didn't matter what kind of political order they chose. The organization that was supposed to protect them from outsiders and order their civil affairs had become the problem. Government wasn't separate and pristine. It was a tool of the people who already had power."

"That's a mouthful."

"We're like that. There's a famous quote from Thoreau. All machines have their friction, but when the friction has its machine, it's time to get a new machine."

"Uh huh."

"My father is the friction having the machine. When he—an agent of the organization that is supposed to protect the smallest and weakest, uses his position to prey on them, and to silence those who might stop him—at that point, *government* should take him down. If not, the people must. When the machinery is so big that the smallest have no redress, government has failed. Not politics. *Government*. And that's when it's time to go back to the drawing board."

I ponder her words. Is she due for an introduction to Barrett?

Is she already part of Barrett's organization?

I say, "How did you learn about the boy?"

"From Géraud."

"...Something I haven't quite understood. How you wound up with him."

"You already figured out that I was working for the other side. The Democrats. If you want government to work, you go with the people who believe in government."

"How did that lead to getting cigarette burns on your back?"

"It was an affair, to begin with. A maneuver to get back at my evil Republican dad. I read once that every time his mother made him mad, John Lennon would tear her curtain just a little bit. He was powerless to do anything real, but he had to do something. It was like that for me. Géraud hit on me at a function. I was there as the senator's daughter. Secretly of course, I took notes to carry back to a group I was part of called *Renaissance Resistance*. We were the kids of Republicans who collected information we learned from hearing our parents talk about strategies and stuff. It's a national organization—but organized in cells. We funneled what we learned to 529s that ultimately got the intelligence where it was needed."

"Wait a minute. There's a group of senators' kids who are spying on their parents?"

"There always has been. The Democrat kids do it too. The Internet makes it easy. So after this dog and pony function is over, my father asks Géraud to take me home. The senator had important business to conduct, you know, for the people. Géraud drove me home and put the moves on me. He's not entirely bad looking, and I was just back from Kenya. Full of rage."

"And Géraud just decides to burn you?"

"No. I felt awful and told him it was a one night thing. He wanted more and since he didn't have the time to follow me around, he hired an investigator. The next thing I know, Géraud is in my house explaining that if I don't go along with what he says, he brings down not just me, but Renaissance Resistance. Whatever we do tonight has consequences beyond me and you and the boy."

"None are more important than the boy." We are silent and she wraps her arms around her folded knees. I continue, "When we were in the hotel, you had his room key."

"A woman is more likely to survive a male by using her brain than her brawn.

I think of the Amazons but say nothing.

"I didn't fight him," she says. "I courted his trust."

"So," I say. "Once he figures you can't fight him, he becomes a sadist. The burns. And one day he mentions your father and the Indian boy?"

She nods slowly. "Pathetic, huh? That's why I'm going to bring him down."

"Why did you go to the battered women's shelter where you saw Keith?"

"I didn't know what they did. Part of me wanted to find another way out. Run somewhere. Burns hurt, you know? And I thought I could forget about the boy. You can't save everyone—but I couldn't forget him. The women's shelter does the best they can, but only for the women who find them. And I imagine it is the same for children's shelters. They're only there for the kids who find them. The rest are lost; their futures are written. Prostitution, drugs, disease, death. But Keith led me to you, so maybe there was a bigger reason for me to go to the shelter than I thought. Maybe when I was giving up, God was using that to take me one step closer."

"I didn't figure you for a religious girl."

"I'm not. But if God is all that, maybe he can find a use for a girl who doesn't believe in him. Maybe that's the beauty in it."

A few minutes ago she said I don't know her. I know more now.

"So, what's the plan?" she says.

"Géraud probably brought the boy in through a back entrance before the hotel locked it for the night, and then exited there while you watched the lobby. Let's get the videotape, and we'll know what to do."

She's quick to her feet, and offers her arms to help lift me from the curb. I clutch her wrists and she leans back. There's reed-like strength in her. We cross the lot holding hands, arms swinging a short arc, our feet in step.

"When this is over, I promised myself I would go away for a week," I say. "Get a hotel in Prescott overlooking the town square, and sit up there and sleep. Maybe do something slow and useless, like read a newspaper. No coffee for a week."

"Sounds wonderful."

We enter the hotel. The man at the check-in desk is grinding his fists into his eyes. We're almost to the elevator before he drops his hands and he stiffens. His gaze follows us to the glass elevator. I press the button for the third floor and the man is still watching. Is he the one I threatened on the telephone the day Mike and I installed the camera equipment? It can't be—that phone call was during the day. Even if I'm wrong, he wouldn't know my face.

"What was that?" Ash says. "He didn't call anyone; he just stared."

"Perhaps he isn't aware that I'm a guest."

The elevator door opens. Motioning Ash to stay put, I peek around the corner and check both ways. The hall is empty. I take her hand and we walk quickly to the room. I slip the key card through. There's a click and the little light goes green. I push the door open.

The VCRs are gone.

"Where is everything?" she says.

"I don't know."

We step inside. The door swings shut and I have a sudden claustrophobic sense like someone has been here recently, and still might be. I smell odd cologne. Footprints cross the freshly vacuumed carpet. I press my index finger across my lips and guide Ash against the wall. Creep to the bathroom, then come back to the closet. Open it. Empty. I step back, slowly take in the room. Where the VCRs had been, I see the room's alarm clock. It flashes 12:43.

I grab Ash by the hand and rush to the hall. "We have to get to Géraud's room."

"Why?"

"Do you have the key card?"

The elevator is still on our floor. No wait. I drag Ash inside and mash the button. The doors close. We elevate to the sixth floor. "Do you have the key?"

"In my pocket. What's going on?"

"Géraud got into the room. He used our equipment to catch us coming back for the tape."

"He wouldn't be able to use it for anything. Legally, I mean."

"I don't care about that. He's got whatever tapes of the senator and the boy we managed to make. He's got our evidence."

The chime rings and the elevator door opens.

"But I spoke when I entered the room," she says.

"I doubt Géraud is waiting up watching the video monitor. Not when he has to fly back to Washington with your father tomorrow. That's what the camera is for."

She leads me down the hall. Stops at a door. Inserts the card into the slot, and pulls it.

Red light.

She does it again.

Red light.

"He changed the key," she whispers.

I pace. Glance at an axe on the wall behind Plexiglas. I scuttle toward it.

"Pst!" Ash furiously motions me to her side and stations me behind the jamb. She raps on the door.

Géraud's muffled voice comes from inside. "Who? What?"

"It's me. *Want something?*"

The chain slips and the dead bolt snaps. The door eases open and I explode through the gap. There's a loud thud; wood collides with his toes or forehead. I shove the door the rest of the way open. Géraud crouches on the floor. He leaps at me. I jab his neck and he goes down. He sprawls on the carpet and I make a saddle of his back.

Ash closes the door. Locks it.

"Pull the belt from his pants, there on the chair."

She whips it free and goes to his feet. Wraps his legs twice and cinches the belt. Géraud mumbles.

"Get me the iron in the closet," I say.

Ash hesitates.

"Now."

Ash brings it. I place it on the carpet, snap the cord free and tie Géraud's hands behind his back.

"Can he breathe?" she says. "With you sitting on him?"

I get up.

Ash turns to the television and VCRs. "How does this work?" she says. She presses play and the television screen goes snowy. "Nothing's on the tape," she says. She presses fast forward and the snowstorm becomes a blizzard, but there's no image of her old man. No evidence. She sits on the side of the bed. Slumps with elbows on her knees. A sob escapes her.

Was the boy all made up?

"Géraud?"

He groans.

"When did you take the video equipment from my room to yours?"

He says nothing.

I take his middle finger. Bend it backward until I hear a sound that indicates a little more pressure will make the bones inside sharp. "Géraud?"

Nothing.

His finger snaps and he screams, "TODAY! This afternoon!"

So there is no tape of the senator with the boy. No video evidence. Letting it go an extra day was for naught.

"But Cyman was here tonight?"

"One last time," he says, "before going back to D.C."

"How did you get into my room?"

Géraud hesitates. I take his index finger. Bend it back.

"The manager made a duplicate key."

"Why would Cyman want a video of me looking for the VCRs?"

"Cyman doesn't know anything. I wanted the video. Me. You know? For the information. That's all. For the information."

Ash leaps from the bed and slams her heel into Géraud's kidney. He doubles over, fetal position, and she kicks his ribs. "There's one piece of information I want. And if you don't give it to me, I'll break every bone in your body. Where's the boy?"

I hold my breath. Does the boy exist? If Géraud denies it, will I disbelieve enough to argue? All the evidence has been second hand through Ash. She never saw the boy either...

"There's no boy."

She crushes her heel to his kidney again.

"You told me there was a boy! Where is he?" She takes the hand I bent and pushes it farther.

"THERES NO BOY!"

"THERE IS!" Ash screams. She balls her hands to fists and slams them to his temples, bouncing his head from the floor. Over and over. "Where's the boy? I know there's a boy."

Géraud grunts with each blow.

Ash rears back and punches his face. She jabs his eyes, bounces his skull, pulls hair.

"Where's the boy?"

I touch her shoulder and she snaps toward me, suddenly less berserk.

Géraud spits blood. His eyes are closed and his brain rattled. He says, "South Phoenix. Baseline Road."

What?

There is a boy.

"Grab the video cassette," I say to Ash. I lift Géraud by his shoulders. "I'm going to undo your feet and take you to Baseline. You make a false move, the first thing you're going to feel is your right temple shaking hands with your left."

I unclasp the belt securing his legs and realize a split second too late that I'm in front of his knees. His right shoots up and connects with my shoulder. He twists and I tackle him. He lands on his back—on his hands—and screams. I drive a fist into his mouth and look up to Ash. She's holding a gun on Géraud.

"Ash!"

"It was on the dresser."

"Give it to me."

"I think I'll keep it."

"Géraud? You hear that? The woman you burned with cigarettes has your gun pointed at your head. Think you might want to help us find the boy?"

"Atian."

"What?'

"Ah Tee An. His name is Atian." Géraud chokes and blood spills from the side of his mouth. "I'll take you."

I clean his face with a washcloth. He's wearing sleeping shorts and a wife beater tee. I push him to the door.

"Shoes," he says. "I need my shoes."

"Not really. You'll see." I push him into the hall. "I thought you were in the French Foreign Legion."

He says nothing. Ash follows us to the back stairwell. The downstairs door is locked from the outside, so there's no traffic.

"Run ahead, Ash, and get your car. Bring it around. We'll wait at the door."

She takes stairs two at a time.

"He won't talk to you," Géraud says. "He knows his pimp will kill him."

"You're telling me I have to kill a pimp? Is that it?"

"Why do you care? No one else does."

"Géraud—I'm starting to dislike you on a personal level."

We wait a minute at the door in silence and then Ash swerves into the open parking space by the door. I shove Géraud forward and into the back of her car. I sit with him.

"Give me the gun."

Ash passes it back, low, between the seats. I check the chamber and rest it on my lap, the barrel pointing to Géraud's stomach. He smiles.

"You're a real Rambo," he says.

"Go to Baseline," I say. The car jerks forward and in five seconds we're bouncing over a curb and heading southbound on Seventh Avenue. Approaching Baseline, Ash says, "Which way, Géraud?"

"Left. There's a brick building with graffiti on the side. That's where he'll be. Unless someone else has him for the rest of the night."

"Who's the pimp?"

"Louie. I don't know his last name. He sits out front all night long. Got his stable in the house. He calls back when you give him the money, and his woman brings up the kid."

"How much dough?"

"A grand. He charges a premium for—"

"Shut up Géraud. Pull over here, Ash. I want to think."

"No way you're getting the boy. You're not a regular. And Louie sees me in the back seat of the wrong car, he knows something's going down. Plus, he's got all the local cops bought, and he serves a lot of people who can flip your world upside down. Smart thing for you to do is turn around."

I tune out Géraud and remember Colonel Hal Moore. Surrounded, outgunned, he charged. Surprise.

"How big a guy is Louie?"

"Small guy. Like a rat. He'll know there's trouble the minute you open the door," Géraud says.

"What, he's got a drive thru set up?"

"Exactly. And don't think he isn't armed to the teeth."

"Ash, drive. Stop in front of Louie. And then wait out front until I come out with the kid."

I catch her eyes in the rearview. They dip in agreement and she hits the gas. The little four-banger hums and we're on the street again. In thirty seconds I see the building with the graffiti. Ash taps the brakes and pulls over, stops in front of Louie.

I watch his hand as I swing the door open and jump from the seat. His left hand is still but his right shifts to his pocket. I cross to his left and draw a bead on his head with Géraud's .45.

"We need to talk, Louie. Pull your hand out of your pocket. Easy."

I glance to the dark building entrance behind and to his right. It is empty. Louie rests his hands on his thighs.

"I don't talk business with a gun to my head," he says.

"Very astute—you get the sticker. This is coercion. You and I are going inside for a boy named Atian."

"A thousand bucks."

"That's right, Louie. That's what you took off Géraud, in the car there. That's what you'll be giving Atian as a goodbye present. Get up. Let's go."

"Piss off. I ain't goin' nowhere, and the only way you get that boy is if you put a bullet in me."

I lash with my left, since my right arm is wounded. First, to his temple, where a large nerve and artery lurk below the surface. A strong blow will knock a man out. A brutal strike will explode the artery, and the victim will die. Louie fuzzes out. He's still breathing. Slumps over the side of his chair and collapses to the dirt.

I fish a .22 from his pocket. It's a purse gun that probably sounds like a firecracker. I unbuckle his belt, whip it from the loops, roll him to his front, secure his hands behind his back and roll him back on his belly. I pat him down but that's his only weapon.

Ash sits wide-eyed inside the car. I give her the .22, keep the .45. "He'll be out for a couple minutes. If he wakes up, make him lay where he is. Watch his hands. If he works them loose, shoot him. Three, four times, at least." I turn. Stop. "Oh yeah. Same for Géraud."

The building is an old restaurant with a counter on the left and tables on the right. Boxes are stacked everywhere and the joint is lit by a low-watt bulb that hangs globeless from the center of the ceiling. The dining area is long and skinny and at the end, like an old western hotel, is a stairwell with an ornate wood banister. The rooms are upstairs. I climb, pointing the .45 ahead.

"Atian!" I call.

I wait on the top of the stairs. I'm about to creep forward when a door cracks open a dozen feet away. There's no light inside the room and I can't tell what's behind the black aperture.

The door slams and instinct tells me it is Atian. I stand there, steeling myself for anything. If he saw the gun in my hand, he thinks I'm bad news. If I open the door I should expect a knife hurled at my face, scalding water, a boot heel, any damn thing.

"Atian, my name is Solomon Bull. I've come to take you out of here. You don't have to live like this anymore."

There's no answer.

"Atian, I know Louie's a bad man and he keeps you here against your will. I don't know what he's used to trap you, but I'm telling you there are good people who want to help you."

I wait in silence, my hearing growing more acute with each heartbeat, each creak or groan of the foreign building. Wonder if Louie is still unconscious.

"I'm going to open the door so we can talk. I'd appreciate it if you don't throw anything at me."

I reach for the door handle.

GUILLOTINE

All men recognize the right of revolution; that is, the right to refuse allegiance to and to resist the government, when its tyranny or its inefficiency are great and unendurable.

Henry David Thoreau

s I twist the knob, a door farther down the hallway opens. A boy—a wisp—stands in the aperture. He's in his underwear and his hair is shiny black. Like mine. He looks nine or ten.

"You're an Indian?" he says.

"Blackfoot."

"Is that a tribe? Where's Louie?"

"Tied up out front. He's face down in the dirt. He won't be able to hurt you. And I'll take you someplace he won't find you."

Atian is slow to speak. He stands partly behind the door and looks downward and up at me at the same time. "Louie says he has friends everywhere."

"I'm sure he does. But he's also got enemies, and I wouldn't be surprised if Louie has a hard time doing business in a few days."

Atian stares.

"If you like, I'll teach you how to defend yourself against animals like him. Teach you to use your hands and your wits, so you never have to be afraid."

He steps into the hall.

"Go inside and get your clothes. Gather everything you want. I'm going back down to check on Louie, all right?"

Atian nods. Fear illuminates his eyes. Does he imagine me splitting sinew, spinning strands together, and triple winding a bowstring? Does he imagine I'll chuck a tomahawk into Louie's head? Or does he only recognize my skin and hair? Does this little Indian know nothing about his people save the propaganda—Custer being "ambushed"—that makes it onto television?

Atian goes into his room but does not turn on a light. I bound back down the stairwell, cross the restaurant and view Louie, still face down on the dirt. By the time I make it back upstairs, Atian stands in the hall waiting for me. He wears shorts and a tank top. A plastic grocery bag dangles from his closed hand. I reach, urge him forward. He steps carefully, his eyes narrow.

I take his hand and we walk side by side down the stairs. He looks up at me the whole time, transfixed, I think, by my hair.

"Why don't you let your hair grow long?" I say.

"No one likes an injun."

"Did Louie say that?"

He nods.

"Atian, forget everything he's ever said to you."

I turn to the squeak of an opening door. Eyes stare out, low. Another door opens and a girl maybe in her late teens studies me.

"What about them?" Atian says.

"I'll call the police in a few minutes, and they'll be taken care of."

"Why are you taking me?"

"Because we are brothers."

Louie has rolled to his side. He curses. I lead Atian behind his back. Atian stops, watches. He makes no retributive move toward Louie; neither does he shrink.

I pull him along and put him in the front seat. Atian is instantly taken with Ash. She trembles and looks straight forward, as if unable to take in Atian's face.

"Géraud, show me your hands."

He twists—still securely bound.

I circle to Louie and rub the muzzle of the .45 on the bridge of his nose. "Earlier tonight, you took a thousand dollars from Géraud. Where is it?"

He huffs. Bloodshot eyes. "My pocket."

"Which pocket, Louie? I'm not going to fish through all of them."

"Front right."

Keeping the pistol to his head, I withdraw a money clip. Count ten one-hundreds and toss the rest to the entrance of the building. "It's been a pleasure doing coercion with you, Louie."

I climb in the back seat. Ash faces Atian, holds his hand and pats it while tears stream her face. She's freaking him out. He cuts his eyes to me, and to Géraud, and back to me.

"Give me his gun," I say.

Ash places it in my hand. I exit. Run inside, up the stairs to the door with the girl. I give it to her. "Louie is tied up downstairs on the sidewalk. You can get away."

I leave her, knowing a better man would think of something different to do. Inside the car, I say to Ash, "Let's get on the road. We got him."

"It's finally over," she says, and sobs.

Atian removes his hand from under hers, and rests it on top. Ash wipes her eyes, shifts the transmission into drive. The front wheels spit rocks and dirt to the undercarriage.

I get out my cell phone, call 911 and explain that a pimp who sells children is lying tied on the ground, and I give the address.

"You're a regular boy scout," Géraud says.

I drive my fist to his eye bone.

In minutes Ash pulls in front of the hotel and I get out, circle and open Géraud's door. He twists from the back seat. Rolls out and lands on his knees. I leave him tied with the cord from the hotel's iron.

"Don't think this is over," I say. "This was the rescue. The punishment is yet to come."

"I work for a senator who heads three committees and sits on another ten."

"That's kind of why I'm going to saw your head off someday."

I get back in the car. "Pull ahead a block so we can talk to Atian."

Ash parks at an all-night service station. "Are you hungry, Atian," she says.

He looks at his knees.

"This place has burritos. Do you want one?"

Atian swallows.

She smiles and I fear she's going to go overboard, and talk like he's two years old. It's awkward. Ash holds my look and we communicate, somehow. To this kid, adults have created a rotten place to live. But Atian doesn't want us to pamper him, or pretend we've earned trust we haven't. He sure doesn't want the condescension that attends us "understanding" him.

What he wants, I think, is to meet one adult who doesn't hurt him.

One person to serve as a cornerstone.

Ash smiles sadly and leaves the car. He watches her walk to the store.

I pull Louie's fold of hundred dollar bills from my pocket and offer it to Atian. He looks at the money, and back at me.

"You keep it," he says.

"The first thing I want you to understand is that this is yours. You own yourself, and nobody, ever again, is going to take that from you."

"I don't want it."

"Because of where it came from?"

"Yes."

"Then it's up to you to dispose of it. This money will buy all the food you can eat for a month. All the clothes you need for a year. Or it can make some nice flames if you burn it on the parking lot. Whatever you want. Your call."

"Burn it."

"It's not mine to burn. You burn it."

"Got a match?"

I look in Ash's center console. Nothing. "I'll be right back." I dart into the quick mart, grab a book of matches from a bowl by the register, and stand outside Atian's window. I pass the matches inside.

"Right now?" he says.

"It's your money. You want to burn it?"

"Yes."

"I bet Ash would prefer if you did it on the parking lot."

Atian opens the door and kneels on the pavement. He crumples the bills and assembles them in a tight pile on the blacktop. He strikes a match and a small gust blows a C note free. I stamp it and he plucks it from under my shoe. I kneel and shelter the pile with cupped hands. Watching my eyes, he folds the matchbook flap over the striking strip and pulls a match between.

The smell takes me back to smoking Marlboros and shooting pool with a rebel named Forringer. Atian holds the flame to the money and after a few seconds the currency flares.

"Atian," I say, "you're not going to be able to trust anybody for a long time, and I understand that. But I want to make a deal with you."

He eyes me.

"You watch what I do, and you'll see I do what I say. I want you to trust me a little more each time you see me keep my word. Building trust is a two-part operation. I do what I say, and you pay me with whatever trust you think I've earned. Fair?"

"Fair."

"So this is what we have to do. One of the men who... you saw in that hotel back there is a very powerful man. I know a group of people who want to take his power away from him because of what he did to you."

Atian's face is blank.

"I'm going to go away for a few hours this morning. I want you to go with Ash. She's going to take care of you this morning. You can get cleaned up, and sleep. And when I come back to you later this afternoon, I'm going to take you shopping for some new shoes. New clothes. You're going to feel like a rich kid. That's my promise, okay?"

A tinge of a smile turns the corners of his mouth. He doesn't know about the battery of tests he's going to face at the doctor's office.

"Let's get in the car." I stamp on the ashes of the dirty money.

When does recovery begin? How long until the protective measures of his mind blot out the memories? Someday when he is forty he'll think something isn't quite right about me, and he'll go on a mission of self-exploration, and bit by bit he'll unearth the horror he withstood under Louie's employ. Between now and then, he'll spackle over the memories so that he can get on with living. Will he start today?

Ash opens the car door, climbs inside. The smell of steaming break-fast burritos fills the cabin. I'm hungry enough to discern the odors of eggs and ham. She passes one to Atian and another to me. "Your second is in the bag, Atian." She places it on the floor by his legs.

"I'm going to walk back to the hotel and get my bike. I've got business to attend this morning. Regarding a senator..."

She dips her eyes. "Do it."

"Cyman," Atian says. "You don't have to hide what you're talking about."

"I'm going to do my best to make the public aware of what kind of man he is. What he did to you."

Atian looks out the window. He has peeled the wrapper from the burrito, but hasn't taken a bite.

"Okay," Atian says. He bites the burrito.

I squeeze his shoulder, then get out and circle to Ash's side.

She lowers her window. I pass her two hundred dollars. "Get a hotel for the day and leave your cell phone off. Don't let anyone, anyone, know where you are. Do not go to your house. No matter what."

"Okay."

Géraud is not the kind of animal that will slink away, defeated. He's the kind that will launch a surprise attack, and it will be vicious. He'll use a surrogate, since he'll be flying to Washington in a few hours with Cyman. And her father? Family won't stand in the way of his career. If it would have, he wouldn't have put his family in this position.

"Never blame yourself when an evil person forces you to make a tough decision," I say, and lean through the open window and peck her cheek. "I'll call soon and leave a message. Don't turn your cell phone on inside the hotel. Drive around."

She seizes the back of my head and holds my lips to hers.

We part. The sidewalk stretches a block between the service station and the hotel, but the burrito doesn't survive fifty paces. It tastes horrible because they put more potatoes in it than anything else. Who authorized potatoes in breakfast burritos? I want his name.

I catalogue my problems. Katrina is still missing. Rachel has, by now, destroyed my stock accounts. Barrett is probably knee-deep in

Operation Guillotine. And the police haven't discovered the humor in my antics regarding Cyman.

The real issue is Barrett and Rachel. I have avoided telling her anything partly because she's so pushy. But also because she represents deified government: the idea government should be all powerful, all sensing, all present. Might say it turns a fella off. But Barrett?

It's time to see what he has to say.

I climb aboard my faithful Valkyrie and fire the engine. The first gray flirtations of sunrise lighten the darkness, which is never truly dark in downtown Phoenix. My last can of Red Bull is fading but I'm sure Barrett will have enough coffee brewed to raise the dead. Morning traffic on Seventeen north is hit or miss. Some places it's thick, and I wonder what possesses normal people to be awake now. And of course I know what it is: life. The bills.

Presuming Rachel has destroyed my accounts, I refuse to join these morning commuters. Blackfoot Indians don't live this way. Not the ones in my mind.

Why should I?

I'm at Barrett's compound. The gate doesn't open.

I sit, avoid looking into the video monitor on the mini tower to the left of the gate. I want to waive at it, but I've been nonchalant about Barrett's hospitality. Has it been revoked?

After a minute the gate grinds open and I drive through. Dismount, and hesitate at the front door. I reach to knock, but wait. The place is silent—calm.

I look for birds. They usually know what's going on. There are none. The door swings open and Barrett stands there. "Heard something on the scanner a few minutes ago. Brothel bust on Baseline?"

"I called it in after I got the boy."

He takes my arm and the pressure in his hand is acute. He holds my eye.

"That was a fine thing to do. That speech you gave about the little people made sense. We have to remember that, in the coming days."

"The coming days?"

"Enter, son. It's time you learn about Operation Guillotine."

"Before we do that, I need your help to tie this up with Cyman. Indulge me for ten more minutes."

He sighs as he leads me inside.

"I need to see the tape that Mike took from the hotel yesterday."

"Why?"

He lied to me. "There's a good chance the tape has the evidence I was looking for. Footage of the boy."

"You got the boy out?"

"Yeah."

"Let it go."

"Cyman's got to pay."

"Son, Cyman's going to pay. The only thing you can do is drag his name through the mud, but you can't do that without dragging the boy, too. Now if you care for the boy, you have to let it go."

"If I let go, Cyman keeps on doing it. Someone has to make a stand. We'll cover the boy's face. But the world has to know the evidence exists. They don't all need to see it, but they have to know it's real. They have to know there's proof the esteemed Senator from Arizona sodomized a boy."

"You've already got the state in an uproar. Doesn't that satisfy you? Graffiti saying Cyman doesn't sleep with animals? Fliers to every government official in the state saying do your job, take him out. A video, all over the internet, proving corruption. Turn on the news and you'll see every station committed to finding you. And investigating Cyman. You've won."

"It doesn't feel like a win."

"It is a win. You get to move on, still in control of your decisions. Still responsible for your past and your destiny. And the bad guys? They suffer."

"Will he hurt?"

"You have no idea."

"You mean Guillotine?"

"Let's talk shop."

I gulp. If I let the conversation drift away from that tape in the tech room, it is never coming back. But Barrett's arguments have logic. Al Capone went to prison for tax evasion, not killing people. Who cares if the punishment is for the specific crime, so long as it is punishment?

I do.

Because to me, the victory is about facing evil, staring it down, over-coming it, defeating it and demanding as a society that we will not tol-erate it. We will not play word games. We will not substitute or make allowances. Punishment is where the virtuous crushes the vanquished because it has good and truth and virtue on its side. In Cyman's case, justice means exposure, humiliation, prison and torment specifically for caring more about his sexual gratification than the life of his victim.

If I don't make Cyman pay for *this* crime, he got away with it. Even if he rots to death sitting in jail for something else, he got away with it.

"In my world, men like Cyman don't get away with raping kids."

Barrett props his chin on a fist. "You're not going to move on, are you?"

"No."

He stands, leads me into the hallway and stops at the tech room. It is empty.

"I noticed it took a minute to open the gate. Where is everybody?"

"Do you need me to answer that?"

He sits on a wheeled stool and spins in front of a television monitor. Presses the power button. Pushes in a videocassette. The screen comes to life with a shot of Cyman' s hotel room; the video activated by Cyman's shirtless torso moving into camera range.

A frail and frightened Atian arrives at the edge of the bed and Cyman pulls the boy's shirt over his head. Atian's expression is blank.

"You're not going to stomach this very well," Barrett says. "But if you're going to show the world, you better see it first."

"You say that as if destroying him is my moral failing."

"No!" He points into my face with violence that catches me off guard. "No! You want to expose him to society—that won't destroy him. Not like I will."

"With Guillotine?"

"That's right."

I glance back to the television screen and it is repugnant. "Freeze it there."

Barrett presses a button. The shot shows Cyman's face and the body of a child. Atian's face is not exposed.

"Can you capture this to a JPG file and send it to one of these computers?"

"No. But my tech chief can." He pushes the stool and slides to an intercom microphone. "Major Barrett, report to the screen room."

"Major Barrett?" I say.

"My daughter."

"Your daughter is a major?"

"She is a major within our organization."

"Ah."

I study the television screen, wondering if something more explicit might better tell the story. But I'm fighting a strong urge to vomit. The television screen shows obscenity in all its vileness. But the significance I bring to the trope—that's what torques me tight enough to murder.

The old man preying on fragile youth.

White on brown.

Wealthy on poor.

Politician on native citizen.

For a split moment it seems the only thing the white man brought to the continent was a great matrix of exploitation and deception.

Ruining Cyman won't be enough.

Boot heels approach from the hallway. Cyman's daughter arrives in a flash but my mind runs in slow motion. The turmoil of seeing Cyman's abomination has unbalanced me. And while I desire to leap into a television screen and rend the flesh from Cyman's bones, Barrett delivers a shock that shorts my circuits.

Rachel stands in the doorway, pert and smiling. She wears loose jeans and a t-shirt.

"Don't look so surprised," she says. "It makes me question whether you were worth all the effort."

Barrett shrugs. I think of the saying, when you are in doubt, be still, and wait; when doubt no longer exists for you, then go forward with courage. So long as mists envelop you, be still; be still until the sunlight pours through and dispels the mists—as it surely will. Then act with courage.

Rachel knew about my first conversation with Barrett, about when Apple hires a female CEO, not because of surveillance. Barrett told her. She introduced me to Bernard, showed up after Cyman's guys smashed my window, showed up at Desert Dog, and then was with Bernard— her brother—in Flagstaff.

"Nothing is ever an accident," Barrett says. He smiles as if to say, Ain't it grand?

I remember Rachel's words when I caught her in Paolo's apartment. "You'll have nothing, and you'll be a wanted man. Nowhere to go. Nothing to do. No one to turn to."

"I could turn to Barrett." I had said. "I get the feeling he'd take me in."

And she smiled.

"Does the Treasury even have a group called TFI?"

"Yes. But I'm not in it." She taps a few computer keys and brings up the website she had shown me. Does the name search for her profile. Then clicks on several other links, illustrating they are dead. It's a fake website.

"Congratulations. You made it. Glad to have you with us," Barrett says. "It took a lot of work to find out if I could trust you. Trust is what an organization like mine survives on, and going forward, it'll be more important. I had to put you through every test I could, make sure you had the grit to keep your mouth shut. The raw belief in our purpose."

"Desert Dog?"

"That was about stamina. Every one of my boys has been through it. Fact is, I had to open it up to the public, underground, because the Feds took notice. And using Rachel like that—don't think that's what she does with everybody. But for the mission, and for you, she did her duty. Hell. She's had a crush on you since we targeted you for recruitment eighteen months ago."

"Lucky me."

Rachel smiles. "Don't you have anything to say?"

"I might knock you on your ass."

"Easy, now," Barrett says. "This isn't how we usually reveal our screening methods. But you have baggage... You came here for my help, and I'm explaining why I've been telling you not to waste your time."

"So let's talk politics," I say.

Barrett stands. "U.S. federal and state governments expropriate a third of America's gross domestic product every year. That number was eight per cent in 1929. Milton Friedman said Americans spend—in addition to taxes—another ten per cent of their incomes on government rules and mandates. The Cato Institute puts it at eight hundred and sixty billion a year—more than the entire gross domestic products of Canada and Mexico.

"The tax code is seventy-four thousand pages long. Taxpayers spend two hundred billion dollars each year complying with it. Even

IRS employees don't understand the laws they're supposed to enforce. A General Accounting Office survey found that IRS employees gave incorrect tax advice half the time. On top of that, now they use the IRS to shut down political speech.

"Runaway taxes, runaway spending, and none of it attached to a bit of morality or principle. The Supreme Court says an anti-child pornography statute violates of the First Amendment, but a political ad during the month before a general election is criminal.

"Hank Thoreau said 'that government is best which governs not at all; and when men are prepared for it, that will be the kind of government which they will have.' Does it sound to you like we're moving in that direction?

"He also said that all governments follow the same path—toward oppression. Government doesn't naturally dissolve. It accumulates power until regular folks can't breathe the air without paying a tax. A government guided by the will of the majority has no greater claim to crush liberty than any other government. No institution which gains the uninformed, coerced allegiance of the masses will ever choose to be guided by conscience. The honest individual is left with a decision: am I obligated to the central government?"

"If you're not?" I say.

"Guillotine. My boys, this moment, are set to decapitate the federal government. In one swell foop, all three branches. This isn't a plot to bomb buildings."

He leans back and his chest flexes, almost on its own. This is his moment. The culmination he's been waiting for. This is the speech he's delivered to dozens of men, I bet, and plans to give to thousands more.

"I am part of a network of fed-up citizens, Solomon, who have decided to take action." He glances at his wristwatch. "Very, very soon, five hundred and fifty-seven members of the federal government will pay for their crimes against the people of the United States. Some of our operatives will fail. But most will not. Most are men who have served this nation's armed forces, but who now realize a nation is not merely its polity."

"Soon?" I say.

He nods. "And when they are done, we will link the state governments together—"

"What about the shadow government?"

"Show me a shadow government in the Constitution. It has no authority. None the state governments will recognize. We'll link the states with a new confederation, until each state sends delegates to a new constitutional convention.

"It won't work," I say. "Can you imagine getting California and Texas to agree on gay marriage?"

"Precisely why it *will* work. Neither California nor Texas wants the other to have any say in their goin's on. These new articles of confederation will allow the states to band together for defense, but little else. We've taken the constitution and updated the language so the socialists and plutocrats can't distort it to forever extend the police state."

"You're still going to have oppressive government. Now it will be the states."

"Maybe, but politicians misbehave less when they're close enough the mob can hang them. In a half hour, the central government will be empty buildings. The continuity is the people, and remove them, you have no institutions. It'll take time to rebuild, to elect new leaders. The states will have the liberty to escape the union if they choose, and redraft a constitution that restores their sovereignty and primacy. There doesn't have to be a war that kills citizens. Just politicians. What's the loss?"

"I didn't sign up for this."

"You have no choice."

"I'm leaving."

"You can't get off a warning in time to jeopardize the mission. The FBI needs a six-month lead to connect dot A to dot B. So take your time, and when your free will guides you back, we'll be here."

A barely-prescient vision flashes through my mind, and steals my wind like a sledge hammer to my gut. Washington D.C., smoking, brightly illuminated by sunlight. Flash-news bulletins that the president has been assassinated, and a panicked announcer stating his newsroom is drowning in a sea of headlines, each involving the name of a senator, congressperson, or Supreme Court justice.

I exit the tech room, cross the foyer, open the giant front door. I stand in front of the gate with my back to the house, almost feeling crosshairs on the back of my head. But the gate motor hums and the giant slabs shift sideways and stop when the gap is big enough for a Blackfoot on a Valkyrie to pass through.

THE END

From the Author

S OLOMON BULL is fiction. There is no Senator Cyman, nor is there a senator I'm aware of who engages in the crimes I attribute to Cyman. Certainly, not one of Arizona's former or current senators. That would be a little obvious, wouldn't you say? Also, I wanted to mention that Solomon Bull's character... this guy is a piece of work. Boy. Solomon is so... opinionated. Arrogant. I don't know where he gets it, but I apologize for him. Also, truly, don't try to trade stocks using Solomon's formula. You'll almost certainly lose money.

True story: after the rough draft I had to go back and delete 93 F-bombs and 173 other four letter words. (Actually quite an experience, having to find words outside my lexicon of profanity, which I've spent so many years polishing.) I left one F-bomb in place, where Barrett fails to recognize Yoda, because I couldn't make the humor work without. Regardless, I hope neither my profanity nor lack thereof was offensive.

Solomon Bull is an Indie published novel. Sure, the cover says **Hardgrave Enterprises**, but since we're being totally exposed with each other, that's just a name I took from the evilest sombitch I ever wrote, Angus Hardgrave, who mused about creating a backwoods business empire of distilling moonshine and fighting pit bulls. He called his empire Hardgrave Enterprises, and one year when I was figuring out my taxes, I gave my writing business the name because frankly, it sounds cool.

Regardless, *Solomon Bull* is an Indie published novel. It has no significant marketing budget, no publicist, no team of Big Six publishers trying to figure out how to earn back the two million dollar advance they paid me. In short, this book will pass away more quickly than most unless its readers keep it alive.

How? By spreading the word.

Before I mention a few things that are helpful to authors in general, let me point out that *Solomon Bull* is a moral story, as were *Tread, My Brother's Destroyer, Cold Quiet Country* and *Nothing Save the Bones Inside Her.*

I believe in absolute right, meaning I believe a divine being created right and wrong and that in the end, right will prevail. God will prevail. Each of my novels rests on the foundation that evil is real, wrong is wrong, and the struggle to defeat it is a heroic struggle, whether the outcome is secure or not.

I don't subscribe to hopeless writing. I love noir because the darker the dark, the lighter the light. I hope that's what you take away from all my work... that the impossible fight is always worth fighting.

If you found value standing beside Solomon Bull as he overcame his internal and external foes, please consider doing the following:

Tell a friend. Tell ten, or two hundred, that you enjoyed *Solomon Bull.*

Go on Twitter, Facebook, or some other social media forum and spread the word.

If you belong to a book club, suggest this title.

Follow me on Twitter (@claylindemuth) and consider retweeting some of my tweets. Or friend me on Facebook—I accept all requests.

Don't stalk me. You stalkers freak me out. Write to me. Sure. But don't show up at my house. Enough already!

Here's the biggest help: write a review on Amazon or Goodreads. Even a couple of lines about what you enjoyed about the story can help others decide. One of the most difficult obstacles for a small-press work to overcome is the reader's worry that the work will be inferior, poorly formatted or edited, or just boring as hell. An effective review might address some of those concerns.

Write a blog review, or contact a blogger you know who is on the lookout for Indie creativity.

Or, if you know someone in media who likes to interview authors...

Whatever you do, please know that I am very grateful to you for purchasing *Solomon Bull*. I truly hope you found value in it, and I will feel deeply indebted if you help spread the word.

Thanks—ten million thanks.

ABOUT THE AUTHOR

Clayton Lindemuth writes noir because that's where he lives. He runs ultra-marathons. Reads economics. Is a Christian apologist, a dog lover, and eternally misses Arizona. Clayton is the author of *Cold Quiet Country*, *Nothing Save the Bones Inside Her*, *My Brother's Destroyer*, *Tread*, and other volumes not yet released. He lives in Missouri with his wife Julie and his puppydog Faith, also known as "Princess Wigglebums" and "Stinky Princess."

Made in the USA
Monee, IL
25 September 2021